JARROD BLACK

CHASING PACK

TEXI SMITH

JARROD BLACK

CHASING PACK

TEXI SMITH

First published in 2022 by Popcorn Press, a division of Fair Play Publishing
PO Box 4101, Balgowlah Heights, NSW 2093, Australia
www.popcornpress.com.au

ISBN: 978-1-925914-55-9
ISBN: 978-1-925914-56-6 (ePub)
© Texi Smith 2022

The moral rights of the author have been asserted.

All rights reserved. Except as permitted under the *Australian Copyright Act 1968*
(for example, a fair dealing for the purposes of study, research, criticism or review), no part
of this book may be reproduced, stored in a retrieval system, communicated or transmitted
in any form or by any means without prior written permission from the Publisher.

This is a work of fiction. Names, characters, businesses, places, events, locales, and incidents
are either the products of the author's imagination or used in a fictitious manner.
Any resemblance to actual persons, living or dead, or actual events is purely coincidental.

Cover design and typsetting by Ana Secivanovic

All inquiries should be made to the Publisher via sales@fairplaypublishing.com.au

A catalogue record of this book is available from the National Library of Australia.

DEDICATION

To me mam, Margaret,
you'll be glad you won't need your mobile phone for this one.

CONTENTS

01

Throng

"Jarrod," shouted Des, the first-team coach.

Jarrod was miles away, lost in the thoughts of a chaotic pre-season that had seen him start at St James' Park and end up back at the Arena with his beloved Darlington. He looked up at Des, puzzled.

"Warm up," said Des through gritted teeth. He looked agitated.

Jarrod remembered where he was. He stood up and shuffled in front of his teammates in the dugout and leapt up onto the grass. Manager Gary was gesticulating wildly to his players as they toiled in the warm sunshine, unable to make in-roads into the Twente penalty area. An hour of the game had passed, and Darlington were two goals down, in danger of making this final home friendly of a high-quality pre-season a thorough disappointment.

Two minutes later, the change was made. Gav Selley trotted forlornly towards Jarrod, and they clasped hands. Jarrod's appearance onto the pitch at least stirred some applause from the big crowd. There was suddenly a wave of excitement. Last season's player of the season, the man brought in last year to steer the club successfully to promotion from League Two at the first attempt, the player who had landed a dream loan move to Newcastle and was back in town, was now in his usual midfield spot.

He slotted in beside Peter Van Vloten, signed from the visiting team right at the start of pre-season. Part of the deal to bring him to the club was to play a friendly, and a home game with a team with European pedigree was great PR for League One Darlington. Peter's performances hadn't been met with much praise, but he'd been played out of position on the left. Now, in this second half of the final pre-season game, he found himself in his preferred central midfield role, and was now alongside club captain Jarrod Black.

Peter seemed to sense his chance at forming a partnership with Jarrod. Jarrod was immediately on his wavelength, and in their first moment of action together, Peter went in bravely in a tough challenge. Jarrod was hovering just behind him to pick up the pieces, and immediately sprayed the ball out to Connor Naughton. The crowd over on the left rose as one from their seats. The tricky winger teased his marker and slid the ball nonchalantly through his legs as he lunged in.

Peter was already up off the ground and sprinting towards the penalty area, past Jarrod who was anticipating the scraps on the edge of the area. Connor's arrowed cross was perfect for Peter to run in, almost stumbling, to meet the ball with a low header. His joy as the ball whizzed past the Twente goalkeeper and hit the net was clear to see. Centre forward Will Telfer raced over and joined him as he ran away to celebrate with the crowd, the rest of the players, including Jarrod, catching up and jumping on the goal scorer.

Jarrod had played in the team with Peter previously, but they had not been paired in central midfield before. There was a real connection, and Jarrod was keen to explore it further. The next moment came when a long clearance from the Twente keeper came towards Jarrod. He prepared himself to contest the header but heard a booming voice behind him bellowing 'Petaaaaaaar!' and stood aside. Peter flew past him to meet the ball, brushing aside the visiting player and clearing the ball long into touch. Peter turned and ran back past Jarrod, and they slapped hands. Jarrod was loving it.

The crowd was well and truly entertained now, following on from a first hour that had tested their resolve. Sam Basaan's low ball down the right for the latest substitute Roni Verelo had the crowd on their feet again. A feign to pass inside and then a samba-like shimmy from the silky midfielder took him to the byline and he chipped in an inviting cross. The roar subsided as the crowd took a collective intake of breath, before on-loan Anton Broman connected and sent a header over the keeper for a dramatic equaliser.

The young forward—a cause for much optimism since he had caught the eye pre-season after joining from Newcastle as part of Jarrod's own short-term and much-publicised loan the other way—stood in front of Bay 66 with arms stretched out wide, taking the acclaim. It was a great team goal though, and Darlington had looked good value since Jarrod's introduction.

The final whistle wasn't long in coming, the players making their way around the field to give thanks to the supporters for coming down on this Monday night ahead of the weekend's opening league fixture. This had been a good result for Darlo in the end; Jarrod felt that he had done enough to merit a place in manager Gary Hollister's line-up for the first day of the season at Shrewsbury Town. A pre-season return of two wins, three draws and a narrow defeat against highly fancied Championship heavyweights Derby County had given everyone at the club much optimism.

A third consecutive promotion was not out of the realm of possibility. Gary and owner Gerry Lincoln had expressed much more realistic expectations for the season to the media though, and quite rightly. This was a League One containing names such as Charlton Athletic, Huddersfield Town and Birmingham City. Mixing it with that calibre of club would be a big test.

"Well done, lads," said Gary as he addressed the troops in the changing rooms. "That was a very important second half for us, and for our fans too. Well done, Peter, what a good goal that was, and well done, Wes, for keeping them out at the start of the half."

The media throng just inside the foyer of the reception in the stadium was unusually big. Word was getting round of a potential big signing being made that evening. Gary was surrounded but shooed away the pack and suggested that they talk with "the real stars of the show, Peter Van Vloten and Jarrod Black". The two of them were walking together past the crowd when they heard that and turned to each other with a little smile. They stopped and faced the media and smiled again.

02

BetShed

Jarrod had not been back long from his loan spell at Newcastle. His dream of playing at St James' Park for the club he had loved all his life had been fulfilled. Sure, it wasn't in the Premier League, and of course it was a very short loan term, and his place was filled by some very expensive and experienced imports. But it had included a glamour game against Barcelona, and it had involved a dramatic comeback. Nothing would take that night away from him.

The drama that surrounded that game, Jarrod's involvement in the bust of a multi-million-pound betting syndicate, was almost a distant memory. If it wasn't for the almost daily contact with D.I. Allison of the Met Police with updates on the trials of the parties involved, he could have forgotten it completely. The trial of the main offender and foot soldier, Yannick Lefevre, appeared to be going nowhere and the detective inspector was concerned that he might get away scot-free.

The footballing public weren't going to forget it quickly though. He was recognised even more now wherever he went, especially in Newcastle. There had been requests for TV interviews about the betting scandal, but the standard response email sent on Jarrod's behalf by the police was enough to put off any media outlet looking for an exclusive.

One by-product of all the drama was Jarrod's link to betting and money. Advertising and PR companies were all over him. Jarrod's agent, Duddy Freiberg, who had masterminded the loan deal at Newcastle, was still managing Jarrod's affairs in a somewhat unofficial capacity. He provided Jarrod with constant feedback as to the sort of wheeling and dealing that was happening behind the scenes. He had knocked back offers to be brand ambassador for at least two betting companies, and also one from a payday loan company of ill-repute.

Two weeks ago, though, an offer from BetShed—a new player in the crowded online betting marketplace—was deemed too good to turn down. Jarrod had been asked to spend a day at a film studio near London. It was an enormous day. Jarrod had caught a train from Darlington after training on the Sunday afternoon and was met at Stevenage by a car that drove him to the studio nearby. There he had a briefing with the producer and a run-through of what he would need to do and say.

After he had eventually gone to bed at midnight, he was picked up from his accommodation at 6:30 a.m. for a whole day of shooting. The previous six weeks had given Jarrod so many new experiences, so this was water off a duck's back. The one thing that he had found intriguing was the amount of kit and the number of people needed just to shoot an advert. It was like all the gear from the whole of the Arena on game day, shoehorned into a space as big as a village church hall. People stepped carefully around and over mysterious black boxes. Jarrod stood on a small stage with blinding lights shining at him from all angles.

The idea behind the advert was pretty clever—Jarrod was on a stool in front of what he had assumed to be a green screen. He was dressed in a good suit, a Gibson and Brookes—he recognised the name—and it fit him perfectly. He was instructed to type something into the mobile phone he was holding, stumble off the stool as if surprised, and then start walking. He then did multiple shots of him walking at an increasing pace, then jogging. His jacket came off between shots, and his shirt then unbuttoned to reveal a generic football shirt. He eventually ended up in full football gear. The last shot was of Jarrod celebrating a goal, both fists in the air, head back and roaring at the sky.

Jarrod had been told what was meant to be playing behind him on the screen but had been unable to really follow what the director had been telling him. It had all sounded a little contrived, but he had no reason to doubt that it would be very impressive. He was told that he would get a preview of it anyway before it went to air.

Jarrod felt as if he'd made a few friends during the course of that long, long day, and remembered being exhausted when he arrived back home after midnight after a late train journey back up north.

He was given a preview of the ad, about a week ago. There were in fact a series of four different ads, all using the same footage, but all with totally different backgrounds. The idea was that a user of the BetShed app had placed a bet and that had prompted Jarrod to get off to his game, as if given instructions to score the winning goal. The user was in a different country and a different scene each time, but the result was the same: the winning goal. The ads all ended with Jarrod back on his stool as if he were ready for the next user of the app to place their bet.

Jarrod wasn't convinced it was that good. He didn't quite get the message, but the finished product looked slick and the background looked convincing. He was pretty happy with his own acting skills too. The ads were about twelve seconds long—long enough that Jarrod was sure he wouldn't see them at prime time in the ad breaks in *Coronation Street*.

When the ads came out, they were everywhere, especially online. Every time he looked at any website or ventured into social media, he saw his own face. It had kind of grown on Jarrod and after two days of being bombarded with the same ads, he was able to look at it and say that it was a pretty good piece of work. The money that had been offered for the shoot was amazing too—eighty thousand pounds for a day's work, and they'd even paid for everything while he was there.

After the payments had hit his bank account from the spell at Newcastle, this added to make an enormous amount of money sitting waiting to be put to work. Jarrod's wife Marianne had been discussing investing in another house, maybe in Newcastle. Jarrod had always thought he should invest into something back in Sydney but was too afraid of the outrageous prices. Or it could just stay in the bank, and they could live quite comfortably off that for a while when Jarrod hung up his boots. They'd be able to do some travelling when he finally had the time; Jarrod had never been to South America and Marianne had visions of a Kombi van tour.

That feeling of accomplishment was immediately nipped in the bud the following day at training. No one had said anything about the ads until Dec Hines scored a cheeky goal in the small-sided game at the end, and raced into the corner of the field, raised his fists to the sky and roared. Everyone burst out laughing, Jarrod included. A chant of "BetShed, BetShed", just like at the end of the ads, went up and all the players converged on Jarrod, jumping around him. It was as though they had just won the FA Cup.

Jarrod loved this bunch of players. They were all on equal footing; there was no grandstanding by anyone in the squad, or if there was a hint of it, the player in question would quickly be shot down to size. Jarrod was the club captain but there were more confident and over-the-top individuals than himself. He felt as though there was a trust between the players on the field that was there off the field too. Jarrod had enjoyed his time in the spotlight at Newcastle and was enjoying some airtime now, but he knew that his teammates would keep him well and truly grounded.

A video session to watch highlights of their opponents Shrewsbury included a link to an online clip of their last game of last season. Before the game started to play, it cut abruptly to an ad. It was Jarrod's BetShed ad. He put his hand over his eyes as the rest of the squad cat-called and booed at the screen, a shout of "bor-ing!" getting everyone laughing. Keeper Wes Kellehar got angry the next day at his phone and shouted "Bloody Jarrod Black, you've taken over my phone ..." as a pop-up played the ad for the umpteenth time. There was a lot of laughter in the changing room. Jarrod hoped that Wes wasn't being serious.

03

Meadow

The trip to New Meadow for the opening game took longer than Jarrod had anticipated. The leg after leaving the M6 to the stadium seemed to take hours, despite there being relatively light traffic. In the absence of Mitch Short, still on loan at Glasgow Rangers, Wes had started the comical introduction to the host town, a tradition that was revered on Darlington bus journeys. It was some great patter, big on sheep jokes, but he'd done it a little too early. As a result, Jarrod felt a little weary stepping off the coach, when he would usually feel invigorated by the tour guide spiel. He reckoned he wasn't the only one feeling that way.

There was something not right, that was for sure. Jarrod was named on the bench when he was sure that he would be in the starting line-up. Peter was in midfield with fresh new signing Benson Gadriga, the formation much like Monday night's starting eleven that misfired in the last friendly game. Gary and Des were deep in conversation in the corner of the changing room. Benson was still getting to know his teammates after arriving two days ago. He was a player of immense potential that Gary and his scouts had tracked all last season at non-league York City. He was on the radar of Championship clubs too, but the offers were not right for the player. Gerry had become involved as the transfer window approached its conclusion. Armed with the loan payments from Newcastle and Rangers for Jarrod and Mitch respectively, they went in with one last offer and that broke the stalemate. A handsome fee for a non-league part-timer was exchanged and the young midfielder made the short journey to Darlington the next day to get ready for the opening league fixture.

Jarrod had mixed emotions about being on the bench. He was club captain. That didn't mean that he was guaranteed a place in the team, but his presence in the squad was deemed vital. Gary hadn't offered any reason for his omission for this one, other than that he was taking a calculated risk. So many times, a new signing at a club had to be eased into the team after a few weeks, but Gary wanted to make a statement here and Gerry wanted his long-term target to make an instant impact.

The warm-up was a little laboured; at least that's what Jarrod felt. The Darlo fans were out in force, but the usual sun-swathed conditions that heralded the start of a new season were replaced by driving rain. At least the supporters were undercover, and they were in good voice. Jarrod tried to instil a sense of urgency into the final warm-up and made sure that he put in an extra effort in a passing drill where he was trying to intercept. In the changing room after the warm-up, Jarrod felt strange to be in his tracksuit, but still made a point of pumping up his teammates. Connor received some strong words—Jarrod had always thought that he was capable of more and let him know that he should be running at his defender from the first minute.

He had encouraging words for Peter and Benson, instructing Benson to stay close to Peter when the opposition had possession, and to move quickly into position when they won it back. As the players walked out of the tunnel to the tune of 'Catch Me If You Can', Gary put his arm around Jarrod and squeezed.

"You're itching to be out there, aren't you?"

"Of course," said Jarrod. "I hope I don't have to come on when we're losing. I hope we're celebrating by the end of the ninety minutes."

That was a telling statement. It was stinging and was meant to sow a seed in Gary's mind. Jarrod surprised himself with his words. It was almost a veiled threat, the words of someone who would be tutting and shaking their head if it all went wrong. Jarrod felt a little uneasy at his thoughts. Des had an encouraging word as they made their way into the players' seats behind the technical area.

"It pains me to see you on the bench, Jarrod," said Des. "I know how much this means to you and how much you want to be out there leading the team. I think the fans will get a surprise."

Jarrod took his place on the bench in between Roni and Ghali Barbera, and he felt surprisingly relaxed. The first eleven was in position now and a roar started from the crowd, growing in volume until the referee blew to start the game and the roar turned to applause. It wasn't long before the supporters were absorbed in the game, the home team starting at a quick tempo.

The failings that were obvious in the first half of Monday's game were evident here again. There was a gap between midfield and defence, with debutant Benson trying just that little bit too hard to get involved in the action. Anton up front was also finding the going tough, looking forlornly at the long balls played up to him with no chance of beating the central defender for height. At least Will Telfer, last year's top scorer, was involved and was trying to find space for the flick-on.

The party atmosphere in the away end had almost disappeared as Darlo toiled and weathered a storm of attacks from the home side. A litany of telegraphed passes brought groans from the bench, Gary and Des getting fidgety. On the half hour, central defender Raynor Gunn clattered into his man on the edge of the box, a petulant response to some gamesmanship from the opposing centre-forward. After a minute of setting the wall and working out who could and couldn't be in it, the Town left midfielder stepped up and looped a terrific shot over the defenders and past Wes for 1–0. Gary spun around in disgust. Jarrod nestled his chin on his clenched fist. New Meadow was rocking.

Half time in the changing room was no place for the faint-hearted. Jarrod had never seen Gary so upset. Physio Sash was tending to Connor who looked as if he'd been playing in the mud, his hair and face coated with dirt and his shirt ripped at the collar. Gary paced up and down the room, his demeanour changing from angry to pleading. How could they let their fans down with a performance like this? Jarrod was taking this all in. He'd find it useful at the sports psychology course he was enrolled in on Monday at St George's Park as part of his long-running goal to get a UEFA A Licence.

There were no changes at the break, and Darlington responded to Gary's words after half time. Suddenly there was composure, and Anton began to get some time on the ball. The running of Dean Minto and Connor was starting to cause panic in the home team's defence. A long cross from the right by Connor was headed back across goal by Anton and Will lashed the ball against the bar and over. This was more like it.

Benson was toiling with little effect in midfield. The first change saw Ghali replace him in an unfamiliar central midfield role, but once it was clear that the replacement was finding it equally challenging, the second change saw Anton sacrificed, and Jarrod entered the fray. Ghali went up front and Jarrod found his place next to Peter and gave a rallying cry to his teammates around him.

The tempo was immediately raised, and Darlington started to press higher and higher. Defender Freddie Asquith found himself in attack as the away team broke away quickly from a Shrewsbury corner. Jarrod's delicate through ball saw Freddie race clear of the last man and shimmy to dummy the keeper. His lack of experience in these situations though saw him push the ball too far towards the byline and the resulting shot was from such an acute angle that it flashed across the face of the goal and into touch on the far side.

With five minutes remaining, Darlington had been on the attack for the majority of the half. A momentary lapse in concentration from Raynor saw him caught in possession and the Shrewsbury striker picked his pocket, ran through on goal, and showed Freddie how to finish, through the legs of Wes for the decisive second goal. Jarrod was disgusted, but put his arm around Raynor to console him, as the stadium bounced along to the rock anthem that saluted the goal.

Jarrod booted the door when he arrived in the changing room after an extended PR session with the Darlington fans at the away end. Freddie followed him in and booted it again, then Raynor smashed it against the wall with such force that some of the paint flaked off the heavy wooden door. This was not the Darlington team that Jarrod knew and loved. Gary was calmer than at half time. After all, the game was over and there was nothing he could do about the result. He was full of praise where it counted. Peter was singled out for his never-say-die attitude, and Connor's display earned him a lot of encouraging words. But they had lost and were unfortunate to be on the end of a two-goal defeat.

That could have derailed Darlo's season, but Jarrod knew that his teammates had been a little off, even from the moment they stepped off the coach, and he wasn't concerned. The Radio 5 roundup as the coach pulled away highlighted the damning reality of twenty-third place; only Lincoln City had lost by more and were keeping them off the bottom of the table.

Jarrod's belief in his team to bounce back from that opening day defeat was justified. The first round League Cup tie at Barnsley on the Wednesday night was a massive shot in the arm. Jarrod started the game alongside Peter, and he was instrumental in a 3–1 win against one of their League One rivals.

By the time the following weekend was over, and the second round of league games had been played, Darlington were back in mid-table, a 2–1 home win against Plymouth Argyle at the Arena sending them up to the heady heights of fourteenth. They had two wins under their belts and the signs were good for more of the same as they looked to gain a foothold in this difficult division.

Jarrod had cemented his place in the side after those two commanding displays and Benson had to be content with a place on the subs' bench, despite his obvious talent and much-hyped transfer. A victory for experience over youth, Jarrod thought, although he was genuinely concerned that Benson might not recover from his difficult start with the club.

04

Croft

Jarrod had just arrived home from another all-day session at St George's Park and was feeling exhausted. The lack of direct transport links to Burton-on-Trent had given him no option other than to drive and getting snarled up in some heavy traffic didn't help the journey. It was now just after 9:30 p.m. The lights were off in the kids' bedrooms. Marianne would still be up, but not for much longer. He pulled out his mobile phone. It had been buzzing in his pocket quite frequently the last twenty minutes, and he hadn't checked it.

There were a number of missed calls from an unknown number, the same one four times from a London code. He was ready to dismiss it as yet another one of those junk calls asking him to sign up for a mobile plan or telling him that his home internet was suspended, but he saw that a voice message had been left on the final call. An Indian-sounding 'James Thomas' from the call centre in Bangalore wouldn't have left a voicemail message. There were other missed calls and a few other voicemails. Jarrod had to listen to a couple before he got to the one from the unknown number.

"Hi, there, Jarrod," said the voice, the use of his first name instantly making this a genuine call. "This is Stevie Mosseman of Barrowful Productions. We would like to chat with you about a new movie production that we have starting early next year. Please return my call on 0200 8000 4000 any time."

The message had been received only a few minutes ago, so Jarrod had no hesitation in ringing the number. Strange number too; someone must have paid a lot of money to get a number like that.

"Thanks for calling back, Jarrod," was the instant response after only one ring. "Stevie Mosseman."

He accentuated the 'e' in his surname, letting Jarrod know that he was not all moss, just a little mossy.

"What can I do for you, Stevie?" asked Jarrod, still unsure of the context of the man he was talking to. He could be a salesman, an advertising man, he could even be looking for a reference for someone else.

"Your name has been thrown into the ring as the new Harlowe Croft in our next movie *From the Gallows*," said Stevie. "We would like to meet you and have a chat face to face."

"Okay," Jarrod abruptly responded, agitated at the nonsense he was hearing. "Now is not a good time though. I've just arrived home after a big day. I'll get back to you, hopefully tomorrow."

"Oh, right, okay …" stuttered Stevie. "Well, goodnight."

Jarrod hung up with a roll of his eyes and grumbled to himself, 'What next?', before leaping out of the car into the cold night air and jogging quietly over the gravel to the front door to let himself in.

05

Licence

It wasn't until the next morning that Jarrod thought about it again. He was on his way to training when the hosts of the easy-listening mid-morning show on Radio Teesside had a quick exchange about their favourite Harlowe Croft actor over the years. It turned out that heart-throb Craig Daniels had been dropped as Croft, the lead character in the long-running semi-serious British institution, and that a more youthful Croft was being considered. Youthful would be a loose term, however, as Harlowe Croft had been anything from thirty to sixty in the top-grossing movie series over the years.

Jarrod drove through the gates and found a spot. The seed of curiosity had been sown in his mind, and he quickly googled Craig Daniels and started reading. It was true all right: the onset of wrinkles and his increasingly baggy eyes had caught up with the actor. He was also no longer in shape, his larger frame belying the mystique of Harlowe Croft. Croft was always a slim figure, quintessentially English, who wore a suit well. It was time for a change.

There were many names thrown around; Murat, from the light entertainment duo Murat and Andoni, was in there. He did cut a slim figure, but his accent might be too strong to disguise as a Londoner. James Milner, the ex-Liverpool player, was also a name that Jarrod recognised, that chiselled chin a striking feature in anyone's books, but not the perfect fit physically. Needless to say, Jarrod's name was not in the frame, and he was pretty sure it wouldn't be at any time in the near future.

He was just about to step out of the car when a further thought about how much these actors got paid flashed across his mind. With one foot on the ground and his leg keeping the door open, he disappeared down another internet rabbit-hole when the first figure of $15 million per movie popped up. That dollar amount, in US dollars, he assumed—wow, that was a lot of money.

He realised that he should make tracks to training when his leg was starting to get a little numb from the car door.

The morning training session was a light jog and preparation for the evening game at home to Bristol Rovers. Jarrod had missed yesterday's late afternoon training session and was keen to get his muscles moving again after way too long driving there and back to the Midlands. He breezed through the reception area with a wink to the young receptionist who was on a call and raced up the steps and past Pauline's office. Pauline, the head of media at the club, noticed him dashing past and called after him.

"Jarrod! Jarrod!" she shouted, Jarrod not realising until the second shout. He stopped and backtracked, poking his head around the door.

"Pauline! Did I hear you shout my name?"

"Yes, yes, come in. One minute," replied Pauline, pointing at the empty seat opposite hers. Jarrod complied, although he made it look as if he wouldn't be staying there long. He glanced at the pile of newspapers on her desk with the trashy mag on top with Craig Daniels on the cover.

"How was yesterday?" she asked.

"Yesterday was fantastic," said Jarrod, instantly engaged now that someone had taken an interest in his epic UEFA A Licence. "We had a session about the different characters we might come across in a football team. I think I can categorise everyone in the squad now."

"That's good," said Pauline. "Now, when does this end?"

"When does it end?" repeated Jarrod, with a puzzled expression.

"We've got Saturday, Tuesday for pretty much the whole season, especially if we go on cup runs," said Pauline. "Are you sure you've got the time to give to your licence right now?"

Jarrod rocked back in the seat and stared at Pauline. He didn't know what to say. He searched for clues in Pauline's eyes. Was this coming from Gary, the coaching staff? Had Marianne said something? Did Gerry notice that he was away a bit more than usual? This needed a crafty response. After all, he'd stalled so long on this bloody licence, he couldn't abandon it again.

"Oh yes," he finally answered. "It's all about preserving the body at this stage. Taking some time away from the training field is not a bad thing sometimes. I'm still active on these days away, you know, but at least I don't get into game situations and risk injury."

"Right," was all that Pauline could respond with. She was clearly not convinced. Cristiano Ronaldo was fitter than he ever was at Jarrod's age and wouldn't miss a training session. To be fair, Jarrod wasn't Cristiano Ronaldo.

"Can I go?" asked Jarrod with the hint of petulance that such a sentence always carried. Pauline showed her palm towards the door and smiled warmly as he left, holding her gaze as he walked out. That unspoken communication confirmed that it had come from somewhere else, and that Pauline was acting as the messenger. They had a fantastic working relationship, Pauline and Jarrod, and it would be as strong as ever this season.

06

Downpour

Jarrod subconsciously wanted to show the coaching team just how fit and ready he was for the evening game, putting in extra effort and making sure he stuck to his marking task in the defensive drill. Bristol Rovers were blessed with an outstanding midfielder from Jamaica, Chilton Richards, a towering presence in the centre who had terrorised teams in the early stages of the season to help put his team top of the table. Gary and Des were working out who was going to be given the marking job: Jarrod or Peter. Jarrod was in two minds—on one hand he wanted to prove a point and be considered as the man for the job, on the other hand it would be a bruising ninety minutes.

Training was cut short by a heavy downpour, but the sun was almost out again by the time they had run for cover. The squad assembled in the changing rooms, unsure as to whether or not they would be continuing. Gary and Des walked in, and Gary closed the door. He strode over to the whiteboard and started to rub off the previous scribblings.

"Right, lads," he said, using the 'r' to clear his throat and get everyone's attention. "While we're in here, let's run through tonight's starting line-up. Wes in goal."

He started to write with the only working pen, first putting up the formation in dots, a conservative 4-4-2 with a diamond in midfield, then filling in the names against each dot.

"Right back, Steva, in the middle, Raynor and Freddie, Basa at left back," he said, jotting the names down as he said them and then turning to Sam Basaan as if to reinforce something they had talked through together previously.

"Out wide in the midfield four, Connor," he said pointing with the pen. "And Deano. And in the middle, holding in front of the back four, will be Oz, with Peter following the big lad around in front."

Jarrod hadn't heard that nickname for a while and smiled, looking at Peter who looked a little worried about the task ahead, but managing a raise of the eyebrows at Jarrod.

"Up front, A.B.," Gary continued, pointing again with the pen at Anton. "And Will."

Des then took the pen and started to write the names of the substitutes while Gary turned and addressed the team.

"Now, we know that Rovers are a pacy team," he started. "Give yourself a chance, stay on your feet and don't dive in. Steva, you were outstanding last week, I'm counting on you today for another big performance against their left winger. He's fast, but you're faster."

Jarrod was analysing Gary's delivery, thinking back to sessions he had been in at St George's Park and forward to what he would say in a similar situation. It was good to hear Gary talking up one of the young prospects, although Jarrod may have preferred to make it a little less public. The pressure might be on young Steven Horton now, and a poor performance might derail his impressive start to first-team life.

Conversely, it was clear that Gary and Sam had talked about Sam's role today, and that wasn't deemed for the ears of the whole squad. It was fascinating, all this psychology, and Jarrod had become more and more aware of it now that he had studied it as part of the A Licence.

The players were ready to go back out for training, but Gary instructed them that they were done for the session, and they were due back for a late lunch at 3:00 p.m. The two hours' gap that they had now was one that frustrated Jarrod in the early days, but as he got older and his life got busier as the years passed, he was appreciative of the time to be able to run errands and make phone calls. Today would be no different, and he installed himself in the deserted breakout area of the Arena, a space that doubled as a corporate lounge on match days. Out came the phone.

There was a missed call from that London number again, and just as he was heading to check the voicemail, the phone vibrated, and a call came in. Jarrod was startled and instinctively answered it, cursing that his reflexes had kicked in ahead of his brain. This was a number he didn't know.

"Jarrod speaking," he said in his politest manner.

"Jarrod, yes, Jarrod, oh, hi," came the rather flustered response. "Robert Biscotti here from Zion Films, I was hoping to grab five minutes of your time. You may have spoken with my co-producer Stevie Mosseman already."

"Ah, yes," said Jarrod, remembering that he should have returned that call from last night and immediately feeling guilty for being so short on the phone. "Your colleague caught me at a bad time last night."

"Understood," said Robert. "Now, I don't know how much Stevie discussed with you, but you may have heard the news that a new Harlowe Croft is being lined up. It's all over the television today."

"Yes, I must admit, since last night I've noticed it everywhere."

"So, if I was to offer you the role right now and put you on the spot, what would your first reaction be?"

"I'd say I wouldn't believe you," said Jarrod. He had been plagued with junk calls early in his career, people trying to take advantage of him or bait him into agreeing to something that he didn't want or need. "Who gave you my number?"

"Ah, yes, I do apologise," said Robert in a theatrical tone. "My good friend Duddy may or may not have left his little black book open at the right page when I met up with him last week at the studios."

"You know Duddy?" exclaimed Jarrod incredulously, before acknowledging that Duddy knew everyone. "Of course you do ..."

"We've known Duddy Freiberg for years," said Robert confidently.

"He's a football agent, but he's also a very shrewd agent in the film industry. He loves movies. Has he not mentioned that to you?"

"I had no idea," said Jarrod, starting to warm to Robert.

"Now, the movie is going to be shot on location," said Robert. "Either in the States or in your old stomping ground in Australia …"

"Oh …?" said Jarrod as if he was divulging his interest.

"… and we're confident that it will be Australia," continued Robert, seizing on the crumb of interest. "Your name was thrown around a lot. Who do we know who would fit the look of Harlowe Croft, would be at home in Australia and can act?"

"I can act?" asked Jarrod.

"You can. It doesn't take much to see from your post-match interviews and press conferences that you hold yourself well, like Harlowe Croft. Plus, your advertising debut …"

"You are kidding now."

"No, it's clear that you have what it takes."

"Well, I'm blown away," said Jarrod after a moment of silence.

"Think about it. Let's assume that Duddy will be your managing agent. Shooting for the movie is due to begin in April next year, hopefully only just overlapping with the end of your football season by a week or two."

Jarrod was silent for a moment while he processed what he had just heard.

"When do you need to know?" asked Jarrod. "I mean, that's a big call."

"Sure, we'll give you a day or two before we need to cast the net if you're turning down the opportunity. I'd urge you to think it through, and when you have, just let Duddy know that you're ready to talk again."

"If I need to discuss anything, should I give you a call?" asked Jarrod.

"Yes, this is my direct number," replied Robert. "Save it in your phone. Contact me any time, day or night. This is a key decision in the whole process, and we'd like to have it resolved as soon as we possibly can."

That cemented the importance of the call and added an element of urgency.

"Thanks, er, Robert, was it?" stumbled Jarrod.

"Robert Biscotti, Zion Films," repeated Robert patiently and with a hint of a chuckle in his voice. "We'll hear from you soon."

That call prompted a quick Google search on Jarrod's phone. Sure enough, the first entry for Robert Biscotti, even before he had finished typing the surname, was his entry on the Zion Films 'Our People' page. There were links to movie review pages, biographies on other websites. This was definitely a man with a lot of clout. Jarrod saved his number in his contacts list and typed in 'Harlowe Croft next movie' before he was interrupted by a door opening in the corridor and a cheery whistle, unmistakably the trademark whistle of coach Des Davis.

07

Coach

Jarrod glanced up; Des took that as an invitation to come and sit in the seat on the opposite side of the table. Jarrod smiled. He'd always enjoyed his coach's company and warmed to him as soon as he met him last year at the trials.

"J.B.," said Des, using yet another nickname. "A quick word, if I may?"

Des was now sitting opposite with his elbows on the table, his two hands clasped in front of him. It looked serious. The body language didn't look entirely positive, and Jarrod thought back to the brief discussion he'd had with Pauline earlier on. Maybe this was escalating up the chain.

"Hello, Des," Jarrod said warmly. "What's up?"

"I don't know where to start, to be honest," said Des in a low voice, to suggest secrecy.

Jarrod shuffled in his chair as if he needed to get closer to hear him.

"Hartlepool have been in touch …" he started, then paused to see if that rang any bells.

Jarrod was well aware of Hartlepool United. They were considered by the fans to be the main rivals, despite not having faced each other competitively for a number of years and despite Middlesbrough being closer geographically. Going back in time though, both teams were mainstays of the bottom division of English football and as a result faced each other very regularly. The 'monkey-hangers' of Hartlepool still came up in conversation quite often with locals. Jarrod was intrigued. He raised his eyebrows in anticipation.

"Their manager is being courted for the vacancy at Aberdeen," continued Des. "He's an ex-player and he'll definitely take it. Hartlepool have asked me to consider the position."

Des was agitated about being the centre of attention. He had been manager of a couple of local non-league teams before coming to Darlington, so he was no stranger to being in the hot seat. But he was obviously going through the same emotional turmoil that Jarrod had gone through just a few weeks ago when Newcastle came knocking. Jarrod knew that empathising about his predicament would be of no use to Des.

"How good does it feel to be wanted?" he said instead, before following up with a practical question. "What's the timeline for this happening?"

"I was given a heads up two days ago," Des replied. "And they'll have a vacancy to fill later today if everything goes as expected."

Jarrod smiled. Football rarely involved long drawn-out decisions when it came to players and managers. One day you'd be enjoying life, family settled in the area, the next day you could be in a different town, a new club and even a new country. He felt privileged to be the one that Des confided in, but also happy to be able to impart some relevant advice to his colleague. Des would have come to Jarrod probably to make up his mind that he was going to take it. After all, Jarrod had a track record of decisively making and sticking to decisions.

"I'm going to take it," said Des, popping that thought bubble and letting Jarrod know that there was no decision left to make. "It might take up to a week to happen, but if the opportunity arises as it is scheduled to do so later today, I'm throwing my hat in the ring."

Jarrod's eyes had widened further.

"Which means that we will need a coach to take my place," continued Des, who had leaned even further forward and was speaking in a slightly slower and softer voice.

Jarrod pulled his neck back and gave the Ancelotti eyes.

"And Gary would like that person to be you."

Jarrod sat and stared unblinking at Des.

"You're close to getting your licence," said Des. "You've got the right personality to be a leader, you know the game better than most, and you've still got something to offer on the field."

Jarrod was piecing this together in his head. A quick appraisal of what it would look like if this whole scenario, that was all of fifteen seconds old, came to fruition. The shoe was on the other foot now; it was back to Jarrod being the one with the decision to make.

"Wow," said Jarrod before puffing out his cheeks. "Should I wait for Gary to come to me, or is this an official approach?"

"No, no," said Des, shaking his open hands in front of him and sitting back. "Nothing official. I just wanted to give you a heads up that Gary or even Gerry might be looking to speak with you after the game tonight."

Jarrod watched as Des stood up, as if in a hurry to get out of there now that he had that news off his chest.

"Just a heads up," said Des. "See you in an hour or so."

As Des was about to leave the breakout area and go through the double doors, Jarrod intentionally called out loudly.

"Congratulations, by the way!"

Des stopped, turned and raised his finger to his pursed lips before smiling and disappearing with bluster through the doors. As they flapped to and fro before closing, Jarrod contemplated what he had just heard. And then he glanced down at his phone. It was a message from D.I. Allison asking him to call. He tapped the name, which opened the Signal 7 app and started the private encrypted call.

08

Signal

"Jarrod, thanks for calling straight away," said D.I. Allison.

"Detective Inspector," said Jarrod, using his title instead of his first name for a change. "If you ask me to call, I call. What can I do for you?"

"Just a heads up," said D.I. Allison, repeating the turn of phrase that Des had just coined. "Your friend Yannick Lefevre has been released from custody. You'll see it on the news later tonight. He's in London. Just thought I'd let you know."

Jarrod could feel his skin tighten and goose bumps appeared on his arms. By 'friend', D.I. Allison was referring to an integral member of an illegal international betting syndicate that so nearly got away with a most daring match fix that would have changed the face of English football altogether. Jarrod had often thought back to how Newcastle United would look with those millions of pounds ploughed into the club. They would have an Indian corporate backer and an ageing and increasingly stressed-out midfielder ready to sacrifice his soul for the next fix while the police contemplated their next move to make that all important arrest. It was so close to happening and Jarrod was so grateful that it was wrapped up before it got to that stage.

"Shit," said Jarrod. "That's not good. Are you keeping tabs on him at least?"

"We're not allowed to do that these days," said D.I. Allison. "Although unofficially we'll let you know if he's close by at any point."

Jarrod was buoyed by that—at least he would know if Lefevre was out for revenge at any point. Although he had seemingly got away with murder now that he was back out on the streets.

"Thanks, Marcus," said Jarrod, happy to slip back to using the detective inspector's first name. He did feel as though he was a friend after all they had been through.

"Good luck tonight," said D.I. Allison, forever the football fan. "If you can knock off Bristol Rovers, that'll be a huge statement. Catch up soon."

It sounded a little premonitory. If he was going to catch up soon with D.I. Allison, it would not be for a quick pint, but something a little more sinister. The call ended and Jarrod's phone flicked back to the Google search he had been on originally. Robert Biscotti. Zion Films. Jarrod had some thinking to do.

After some time, he took out his phone again.

"Jarrod, my good man," came the deep Scottish voice at the other end of the call. "I was told that I might hear from you today."

Jarrod had called his agent Duddy Freiberg. Footballing decisions were low on the agenda, it was the entertainment business that Jarrod was hoping to discuss. Even after being kept in the dark by Duddy about this movie and his love for films, Jarrod could not bring himself to be angry with him. After all, he was probably a foot taller than Jarrod and one of his over-sized hands would crush his neck in a fight.

"Hello, Duddy," said Jarrod calmly. "You weren't going to mention Harlowe Croft to me? Stevie Mosseman? Robert Biscotti?"

"The movie industry moves in mysterious ways," said Duddy. "There are things that should come from the movie-makers firsthand, whereas the agents should be there to simply facilitate the transaction."

"So, cutting right to the chase then," said Jarrod, doing just that. "What is on offer here? I mean, do you think I can be the next Harlowe Croft?"

"Of course you can. The actors that you see on your screens are either full-time acting professionals who have grown up in the industry, have attended performing arts schools and are destined for the screen. Or they're like you, a good fit for a role but with no acting credentials whatsoever. Even

Vinnie Jones was good. Well, apart from that dreadful *Eurotrip* movie."

"So, give me an indication of compensation," said Jarrod, using the term in an unfamiliar way. "What would I expect to get paid?"

"First indications are fifteen million pounds for the first movie and double that for any subsequent role. Not bad for less than a year's work. It would be quite intensive though."

Jarrod could feel himself starting to feel cold. A sign of nerves.

"Production is not scheduled to start until April next year," continued Duddy. "But you would need to be in preparation by the end of this year at the latest."

"Right," said Jarrod. "So I would be looking at finding a club in Australia then, if I want to play on. I get the feeling that I would need to make a lot of sacrifices for this."

"You don't get a fifteen million pound pay cheque for nothing. They'll get their pound of flesh in return."

"What should I do, Duddy?" asked Jarrod directly.

Jarrod could hear Duddy rustling papers.

"I'll ask for eighteen million pounds. At least that way you'll test the waters."

Duddy was prepared to enter into a negotiation that he had just manufactured himself. Jarrod couldn't help but laugh out loud.

"But if they say yes to anything over seventeen million, then you have to say yes. Deal?"

"Ha ha, deal," said Jarrod, albeit jokingly. "You know that this is not about money for me. I would hate to leave Darlington in the lurch when they need a push at the end of the season. But I guess if the money is right ..."

"You need to talk to your beautiful wife first, Jarrod," said Duddy. "You would be away from your family for a year, or they would need to relocate with you to wherever they make the movie. And it does look like Australia at this stage—the exchange rate makes it attractive."

"I'll do that tomorrow," said Jarrod, glancing at the clock on the wall. "I'll give you a call back. Eighteen million pounds, Duddy. Does that register the same thoughts for you as it does for me?"

"Oh, just total financial freedom and setting you up for the rest of your life, that's all. Speak with you in the morning."

"Thanks, Duddy," said Jarrod. "I am, as always, in your debt."

That spare two hours had almost been used up. Jarrod's heart was beating faster than usual, and he had a slight mania about him. He leapt to his feet and raced over and through the doors, keen to be one of the first in the cafeteria for the pre-match meal.

09

Rovers

Jarrod surveyed the changing room. Wes gave him a wink; Connor was already fully kitted out and was nervously pacing around. Freddie was wrapping his ankle in a bandage, chatting to himself to get pumped for the game ahead. This was a group of players that he loved. He had left them once already and only the lure of his beloved Newcastle United had been enough to tease him away. This time though he had a post-career opportunity to set himself up for life, a move to his home country to potentially put down new roots—it was almost a clean slate. A quick nudge from physio Sash snapped Jarrod from his thoughts.

"Are you getting ready tonight or what?" asked the puzzled Sash. He was used to Jarrod fiddling with his ankle brace at this stage of the pre-match routine. Jarrod used that as the cue to switch back on to the job in hand. No point in dwelling on the maybes and the distant future. Bristol Rovers was the here and now, and this was a big game.

"Just having a moment to take it all in, Sash," said Jarrod with a wry smile. "Getting ready in my head for the task ahead."

"Whatever you say, Jarrod," came the response from Sash, who turned to help Freddie cut the roll of bandage that was putting up a fight against the scissors.

Jarrod got changed and as usual spent way too long fussing over the brace on his left ankle. Sash was straight over.

"Finding it hard to reach down these days, are you?" said Sash dryly, loosening the laces further and easing the stretch fabric part of the tough brace over Jarrod's ankle. Jarrod smiled at Sash. It *was* more of an effort these days to reach down to his ankle, but he wasn't going to admit it.

Gary and Des were deliberating over the whiteboard in the corner of the room. The players were ready to go out for the warm-up. Jarrod could see that they had both been scribbling different ideas on the board. They seemed to be deep in debate. Gary grabbed the eraser and rubbed the whole thing out, then put his arm around Des, who reciprocated, and they stood for a few seconds arm in arm. This might be the start of the goodbyes. Des turned, still smiling, and ushered the players out for the pre-game warm-up, catching Jarrod's eye with a grin when he passed.

It was a warm evening in the North East of England. The sun had gone down behind the stand and the Arena was looking resplendent. With less than half an hour to kick-off, it was clear that this was going to be a big crowd. The club had done their marketing well. League leaders in town with their international stars, Darlington on the back of good wins, a real test of the home team's promotion credentials even at this early stage. By the time the players had gone back in for the final team talk and were in the tunnel ready to appear, almost every seat was filled. The roar that greeted the players was as exciting as Jarrod had ever experienced in his long career.

Darlington had employed a three-pronged attack of Ghali Barbera, Will Telfer and the on-loan bruiser Anton Broman. That went against the expected defensive line-up with a lone front man. Manager Gary Hollister had played his hand. Bristol Rovers had a reshuffle too, reverting to four at the back from the exciting 3-4-3 formation that had propelled them to the top of the table. Jarrod was impressed by Gary's tactics and the fact that it had prompted a rethink in their opponents. He could feel himself getting more and more pumped up as the seconds ticked to kick-off.

The opening whistle was greeted by a raucous cheer and from that moment the noise barely dropped. Rovers had brought a healthy contingent of away fans that seemed to have filled their generous allocation of seats and they were belting out a continuous repertoire of songs, interjected by chants in response from the home team. Chilton Richards received a huge roar when he touched the ball for the first time, laying it off quickly under close supervision from his marker Peter.

The first half flowed from one end to the other, no real clear chances on goal except for a snap shot from Connor from the left that was palmed away by the visiting keeper to a chorus of "oohs" from the home crowd. That was until Rovers pounced on a loose ball from the back by Raynor. The away team's other central midfielder, Nick Bevin, latched on to the wayward pass, dribbled to the edge of the area to draw Freddie, leaving Ignacio Tollerado free to sweep the ball under Wes to score in front of the home fans. Hands were on heads in the home end as the Chilean striker punched the air right in front of them, earning some choice words from angry faces.

The final five minutes of the first half saw Darlington pour forward, Jarrod whistling a shot just past the post from distance, and Ghali teeing up Will who was crowded out before he could shoot from ten yards. The signs were still positive, and Gary's tone at half time was equally positive. There was no kicking doors or throwing teacups. The players went back out in a positive frame of mind and that was reflected in the opening exchanges of the second half.

Powerhouse midfielder Richards raced away with the ball from a tackle with Dec Hines, but there was Peter to slide in with the perfect tackle to send the six-foot-seven Jamaican sprawling. The crowd reacted and so did Darlington, Jarrod instinctively flicking the ball left to Connor who sped off with a gallop down the wing. His electrifying pace, head back and knees pumping, led him to the byline where he steadied himself and rolled in the perfect cross, in between the goalkeeper and the onrushing players. Anton stretched furthest to steer the ball in at the far post. It was a magnificent goal; Anton was quick to celebrate with Connor and point to the name on Connor's shirt.

Soon after, Raynor leapt high to beat Richards to the header, no mean feat for someone six inches shorter, and his massive clearance was picked up by Will. Never one to beat a defender for pace, Will held off the challenge from two players to steal some time and to get himself in a position to cross. By now his fellow attackers had moved into position and Will swung in a long searching cross. The goalkeeper was in two minds, but came to punch, colliding with his own player, sending them both sprawling to the ground and leaving Anton with time and space to control and shoot past the two Rovers players on the line. Another glorious goal for Darlo, this time an element of fortune, but the finish into the roof of the net was sumptuous.

A series of yellow cards and injuries requiring physio treatment then stalled the game as a spectacle, but the crowd was playing its part in lifting the home side to keep the pressure on. Jarrod feigned to clear with distance with five minutes remaining, instead rolling the ball through his player's legs, and he set off with space opening up in front of him. Connor offered the wide run while Steven Horton galloped down the right to join the attack. With both options looking perfect, another feign to play the pass left the defender wrong-footed and Jarrod slipped the ball inside the left-back for Steva to run on to. The keeper advanced swiftly but the young defender bravely got there first and poked the ball under him and just past the despairing dive of the last defender to squeeze inside the post. Steva raced to the home fans, eyes wide, fists clenched, the joy written all over his face. He was swamped by home fans and then by his teammates, even Wes making the journey up-field to join in the oversized celebrations. This was another moment that gave Jarrod immense satisfaction, seeing a player who had come through the youth set-up score their first goal for the club, and to win the game against the league leaders.

The final whistle was greeted with delight by the fans and more restrained emotion from the home team as they shook hands graciously with their opponents. Raynor jokingly picked up substitute Roni Verelo so he could shake hands with the giant Richards, and the whole team then made their way over to Bay 66 to join the party in the home end. Jarrod stood from a safe distance and took it all in. Steva was mobbed, posing for selfies, signing shirts; Anton was loving it too. Jarrod looked up into the crowd. In the midst of the departing fans, there was a familiar figure standing with his hands in his pockets, smiling. Jarrod wasn't sure at first but then it hit him as he made out the scars across his cheeks.

It was Yannick Lefevre.

As soon as he realised that Jarrod had seen him, Yannick pulled his hands out of his pockets and clapped slowly. He continued clapping as Jarrod turned and was uncharacteristically one of the first players to leave the scene of a majestic victory. Jarrod had an empty feeling in his stomach and could sense his heartbeat quickening and his fists clenching.

He was collared for an interview as he walked towards the tunnel, not forgetting to applaud to the remaining fans in the main stand. He was almost going to brush away the interview but regained some composure and stopped with a smile with the cheery journalist. He had been spooked but was not going to let it spoil the feeling of elation that had enveloped the Arena. The endorphins and adrenaline were all combining, and Jarrod was buoyant in the interview before bounding across to the advertising hoardings to rejoin his teammates who were making their way slowly to the tunnel via a series of high fives and photo opportunities with the fans.

10

Wobble

As soon as all players were accounted for in the changing room, Gary closed the door.

"Lads, lads," he said, trying to attract everyone's attention. "LADS! What a second half. That was as good as anything we served up last season; we've found our groove, haven't we? We've remembered just how good we are. Peter, that was a fantastic performance, Connor that was possibly your best game in a Darlington shirt, and Steva …"

He turned to where the young defender was sitting.

"… what a run, what a goal, what a moment. Steven Horton has arrived!"

The players again all rushed to congratulate him, as if he'd scored again. Everyone was jumping around; it was a golden moment. The players eventually got back to their places in the changing room, some starting to strip off their shin pads and socks.

"We've got some news for you all that we want to share too," said Gary. "Des …"

Des moved forward to address the troops.

"I need to make an announcement," he started. "If I don't talk with you now, I don't think I'll get another chance."

There were puzzled looks between players. Jarrod knew exactly what was going on.

"This evening, I have accepted the role of Hartlepool manager in the National League," continued Des.

There was silence. This was shocking news.

"This has been a very difficult decision for me," he continued. "But I know that I am leaving behind a team that is firing on all cylinders and ready to make an assault on promotion again."

There was a hint of a wobble in his voice. Wes stood up and walked over with an outstretched hand, which Des shook and Wes went in for the hug. Jarrod had the urge to clap his hands and the whole room erupted again. "There's only one Des Davis" rang around the room, even Gary joining in, and the players were all on their feet saluting as they sang. A lovely moment.

Jarrod arrived home that night to a big hug from Marianne. She had heard the news of the big win and the news of his coach leaving. Jarrod needed that hug. There was so much more on his mind than that, but it could wait until the morning when he had a clear head. He stood at the bottom of the stairs in an embrace with his wife. Normally this might turn into something else, but Jarrod was just happy to have the support of his partner to give him some strength to face it all. They walked up the stairs hand in hand.

11

Strong

Marianne breezed in from dropping the kids at school. Jarrod had taken the advice of his own body and slept on through the morning rush, only rousing when Aneka raced in and jumped on the bed knees first to say goodbye. Marianne clanged around in the kitchen, putting plates and pans in cupboards while the kettle came to the boil, and that was enough to get Jarrod out of bed and downstairs.

"Hi, honey," said Marianne with a big smile. She was on a mission and was full of energy.

"Good morning," Jarrod replied, wiping crusts from the corner of his eye with a knuckle. "Oh, how I needed that. Thanks for letting me sleep on through."

"So, what's happening with the coaching job at Darlington?" asked Marianne.

Jarrod looked at her, as if alarmed.

"What do you mean?" he asked.

"Just wondering if they would ever ask you to take on the role of assistant manager," she continued. "I mean, you've been doing your licence. It would be a logical step, no?"

This was very perceptive of Marianne and Jarrod didn't know whether to be wary or incredibly impressed.

"Has someone said something to you about it?" asked Jarrod.

"Oh, it's just been talked about a few times in the past when I've been at your games. You know, Pauline was talking about it only last week when you came back from your course."

"Right," said Jarrod. "Well, let me fill you in."

"Tea or a coffee?" asked Marianne.

"You'll need a strong coffee for this one, I reckon," said Jarrod.

Jarrod sat down at the kitchen bench, while Marianne prepared the coffee, somewhat of a role reversal, and she remained standing, leaning against the counter behind as she took her first sip. Jarrod proceeded to tell Marianne about his discussion with Des yesterday. She looked genuinely delighted for him.

He then went on to tell her about his conversation with D.I. Allison, which saw her smile fade away. She had been spooked by the creepy Yannick Lefevre on holiday only a couple of months ago, and despite the reassurances that the police were watching his every move, the concern was etched on her face. Jarrod didn't say that he had seen him last night. He weighed up the pros and cons of telling her and decided that she didn't need to know that final detail.

He saved the most outlandish story till the end. Starting with the phone calls and the discussion with Duddy, he got to the point and asked Marianne if she understood.

"So, you know Harlowe Croft, right?"

"Of course. Craig Daniels. Hot."

"Well, he's apparently not so hot right now, and they're looking for a new Harlowe Croft actor. They've asked me to play the role. Shooting starts in April next year, probably in Australia."

Jarrod wasn't sure what the reaction would be.

"Ha ha, nice one, Jay Jay," said Marianne. "Do you think I was born yesterday?"

Jarrod stared at her with wide eyes until she realised that this wasn't a joke.

"WHAT?" she exclaimed. "You're the next Harlowe Croft? No way…"

"Yes way," said Jarrod, as Marianne walked around to the other side of the bench and stood next to him.

"You're joking," she said again. It was a totally unbelievable story after all.

"What do I need to do to convince you?" asked Jarrod.

"I don't know. I believe you," she said with increasing volume and excitement in her voice.

Jarrod pulled out his phone as if to show her something then realised all he had was a couple of calls in his call history from random numbers. He did remember saving the very first voicemail he got from Stevie Mosseman as it had a phone number in it. He rang his voicemail and flicked through a few messages before playing the message on loudspeaker.

Marianne's hands grabbed Jarrod's arm.

"You're going to be a movie star? You are going to be the next Harlowe Croft? Is this for real?"

Jarrod and Marianne stayed at home that morning. Jarrod didn't have to be anywhere until early afternoon and Marianne turned down a coffee with one of the mums from school so they could talk. Jarrod had three, maybe four options.

"So," he said, opening his left hand and pointing to his thumb with his right. "Option one, I stay at Darlington as a player and complete my coaching badges before I look at accepting any coaching role."

Marianne nodded.

"Two," he said, sitting up straight in the stool. "I stay at Darlington and take the player coach role, while also finishing off my licence."

He thought for a second.

"That sounds like a busy option."

Marianne gave the hurry-up signal.

"Option three. I take this opportunity to become a movie actor, and go off to Australia, or wherever the filming is taking place, and I'm away for the best part of a year."

Marianne rocked back on her stool at that point. Jarrod took that as a cue to move on to the next option.

"And option four: this movie opportunity is in Australia, and we all move over there. I get a club over there and play while I finish off my badges and then filming starts."

"Let me stop you right there," said Marianne. "Why didn't you start with that as option one? That's what we should do. We all love it here, right? But we've loved it every time we've gone to Australia, and you've always said it would be a great place to bring up a family."

Jarrod was taken aback—Marianne had loved her time over there on holiday, but moving to another country, and a country so far away from everything they knew as a couple and as a family, was a different proposition. He then remembered that Marianne herself had made the move to England and that they had already moved the family from Gateshead to Darlington. They were quite practised at upheaval. The journey to the Pyrenees to see her family took the best part of a day, so what was a few more hours on a plane?

"You're already there, aren't you?" asked Jarrod. He stood up and lifted Marianne onto the bench in front of him. They kissed passionately, which led in turn to quite the scene on the big couch in front of the fireplace. If this was what turmoil and worry felt like, he was up for more.

12

Exotic

"Ah, shit, look at the time," chuckled Jarrod as they lay entangled in each other. "Training in forty minutes, where did the morning go?"

He leapt to his feet and searched for his clothes, before running up the stairs to jump in the shower. He heard Marianne coming up the stairs as he reached for a new towel from the laundry cupboard. The sight of his wife, naked, hair ruffled and flushed in the cheeks, Jarrod couldn't help but stop and watch as she calmly walked up the stairs and past him with a cheeky smirk and disappeared into the bedroom. He'd hit the jackpot with Marianne, he thought. The coolest chick, the exotic French-ness, a fantastic role model to her children and a perfect physical and emotional match in the bedroom. She had also been through a huge breast cancer journey this year and had the scars to prove it, but her hair had grown back sufficiently to get styled in the slicked-back, shaved-around-the-sides look that a warrior princess might sport in a superhero movie. Jarrod found her more and more attractive as the years passed. He just couldn't believe his luck in finding the right partner at the right time. If there was someone he wanted to go through the next phase of his life with, when playing football was replaced with something else, it was definitely her.

Quickly showered and finding all his training kit, he afforded himself a quick cuddle with Marianne before racing out of the house to the car. The gravel danced off the wheel arches as he showed his haste to get on the road to the Arena. He was now in his office. This was where he had become accustomed to making all his life's big decisions—in the car. It was quality time with his phone, and he put that time to immediate effect, ringing Dad. The phone rang a few times before he answered.

"You have to be joking, Jarrod," said Dad with a croaky voice. "If it's not Anna ringing me at all hours of the day, it's you ringing me at 4:00 a.m.!"

"Ah, thought you might be up already. The older you get, the earlier you get up out of bed, isn't that right?"

"Cheeky bast—" said Dad, before realising that he was on speaker and there might be others in the car. "You're ringing for a reason, aren't you?"

"This is a bit mad," said Jarrod as he concentrated on passing a couple of cyclists with enough room. "But what would you say if I were to star in a movie?"

"A movie? What kind of movie?" asked Dad, who sounded sceptical.

"A big-budget-box-office-smash kind of movie," said Jarrod. "You know Harlowe Croft, right?"

Of course Dad knew Harlowe Croft. It had been around for years and years, since when Dad was courting Mum, and it had become an international phenomenon that transcended language and culture.

"Harlowe Croft? 'Straight glass, no water, no ice', that guy?"

"The very same."

"You are joking, right?" said Dad, sounding less croaky and more engaged than before.

"Why does everyone think I'm joking?" exclaimed Jarrod. "Why wouldn't I be a good fit for the role?"

"You're not joking, then?" asked Dad.

Jarrod filled in his dad about the opportunity that had fallen his way, about the chance to become a coach with Darlo and also about last night's game. He had already arrived at the Arena and was still sitting in the car as he watched his teammates arrive and walk over to the entrance. Dad sounded enthusiastic about each of the scenarios. He seemed most keen for him to complete his licence, in the same way that a father would be keen for his son to finish his studies before heading off into his first full-time job.

"Dad, you've given me great input, as always," said Jarrod to wrap up the call. "I'll ring Mr Leonard later today. This is all off the record, as you can imagine. Training's due to start soon, so I can't be late."

"Okay, son, pass on my love to Marianne and the kiddas," said Dad. "Harlowe Croft … heh heh …"

The phone went dead. Jarrod still didn't think Dad believed him. He did make a mental note to call Mr Leonard, his first agent when his career was starting out, someone who had been a mentor and a Mr Fixit during his and his sister Anna's career. Just as he was getting out of the car, his phone pinged. It was D.I. Allison. He couldn't ignore this one.

"Detective Inspector," said Jarrod. "Good to hear from you."

"Hello, Jarrod," said D.I. Allison. "Good performance last night, well done in knocking off the league leaders."

"Thanks, it was a great result. Look, I'm due in at training right now …"

"Jarrod, we have reason to believe that Yannick Lefevre is in the area."

"Yes," said Jarrod, trying to keep his emotions in check, "I know. He was at the game last night. I saw him in the crowd."

"You're joking."

"Why doesn't anyone believe me at the moment?" asked Jarrod. He was agitated.

"Sorry, Jarrod," said D.I. Allison, composing himself. "What I meant was, are you sure it was him?"

"Oh, I'm sure all right," confirmed Jarrod. "Scars across his cheeks. Tall. Wild black hair. It was your man, for sure."

"Keep your eye out. And if you see him again, can you please let me know as soon as you do?"

"Ah, yes, sorry about that. Lots happening at the moment. I'll fill you in when I know more. Gotta dash."

"Intriguing," said D.I. Allison. "Take care, Jarrod."

13

Beckoned

Jarrod sprinted to the front entrance of the Arena and his shoulders slumped immediately when he saw that he was three minutes late. Perhaps no one would notice. He breezed into the changing room and the whole squad was there. There was a big cheer. They were all pointing at the top of their wrists. He wasn't going to get away with this. That would be a hefty fine into the coffers for the end of season. Jarrod didn't even put up a fight and took his place and started to get changed as his teammates started to file out on to the field.

The turf at the Arena was unreal—despite training on it often and despite it being used for rugby games every other week while the local rugby club built their all-purpose boutique stadium nearby, the surface was as good as any that Jarrod had played on. The longer grass, maybe a requirement for the oval ball game, was like a cushion underfoot, and any grazes would not be from the dirt or from the uneven surface, it would be from the grass, like a burn.

This training session was quite intense, even though they had played the night before, and they were put through their paces by Gary himself, with strength and conditioning coach Andy Willson taking a more active role in the absence of Des. Andy was used to being involved in the rehabilitation of injured players and focusing on individuals, but he was out here with the group and seemed very comfortable with the role.

The session ended, as it often did, with a full-field game. Gary had entrusted two of the players, a midfielder from each team, with a scenario that they would need to manufacture. The other players didn't know what it was. It was designed to address an issue from the last night's game, or from previous games, that they needed to work on. Gary had done this in the past and it had engaged the players so well. When the situation did occur, they would yell out "stop!" and have a chat about it to make sure everyone could see it. Jarrod was intrigued. It was straight from the Pro Licence handbook, and when it was done right, it was an instant learning tool for the whole team.

Gary left Andy to it. He walked over to Jarrod and beckoned him over to the sideline.

"Jarrod," he said, turning to face his midfield man. "I don't know if the timing is right for you, but we have a coaching vacancy here at Darlington. Des is training with his new club this afternoon; Andy has stepped up today, but we need a full-time coach to take the place of Des. I'd like you to be that new coach."

Jarrod looked at Gary and felt obliged to feign surprise. He couldn't bring himself to do it though.

"Des mentioned it to me," he eventually said. "And I was getting worried when Pauline pulled me up on being away at my course."

"Ah, yes," said Gary. "I did talk with Pauline to try and find out how long you had to go on your licence. I think she may have taken it the wrong way."

"I think so too," said Jarrod.

"Anyway," continued Gary. "The offer is there. Initially I would like you to be player-coach, at least for the rest of the season. Then we can work out what happens next when we reach May and we know where this club is going."

"I'm flattered."

"But are you interested?"

"Of course I'm interested. You might just need to give me a day or two to mull this over. Andy's doing a good job today, he seems to be the right sort of character for the role."

"Andy's too precious to us in other areas. But yes, I agree, he's engaging the players very well. Tell me, you've got another six months left of your Pro Licence, right?"

"Graduation in April at this stage."

"So why don't we give you some first-hand experience while you finish that off and we can make you full-time player-coach once you've completed it? It'll give you a reason to complete it—if you're anything like me, you'll get distracted, and it'll take you another three years to finish it otherwise."

Jarrod laughed. It had already taken him so long to get this far, and he had enjoyed having a little more time to give it since his return to Darlington. To finish it would be a massive achievement.

"Let's talk on Friday about it," said Jarrod, giving himself a tiny two-day window to get things in place and make key decisions about his future. He had never had the luxury of so much time, but then again, he had never had this much on his mind.

He shook hands with Gary and ran off to rejoin the game.

14

Perceptive

"Mr Leonard!" exclaimed Jarrod when his old agent answered the phone on the second ring. Jarrod was once again in his 'office', ready to drive home.

"Oh, Jarrod, such a pleasure to hear from you," said Mr Leonard. "Are you settling back into life in Darlington?"

"Darlington is fantastic. There's always a but though."

"Right …?"

"I have an opportunity to return to Australia."

"An opportunity?" enquired Mr Leonard. "You coming to play for Sydney FC?"

"No, no, it's a … er … business opportunity, but I would still want to play football at a good level."

"Well, there's a change of direction I never saw coming," said Mr Leonard. "I had you down as someone who would move into TV punditry. And then after you're fully qualified, off into coaching."

Jarrod paused while he processed what he'd just heard. It was how he had hoped it would unfold too.

"Well, let's say that remains a possible path," said Jarrod eventually, the pause hopefully attributed to the delay in the line. "But as it stands there is a very big possibility that I'm going to be in Australia maybe from the end of this year and for the rest of next year. But I'm not ready to end my playing days just yet."

Mr Leonard had never heard Jarrod so definitive. Jarrod had always come to him for advice on what to do.

"Okay, so you're not at liberty to tell me what this opportunity is," said

Mr Leonard perceptively. "But you're looking at the possibility of playing in Australia next season?"

"That's about it," said Jarrod. "I'm not able to disclose any details at this stage, Mr Leonard. The annoying thing is that I don't have any knowledge of the Australian scene, to be honest. The landscape has changed so much since I was there, and I'm hearing that the national second division is joining the A-League this year. I was hoping you could point me in the right direction, if you can't help me yourself."

"You've caught me at a good time, Jarrod," said Mr Leonard. "This Division 2 has sent a lot of business my way. I was hoping to retire soon, but we've got fourteen clubs crying out for new talent, an actual transfer system that generates money for the clubs, and a lot of funds coming in from a new TV deal and some incredible sponsorship deals. It's a good time to be an agent. Where are you thinking?"

"Where am I thinking?" asked Jarrod, "Good question. I'll have to find out where I'll be based. Let's just say I'm interested to know what the process would be. Would you be able to represent me as my agent in Australia?"

"Yes, Jarrod," said Mr Leonard, after his own dramatic pause. "Yes, I would."

"Thank you, Mr Leonard," said Jarrod. "I'll be in touch very soon with some more details."

Jarrod was still in the car park. He had driven across to the gate but had pulled over at the side to concentrate on the call. He contemplated the next call, then drove off through the gate and on to the road back home.

15

Military

Jarrod boarded the train at Darlington bound for Kings Cross. He found a spot for his Football Australia-branded suitcase and walked into the first-class carriage, up the aisle to his seat. There was Jan Haratounan, Socceroos teammate and Hearts forward, sitting asleep in the window seat with his head leaning awkwardly on the window. Jan and Jarrod had shared a room in their last Socceroos adventure that took them to Prague and Geneva for two top-class friendlies, and they had done some sightseeing together too. Jarrod gave Jan a nudge with his knee as he put his backpack above his head in the luggage rack.

"Terminus, terminus, all passengers disembark," said Jarrod in a voice that was very much like the Fat Controller from *Thomas the Tank Engine*.

Jan's eyes opened and he stared at Jarrod for a moment then broke into a smile.

"Ach, you had me going there for a moment," he said. "Just catching up on some much-needed shut-eye."

"How's your season started?" asked Jarrod, who hadn't caught up yet after the Saturday fixtures.

Darlington had won again, this time brushing Oxford United aside on the road, a 2–0 win lifting them into the play-off places. The long coach journey home saw the team bus arrive back at Darlington late at night and Jarrod had felt compelled to get up early this morning and head into the gym at the Arena for an hour to loosen up. It was now just gone midday and Jan would have been on the train for an hour and a half already.

"It's started very well, Jarrod," said Jan. "This could be the year when the Jambos bring the league trophy back to Edinburgh."

"Wow, that would be a turn-up for the books," said Jarrod, whose knowledge of Scottish football history didn't extend beyond the dominant Glasgow teams of Celtic and Rangers and the mighty St Johnstone who he'd trialled with back in his youth.

"Did you win yesterday?" asked Jan.

"Yes," said Jarrod with enthusiasm. "We beat Oxford United at their place and we're humming now. I take it you won too."

"Aye, we did," said Jan in his Scottish Australian accent. "We beat Rangers at Ibrox 1–0, goal to Haratounan. Say, what happened to you after I saw you last? Sounds like you had a bit of an adventure."

Jarrod looked at Jan and nodded with his eyes wide open.

"Unbelievable, it was," said Jarrod. "I was roped in as a man on the inside for the police under the pretence of a transfer to Newcastle. Got involved in some seriously shady stuff and the police made loads of arrests. It's still all going on now. Still, I got my moment in the sun, and got to play against Barcelona at St James' Park. What a thrill."

"Oh yeah, that's your team too, isn't it? Boyhood dream fulfilled. What's the next thing on your bucket list?"

"Hey, steady on, I'm not that old. Plenty of dreams still to come true. Starting with these two games. What do you know about Lebanon as a team?"

"Not much, mate," said Jan. "They've never been to the World Cup but they're getting closer. I can imagine it'll be a stadium full of crazies."

The train journey went so quickly, the two friends locked in conversation until Peterborough when James Bain, a young Cambridge United player who had signed during the transfer window from nearby MK Dons, joined them and they chatted all the way to Kings Cross. The journey wasn't over yet—this was the first part of an intricately planned Socceroos trip, and they were to meet in a café in the station. Jarrod found this planning almost military, and players were to text in their arrival times at each point on the way. Jarrod could envisage team manager Rhett sitting in a control room plotting out each of the players' movements and reacting to any delays and missed connections with ruthless efficiency.

Jarrod's group was meeting with two more players at Kings Cross who were due to arrive in fifteen minutes, then they would catch a tube to Paddington to meet another player before the final destination at Heathrow Airport at the priority check-in counter. That's where they would meet with the rest of the UK-based players.

The journey was seamless. Jan knew this route very well after his numerous Socceroos trips. They met up at Heathrow with two players who lived within driving distance of the airport and once they had gone through the priority gate at customs, they assembled in the Qantas lounge with even more players who had flown in from nearby cities in Europe. Mike Jerszek, the Socceroos coach, greeted the incoming group of players with a handshake. Jarrod spotted Ed Charrah and bounded over to say hello. This was real therapy for Jarrod, who had been feeling the weight of the key life decisions that were being made.

16

Financial

Game one of this two-game international break was a trip to the Camille Chamoun stadium in Beirut, to play Lebanon on Thursday evening. This was seen as the toughest of the two games, the home game with Kyrgyzstan on Tuesday in Melbourne being a game that was earmarked for a goal-difference-enhancing three points. The overseas-based players would then fly out on Wednesday morning for a gruelling return leg that would see them land, thanks to the different time zones, on the evening of the same day back at Heathrow. Jarrod had no qualms about doing the journey. He was loving the late renaissance of his Socceroos career and felt as though he had an extra reason to be on the plane ultimately bound for Australia.

Jarrod grabbed a copy of *The Times* on the way onto the plane from the rack of free newspapers, knowing that it would have a full wrap of the weekend results, but didn't get to open it until well after take-off. The Socceroos players were in business class for the first leg to Dubai, which Jarrod loved, and they were all excited to be on the plane together and able to relax and chat. They all ended up around the horseshoe-shaped bar area with vodka and gin-based concoctions disguised as soft drinks, and the first two hours of the flight went very quickly.

Settling back into the comfortable reclining seats, Jarrod took out his newspaper and noticed a small piece on the front page:

TWO RELEASED AS FA AND POLICE MISS THEIR TARGET

Jarrod's eyes scanned the piece, and he could feel his face reddening. He flicked through the pages to find the rest of the article. Jens Lermann and

Murtaka Chiya, instrumental characters in the match-fixing scandal that Jarrod had helped to uncover, had joined Yannick Lefevre in being released from police custody. This was outrageous, thought Jarrod. How could that happen? They were both one hundred percent guilty as far as Jarrod was concerned. There were other players in the crime, so perhaps all blame had been pinned on one unfortunate soul. Jarrod read on and saw that Viktor Andreyev had been refused bail and had been charged under anti-corruption laws that had recently been passed. He looked like the fall guy.

Jarrod had four more hours of a flight to Dubai and then a shorter hop to Lebanon, and he was now fidgeting in his seat, unable to concentrate on any of the in-flight entertainment or the football scores from the weekend. His mind was whirring. What did it all mean? He didn't get any sort of relaxation until the last half an hour when they were due to land, when he fell asleep.

The stop in Dubai was scheduled to be very short, the players being transferred via a minibus to the terminal and escorted without customs checks to another area where they awaited a charter flight for the remaining four-hour flight to Beirut. Jarrod had relaxed a little by now but was using the time at the gate to read as much as he could about the match-fixing situation. They were still in the waiting area two hours later and questions were beginning to be asked of Mike. The plane was there, ready to go, but they weren't boarding. A set of double doors opened soon after, and all the Australian-based Socceroos walked through to the gate in a noisy pack. The players who had been waiting patiently suddenly found their energy and there were hugs and handshakes as the two sets of players greeted each other. Team manager Rhett was quick to make his first announcement.

"Hello, everyone," he said, clapping his hands to get everyone's attention. "We're all here now, well done for making it to Dubai. We now travel together as a squad, and we go to Beirut together as one. Enjoy this final leg of your journey."

The players were buzzing now. Rhett looked like a man with a big weight lifted off his shoulders. There were twenty-two players from all corners of the globe, even Stef Rodovic who had signed to play in the MLS with Inter Miami. His journey would have been the longest of them all, but he looked as fresh as he always did.

The flight now boarded, Jarrod was sitting next to Kareem Al-Hussein, the Socceroos number one keeper and an A-League champion with high-flying Adelaide United. He was on various panels of player organisations in Australia and an ambassador at the PFA. Jarrod had hoped he would get to talk with him at length, and luckily Kareem was in a chatty mood. They caught up with family talk, news of comings and goings in the A-League, and Kareem was interested to hear about life in the lower leagues of English football. The chat turned to the structure of Australian football, something that had greatly interested Jarrod and was now pertinent to his situation. Mr Leonard had already suggested that it was boom time in Australia, but Kareem stoked that even further.

"Ever since the A-League had a shake-up," said Kareem, "the quality of players coming in from overseas has been outrageous."

"What do you mean? There's always been good players coming in. Dwight Yorke, Del Piero, Diamante: there are three names I can give you."

"Yes, but now that Division 2 is starting for real this year, we have fourteen more clubs with marquee positions ready to fill."

"They don't still have that ridiculous marquee nonsense, do they?" asked Jarrod.

"Ha ha, yes, we do," said Kareem. "And you know what, it's a great idea. We've got our own Financial Fair Play rules in place so clubs can't buy up all the best players, but there's always two spots in each club for two massive signings. No restriction on cost, no restriction on wage. Clubs can afford it too; there's big money now that we've got new sponsors and a new TV company."

"A new TV company?" asked Jarrod, surprised that there was another player in that marketplace after Paramount Plus had stormed the castle.

"Yes, Lermann Sports has just taken over everything," said Kareem excitedly, happy to be bringing some fresh news to his teammate. "They just signed the deal yesterday, or today, whatever day it is now."

"So, no Optus or Fox?" asked Jarrod.

"In the end Optus was outbid by Lermann, or LF Sports, as it's known. It's a betting company," said Kareem.

"Far out, that's healthy competition," said Jarrod. "That sounds bloody incredible, in fact."

"It is, it is," continued Kareem in his excitable manner. "We're not just talking tens of millions of dollars either. This is serious. Football arrived in Australia after the Women's World Cup and the whole country is getting into it."

Jarrod and Kareem continued their chat right until they got off the plane in Beirut. Jarrod asked Kareem whether he would entertain coming to Europe for some experience.

"Are you kidding, Jarrod?" said Kareem as they congregated with the rest of the players in the Arrivals Hall. "This is the golden generation for football in Australia. You're the one who should be coming over to ride the wave."

Little did Kareem know that it was music to Jarrod's ears. Jarrod had a spring in his step for the rest of the journey to the hotel, and once he'd checked in and settled into his room with Jan, he had almost forgotten about match-fixing and people being released from custody. It didn't take long for his attention to return to it though; the front page of the international business newspaper in the room had its leading story titled:

LF SPORTS FREE TO INVEST IN AUSTRALIAN SPORT

Jens Lermann had been released from custody, and his company LF Sports, part of the Chiya Inc conglomerate of companies out of India, was set to pump over USD 100 million into its coverage of Australian football. Those names, it was no coincidence. Murtaka Chiya, the svelte Indian businesswoman who had tried to raise the funds to buy his beloved Newcastle United with dirty money, and Jens Lermann, the Scandinavian-sounding businessman from the North East of England. Jarrod shook his head in disbelief. A quick Google search on his phone revealed LF Sports was indeed yet another company in the betting space. This all looked incredibly shady.

17

Lebanon

Beirut was nothing like Jarrod had expected. It was cosmopolitan Europe with a heavy slice of Middle Eastern charm. Jarrod was ready for strict security and guns everywhere but was surprised when they were given freedom of the hotel and the surrounding area. This was though a city where the car was king. The French and American influences here were obvious in the street names, and there were cars parked everywhere and anywhere the closer they got to the tourist areas. The training facilities at the American University were a little basic and one of the synthetic fields was exposed to the sea, but coach Jim Grant had been assured that it was good practice ahead of Thursday for the conditions inside the main stadium.

The players warmed to their surroundings. It gave the feel of being in camp in the army. Everyone was pulling in the same direction, and no one was game to play up or go walkabout in the unknown streets of the city. When it came to game time, the players were focused and looking sharp in the new Socceroos kit that was making its debut that night. As predicted, the stadium was in a frenzy before they walked out for the warm-up. There were just shy of fifty thousand people in the stadium and a small pocket of Australian fans bedecked in their yellow shirts and scarves. The volume was high as they left the field, but nothing compared to when they walked out onto the field for the game. Jarrod sung the wrong words in the national anthem, forgetting to substitute the 'young' for 'one' which made him wince and lose his concentration as the camera panned across him.

The Lebanese national anthem was something else. The roar of the crowd and the upbeat military trumpet that accompanied the singer made the hairs stand up on Jarrod's forearms. This was a country united, and the atmosphere that it created was electrifying. The players were in place, Jarrod having been called up in his favoured deep-lying central midfield position, and the whistle sounded to unleash a wall of noise.

The first five minutes were enough to take your breath away. The pace was unrelenting, and the crowd reacted to everything the Lebanon players did. Kareem dealt with an early cross, and two corners in quick succession in the opening minutes were well dealt with by the Australia defence. Jarrod ran as much as he had all season in the first fifteen minutes of a game, and barely had a touch. A tough tackle from midfielder Dane Radzinski was adjudged to be within regulations and Dane continued with the ball despite the vociferous protestations of the Lebanese players. He evaded a reckless lunging tackle to square the ball to Jarrod who had kept up with the surprise break. Jarrod let the ball roll through his legs, collecting a fierce shoulder-barge to the chest for his troubles, leaving Jan to run on to the ball with the referee waving to play on. There was time and space for the cross and up rose Ed to power a header under the bar and in for 1–0. The Socceroos players raced to congratulate him, Jarrod still recovering from the hit and being helped to his feet by the player who had collected him. They had their breakthrough, smash and grab, but they had seventy-four minutes to go. Even the most experienced time wasters knew that it was about an hour too early to start that charade.

Instead, Mike instructed his players to take the game to the hosts to try and force another. Jarrod sprayed a ball wide for Mitchell Moore, who jinked around his man and set off down the line. Jan raced towards the box, Ed hung at the edge, but Jarrod had set off on a deep run to the far post. Mitch lifted the ball beyond the last defender and Jarrod reached out with an outstretched right leg to hook the ball back over the keeper and into the corner of the net for 2–0. What a goal! Jarrod was feeling it after making that lung-busting run and on the back of that big hit he had taken earlier.

There was no way he was going to let anyone know that he was struggling for breath, and instead took the opportunity to balloon a clearance out over the athletics track and into the stand with his next contribution.

The half time talk centred around impetus and momentum. Mike wanted a third goal to kill the game off, whereas captain Nikos Galanos was concerned with keeping the clean sheet and not giving the hosts a sniff at goal. Despite their early dominance, Lebanon had not tested Kareem. No changes at the break, and Jarrod had a quick massage of his tender ribs from physio Alex Covac before the players returned to the field for the second half.

What looked like some ultra-conservative defensive play from the visitors was craftily designed to draw out the Lebanon team and stretch the play. Nikos turned the ball back to Stef when he had all the room in the world to go forward, and Stef feigned to lose control of the ball to draw in a challenge. With that, the Socceroos were off, and a swift ball forward to Ed saw him lay the ball off to young winger Miles Carter. He followed orders and went for it, touching the ball around his man, and racing towards goal. The temptation to offload to Jan in the middle was ignored and Miles smashed a shot from the edge of the area that flew past the outstretched arm of the Lebanon keeper for a majestic third goal. The players swarmed around Miles, scorer of his first goal for Australia on only his second appearance. Mike was now ready to close up shop, and both Nikos and Jarrod were ordered to drop deeper.

The positive from the rest of the game was that Australia controlled the play. There was limited attack, but their staunch defence won plaudits from all the pundits and commentators watching. The post-match interview by Mike demonstrated a manager full of confidence in his players, and he singled out Stef and Jarrod for their patience and organisation in the middle of the park. Jarrod and the rest of the team had made their way over to the away fans and were offloading shirts and taking selfies. This had been a fabulous result and Jarrod was feeling 100% part of the first-team squad, as well as feeling a little tender around his rib cage.

That evening, Rhett had organised a full-on Lebanese feast at the hotel, following the previous two days of carefully prepared standard Australian fare. It was a fantastic idea, and the players were all relaxed and enjoying themselves. This was as good as any bonding session that Jarrod had ever known. The three points they had achieved tonight and the manner in which they had disposed of the home side: that was the mark of a professional team. Jarrod could feel himself becoming more and more ingrained in the Socceroos way, and with all the talk of the A-League from the home-based players, he was sure there were some key decisions ready to be made.

18

Pride

"We're coming over," said Marianne.

"For real?" asked Jarrod.

"We're at Newcastle Airport now," said Marianne excitedly.

Jarrod and Marianne had discussed making the trip to Australia together, but the timing wasn't ideal with the kids just back at school and with Jarrod effectively in camp. Marianne though had done all the spade work and had organised the most direct flight from Newcastle to Melbourne via Dubai. It should have been no surprise. She had often done things on a whim and following her recent brush with cancer she had a newfound zest for brand-new experiences. This was quite an undertaking though and she would have been planning it way before Jarrod had left.

"Wow, you might beat me there, we're just leaving now for the airport in Beirut," said Jarrod. "Did you see my goal?"

"Your dad sent it to me this morning," said Marianne. "Wasn't exactly live on TV here. Nice finish!"

Those were two words that Jarrod loved hearing. Words that showed an understanding of the game, words that showed that football was in her blood. Jarrod could feel his heart rate increase.

"Can't wait to see you," he said. "See you in Melbourne. You've told my dad, haven't you?"

"Of course."

Jarrod raced back into the foyer of the hotel to see that the players had disappeared and there were only a few bags left over. The bus had almost boarded, and Jarrod raced to join the stragglers at the door. They were off to the airport moments later, leaving behind good memories of a trip to another country he would have never visited if it weren't for football, but one he could see himself going back to.

The flight back to Dubai was on the same plane that had brought them there, or at least that was what it felt like. Boarding at the gate at Dubai onto the monster A380 in business class, the feeling of community and pride of getting on a plane bound for Australia was stronger than ever. There were only a handful of passengers not in their group, an ageing couple and another two businessmen who were already on the champagne before take-off. They effectively had business class to themselves again.

The quality bonding time was just what they needed, but they knew that past incidents on planes involving the national teams meant they had to be well-behaved. The players all knew each other from previous games and camps, but these hours spent together were priceless. They were meant to be resting for the first six hours, but Jarrod was full of energy and was in conversation with coach Ollie Rescher in the bar area at the back of the cabin.

"Have you had any thoughts about where you want to finish your playing career, Jarrod?" was one question that Ollie threw in.

"Do you have any recommendations?" asked Jarrod, who knew that Ollie had been a top player in his native Germany and in Turkey before finishing his career at Perth Glory, playing until he was thirty-eight. He had since lived and worked in Australia and was a good yardstick for Jarrod.

Ollie thought for a moment. "I'd say, play until you can't play anymore," he said. "Don't let them tell you you're past it. If a club wants you, and a manager wants to play you, you're good enough and you're better than someone else in your position. Don't give it up just because you're getting old; give it up when you're ready."

"Sound advice, Ollie," said Jarrod, who was, in reality, fishing for someone to validate his potential move to Australia. "I see that a lot of players are staying in Australia now, and some are being attracted back now that the leagues have changed."

"Oh yes," said Ollie. "If there was ever a time to be a Socceroos player based in Australia, it's now. COVID-19 changed all that, and now that we've got two divisions and a transfer market, the landscape has changed completely. People actually want to come and play in Australia to further their careers!"

This was a revelation for Jarrod. The era of players making it their career goal to head to Europe was over. Sure, the money was lucrative elsewhere, but it seemed to Jarrod that Australia was catching up and the quality of living in his home country was a big drawcard to players looking for a better life for themselves and their families. Could it be that Harlowe Croft had just presented him with the opportunity of a lifetime?

19

Stark

The squad touched down in Melbourne at some ungodly hour of Saturday morning. The sun was nowhere to be seen. The terminal building was busy though, with a number of flights arriving and departing at the crack of dawn. The heat of Dubai, the pleasant warmth of Beirut and the sunshine in London hadn't prepared Jarrod for the biting wind and horizontal rain that lashed the windows of the terminal. The players were joking with each other how it was good to be home; Jarrod, though, knew that it was no joke. The reality of early spring at Tullamarine Airport was a reminder that it wasn't all thongs and barbies in Australia.

The players raced through the five metres of weather to board their bus right in front of the terminal building. A lone photographer was there in his wet weather gear capturing the moment. It was stark. The smell of rain was thick—it had obviously not been raining for some time and the dead grass in the fields as they made their way along the freeway was a testament to that.

The Pullman Hotel at Albert Park was beautiful. Jarrod had forgotten just how good hotels were in his homeland. No pretence, just good-looking décor and well-designed layouts. This would be their base for the next four days. Training would take place at the nearby Lakeside Stadium, home to South Melbourne FC, a club that Jarrod knew about through his old friend and teammate from his Parramatta days, Danny Zorbas. Tales of twenty-thousand crowds and a history that included games in the Maracana against Manchester United and the likes made the club, with a heavy Greek influence, a romantic feature of the Australian football landscape.

The hotel still proudly displayed its claim as the home of the Matildas for the FIFA Women's World Cup, which brought Jarrod's sister Anna into his thoughts. This was her town. She had made her name with a premiership at Melbourne City and had starred in a fantastic World Cup that catapulted her as one of the top female sports people in the world. As the players were being allocated rooms at the front desk, with Rhett making last minute adjustments to the names, Jarrod pulled out his phone and called Anna. It would be a reasonable time over there, Jarrod hoped.

"Oh my goodness," came the cheery voice, laden with sarcasm, at the other end. "Is that my brother calling me on the phone?"

"Go on, guess where I am?" asked Jarrod.

"Ha ha, you must be in Dubai, no?" said Anna. "No, you're in Melbourne!"

"At the Pullman, no less," said Jarrod. "You know the place well, eh?"

"Oh my god, yes," said Anna. "We stayed there for a night during the World Cup. You're not far from my apartment! Are Mum and Dad there too?"

"Not yet," said Jarrod, not sure what Marianne had organised. "But Marianne and the kiddas are arriving today too. Family reunion!"

"Argghhh!" roared Anna down the phone. "How come we can never meet up all together? Not fair!"

"You'll be pleased to hear it's thrashing it down with rain here too. Welcome to Australia. I can see why you left Melbourne."

"Ah, I miss it so much. Hey, how many tickets can you get? Get as many as you can. I've got some people who would love to see you play."

"I'll have a go at getting some; I'm already looking for five!"

"Good goal too, bruv. Prolific in your old age."

"Thanks," said Jarrod, already starting to realign to the sisterly ribbing and able to distinguish between what was genuine and what was sarcastic. "Got to keep up with you in the goals column for Australia."

"Gotta go, Jarrod," said Anna abruptly. "At training and it's serious! Talk to you when you're with everyone. Love you!"

Jarrod instantly felt at home, even though his sister was somewhere in the North West of the USA. Jarrod and Jan had been paired together again, much to their delight, and Jan had already beckoned Jarrod to the lift where he'd finished the call. Jan put his arm around Jarrod.

"Brits abroad," he said. "That's us."

Little did he know that Jarrod was preparing to chuck it all in and return home to his country of origin.

20

Happiness

Jarrod's phone beeped. He had been snoozing while Jan was crashed out. They had until 1:00 p.m. when they were due to meet for lunch on the club floor. Jarrod picked up his phone and saw that it was only 10:00 a.m., so he'd been in bed for only an hour—the sleep was meant to recalibrate his body to adjust gradually to the time difference, but he wasn't feeling tired. It was a message from Marianne. They had arrived in Melbourne and were booked in at the Park Hyatt. Jarrod knew that was way above any budget that he would have set for himself, but at the same time, he also knew that there could be a big pay day coming his way. He'd let this one pass. Jarrod quickly got changed into his civilian clothes and sneaked out of the room. There was no chance of waking Jan anyway.

He flicked Rhett a message in the lift down and darted through the reception area and through the front door to the solitary taxi at the rank. He was at the Park Hyatt in ten minutes. After struggling to find any form of payment before realising he could pay with his phone, he jumped out in the decadent entrance to this magical palace.

"Dad!" came the shout. It was Sebastian, who had jumped out of another taxi that hadn't yet come to a halt. He raced over to Jarrod who was still looking around to see where his son's voice had come from. He was tackled seconds later, grappled into a big hug. They were in an embrace when there was a thud as Aneka joined the melee. It had only been a few days, but Jarrod knew that after being confined to an aeroplane for the best part of a day, they would be full of energy. Jarrod peeled the kids off and rushed over to the taxi, where Marianne had opened the door but was still inside. Her long legs appeared first, and she gracefully stood up out of the vehicle. Jarrod loving seeing his hot wife. She was a little flustered having lost sight of the kids and on the back of twenty-four hours in transit but smiled the broadest smile when she saw Jarrod bounding towards her.

"Ta daaah!" she shouted. "We made it!"

Marianne's hair was still very short, a by-product of the chemo that she had endured during her battle with breast cancer, but it accentuated her long neck and highlighted her shoulders and her sexy figure. She was well wrapped up too for the weather but was a picture of health. Jarrod instructed the kids to grab a bag each, all of them on wheels, while he took all the smaller bags and checked the back seat of the taxi for any stray items. They walked towards the main entrance and were immediately served by a porter who took their name and loaded up a trolley with their belongings. As they walked through a further set of doors there was a commotion. There was Mum, spring-loaded and having just popped to her feet—she was bundling through the big chairs and causing a racket, while Dad took a longer route and then paused to let Mum get in first for the hug with her son.

"No way!" said Jarrod excitedly as Dad lifted Aneka off her feet and Mum turned to grab Seb in for a three-generation huddle.

"Ha ha, surprise," said Dad. "Who would have thought we'd be meeting here, eh?"

Jarrod was elated. His grin was almost painful. It had been some time since he had seen Mum and over a year since Dad was in the UK to see his debut for Darlington in a pre-season friendly at the Arena. Emotions were high, and the group was subtly ushered to the side of the entrance by a porter to make way for a growing crowd of people who were blocked by, but enjoying, this scene of utter happiness.

Jarrod looked up and caught sight of a figure at the bar, bringing a coffee cup to his mouth. The wild hair, the tall, thin frame, the scars below his eyes. It was unmistakable. They caught each other's eye and Yannick nodded in acknowledgement. Jarrod looked away as Aneka jumped excitedly just below him and nearly knocked his teeth out. When he turned back, Yannick Lefevre had gone. He was going to see a lot of him, thought Jarrod, before he refocused on his family reunion.

21

A-League

Jarrod was caught somewhat between his official duties as a Socceroos player and having his family all together. He let Coach Jim know, and Mike Jerszek took Jarrod aside at the training session on the Saturday afternoon to discuss it. Jarrod would be able to spend the mornings and evenings with his family, but there were certain obligations that were non-negotiable. The first of which was after training, when the whole squad was due at AAMI Park to attend the A-League game between Melbourne Victory and Western United, somewhat of a local derby. The 4:00 p.m. kick-off was perfect. They would take in the game and then Jarrod would meet up with his family for dinner. Marianne and the kids had no plans other than to rest and enjoy the hotel facilities for the remainder of the day, Jarrod's mum and dad taking the kids for lunch so Marianne could get some sleep.

Jarrod had shamefully never been to an A-League game since he had left to go and live in the UK. His memories of Sydney FC games at the cavernous Sydney Football Stadium were of watching down from his seat in the stands as the nutters in the Cove, including a lot of his mates, covered each other in beer with every goal. There had always been good quality players that were perhaps past their best mixed with up-and-coming local talent, but the pace was slower than Jarrod was now used to, and the ebb and flow of the game had never seemed to match the choreographed chants from the crowd. So, Jarrod went into this game as a bit of a football snob, hoping for his expectations to be exceeded.

Those memories were still with him as the group took their seats up behind the substitutes' benches, all very conspicuous in their navy-blue tracksuits. Jarrod had been handed a green and black Western United scarf outside by a fan on the one condition that he wore it at the game. The chill of the afternoon hit as the sun disappeared behind the stand and Jarrod was happy to be wearing any sort of scarf. He was ready to be entertained.

The atmosphere was very much like a Darlington game. The stadium was almost full, so there would have been more here than at a full Darlington Arena. The away fans were segregated, which Jarrod remembered not being done very well in the past. That created an 'us and them' scenario that Jarrod felt was crucial to creating the right mood for a game. The pitch of the seats didn't quite allow for a cauldron-like amphitheatre like some of the venues he'd played at, and the view from the seats further back might not have been perfect. As kick-off approached though, the fans started their chanting, and Jarrod could have been at a sold-out MK Dons or Walsall game. Manager Rhett had done some homework too and had briefed the Socceroos squad on what to expect— home team Victory sitting in third, Western United near the foot of the table, but the visitors on a rich seam of goal scoring.

The game kicked off to a raucous roar from all sides of the stadium. The entertainment on the field was matched only by the antics off the field. The Western United fans had a dazzling flare that was wafting smoke across the field, and they were bouncing up and down in silence, maybe just to keep warm, before bursting into song. The visitors scored after twenty minutes and the fans in the away section went crazy, the goal scorer being mobbed by his teammates right in front of them. A second goal from distance just before half time had the crowd around them tutting as the roar came again from the visiting fans in green and black.

The Socceroos players were ushered inside the stadium at the break and into a lounge area. There were lots of smartly dressed people in there and the players were encouraged to mingle. Jarrod was accosted straight away by a middle-aged gentleman in a Melbourne Victory crested jacket. He introduced himself as Tony Di Paolo and explained that he was involved in the ownership group at the home club.

"Jarrod," said Mr Di Paolo. "If I told you that we had a mutual friend in Manny Leonard, how would you react?"

That was a great line, thought Jarrod, and he made a snap decision to play this one with a straight bat.

"I would be very interested to know what your next question would be." It was almost a Harlowe Croft response.

"Melbourne Victory are looking for a defensive midfielder. You can probably see why," said Mr Di Paolo.

"The game is quite even, don't you think?" remarked Jarrod. "Just wait and see how the second half goes. The urgency to sign a defensive midfielder might not be so strong at the final whistle."

"I like you," said Mr Di Paolo. "I'll be speaking with Manny again soon."

Jarrod excused himself to make his way to the gents. That was quite the discussion he'd just had. It felt like he was back in the underworld in the match-fixing scandal. These people just didn't communicate like regular people, never actually mentioning what they were really talking about. Jarrod was washing his hands when a gentleman walked in.

"G'day, Jarrod," the newcomer said, already in full flow at the urinal.

Jarrod wasn't practised at urinal etiquette and wasn't sure whether to engage with the man or wait until he was ready.

"Good to see you in Australia," continued the man, turning and buttoning up his fly. Jarrod had no idea who he was.

"I don't believe we've met," said Jarrod, not offering a hand until the hand washing and drying routine was done. It was another strange encounter.

"We haven't had the pleasure yet, no," said the man, shaking Jarrod's hand. "Dalton Piercey, Australian Federal Police. I'd just like you to know that we're here and we have been briefed by D.I. Allison about your *situation*."

"Oh?" said Jarrod, checking to see if any of the cubicles were closed. They weren't. They were alone. Jarrod didn't realise that he was in a specific *situation*.

"If you have any issues or concerns when you are here in Australia, please do not hesitate to call me. Here's my card. You have nothing to be concerned about for now."

He handed over a card and wished Jarrod a good evening. Jarrod stood by the hand dryer for a moment and read the card. This was for real. What on earth was happening? His instinct told him to run after this Dalton character and find out more, but he resisted. He walked out of the bathroom and back into the throng. Dane was there and introduced Jarrod to a Western United director, who was very impressed with Jarrod's green and black scarf.

Jarrod had read the game well. The second half turned out exactly as he expected. Victory pushed forward immediately and got an early headed goal from a simple cross from the left to bring the crowd back to life after the break. The crowd lived every moment of the game. Once seventy-five minutes passed, the urgency set in, and the home team found another gear. A stray pass from a Western United defender was seized upon by a Victory midfielder who advanced, feigned the pass and galloped right through the middle to plant a delightful shot from just inside the area to beat the advancing goalkeeper. The crowd all around rose, and Jarrod rose too. A great goal, and that would set up the grandstand finish. The game bounced from end to end, Western United's right-midfielder having the best chance but blazing over from ten yards. The game ended all square. The entertainment had been terrific. Jarrod had joined in with the crowd with their shouts and had been thoroughly impressed by what he saw.

The Socceroos players were invited to stay behind and meet up with their A-League counterparts, but Jarrod had forewarned Rhett that he would be leaving straight after the game. After making sure that he had found Rhett to say goodbye, he raced out of the stadium and followed the crowds along Olympic Boulevard until he spotted a taxi that would take him the short journey to the restaurant closer to the centre of the city. He pulled up at the chic-looking restaurant, not quite his style, and walked through the door. The family were all there at a high table, and there were some unfamiliar faces there too. Jarrod did the rounds of the table, giving out kisses and hugs even though he'd seen the family already this morning. When he got to Mum, she introduced the new faces.

"Jarrod, I'd like you to meet Dana and Milena," said Mum.

"Yes! Anna's friends! I remember Anna talking about you both," exclaimed Jarrod excitedly. This was amazing. If Anna had walked in hand in hand with her girlfriend Elin, it would have completed the picture.

Jarrod found the spare seat and wedged in between Marianne and Dana. The evening got off to a great start. Aneka lifted her iPad onto the end of the table, turned it around, and flipped the cover so it made a stand. It was Anna. And there was Elin. It was a beautiful moment. Aneka was almost in tears talking with her long-lost auntie.

The rest of the night was fantastic, Dana and Milena were the life and soul of the party, and when they eventually had dinner, it was late. Jarrod knew he had a curfew, but he took it right to the limit and made his way back to the Pullman after saying goodnight to the family in the foyer of the Park Hyatt.

22

Plough

Jarrod continued to see his family throughout the next two days in between training sessions, and did the tourist basics around town, taking in the markets, riding incognito on trams. Mum and Dad were loving being around the kids and took them on a couple of side trips to let Jarrod and Marianne have some time together. The weather put on a show for them too. Jarrod was delighted to be able to showcase his country to his family and for them to be enjoying it as much as he did.

On the Monday night, Jarrod only had an hour with the family, tagging along to the end of the evening meal after the 'minus one' training session at the Docklands stadium. He knew he wouldn't get any more time with the family after this and gave out as many hugs as he could. Tuesday would be busy, and he would be flying out first thing Wednesday morning to return home. Marianne and the kids were heading to New Caledonia for three nights to spend time with some of Marianne's distant family members, and Mum and Dad would be heading back to Sydney too.

Jarrod had media duty on Tuesday morning. There were cameras and reporters at the stadium and the whole squad were up for interviews. Jarrod chuckled when he was taken to his first interview—it was Caleb Powell, a Socceroos and EPL reporter for Fox Sports who Jarrod felt was stalking him around the world. Jarrod had given Caleb a scoop just a couple of months ago. He had ridden the wave with that story, and it had given Caleb's career and credibility a massive boost.

Jarrod was compelled to give Caleb a hug. He was a little younger than Jarrod, thirty maybe, still young in the media scene, but he knew how to ask the right questions to eke out a response from his subject.

"Jarrod, thanks for talking with us for the Fox Sports pre-game show. How does it feel to be part of the Australia set-up at such a late stage of your career?"

That was an old question, and Jarrod had plenty of answers from the bank to give, the same spiel he had given maybe ten times already. Caleb continued down this rather safe route for five minutes before changing tact. It was like a Championship winning team toying with one of the sides in the relegation zone and then pouncing when they least expected it.

"Your career has been long and successful in England. You are undertaking your coaching qualifications in England, if I'm not mistaken. When will Jarrod Black the coach or Jarrod Black the manager be seen walking up and down the touchline?"

Jarrod smiled.

"And will that be in England or here in the A-League? Your family are out here in Australia …"

Jarrod's smile changed from genuine to forced within a second. He gave a few words to stall while he thought further about where he should go with this.

"It is no secret that I am doing my Pro Licence at St George's Park in England," he said. "That will give me the option to coach or even manage when my playing days come to an end. As for where and when that will be, that depends on a lot of things. I'm an ambitious man, a pioneering Australian if you like. I'll let you know when the time comes." Jarrod almost blew out his cheeks in relief at that one.

The interview ended with Caleb sharing vision of his goal from Thursday night in Lebanon. Jarrod hadn't watched it properly since it had happened.

"Hey, Mitch does well there," said Jarrod, as his teammate cleverly turned his man and Jarrod was seen lower on the screen starting his run into the space at the far post. "I could see the space in front of me, I just had to get there."

"What were you thinking at this point?" asked Caleb as ball and player looked to meet on the small screen.

"I was thinking it was like an Alan Shearer goal I'd seen from way back. Hit it across the keeper and I've got a chance."

There wasn't a great deal of power in the shot, but its placement was perfect, back across the keeper who was scrambling, and the ball fell just beneath the cross bar into the far corner. Jarrod sat back in the director-style chair.

"Well done, Jarrod, that's a quality goal," said Caleb. "And thanks for joining us ahead of the Socceroos game tonight against our bogey team Kyrgyzstan. Good luck and have a safe trip back."

Jarrod made sure the camera was no longer rolling and the sound engineer had put down the boom. Caleb was unbuckling himself from his audio equipment.

"What do you know, Caleb?" he asked.

Caleb sat down in the chair. He sat for a moment, thinking, and looking at Jarrod before he spoke. "You know, this TV deal, LF Sports, Chiya Inc," he said at last. "It's like an elephant in the room. I just don't understand how they have been able to walk into the Australian media scene and plough in so much money. And no one has asked any questions. These are the same people who were paying players to help fix matches in England."

Jarrod listened intently. He was delighted that this had nothing to do with him moving to Australia or him becoming a global movie star. Caleb would be frothing if he gave him that scoop. No chance today though.

"Allegedly," said Jarrod mournfully, knowing that the police had not been able to make any charges stick.

23

Bogey

A light ball work session followed, and a team meeting over lunch. It was true that Kyrgyzstan were a bogey team after eliminating Australia from the Asian Cup all those years ago, the last time the two had met in a competitive game. Australia had been reduced to nine men and still almost got the result they needed, and that game had gone down in folklore alongside the Iran draw and the Uruguay victory. The team meeting focused on that, and the players were left in no doubt that any complacency or ill-discipline would not be tolerated.

By the time the team meeting had finished, it was almost time to make their way to the Docklands Stadium. They had forty-five minutes before boarding the bus, and Jarrod needed to catch up on a few things. He had contemplated ringing D.I. Allison, but instead chose to call Duddy. He was always up early; he said that it was the curse of growing old.

"Jarrod, my friend," said Duddy. "I hope you're enjoying Australia."

"Hello, Duddy," said Jarrod. "Australia has put on a show for us. I'd forgotten just how good life can be."

"You might be spending a lot more time there soon," continued Duddy. "I've heard back from Zion Films, and they were happy to accommodate your asking price, albeit with a little nudge. They've made their decision too about the destination; they've already acquired some premises in Melbourne and the whole movie is going to be shot on location in Australia."

"Wow. Amazing," said Jarrod, who was banking on that being the decision all along.

"You will be expected in Melbourne at the beginning of December, and you will be contracted for eleven months," said Duddy. "I'll run you through the details when I see you next. If you're back Wednesday night or Thursday morning into Heathrow, I'm in London and I can meet you at Kings Cross and we'll travel up together. Just text me your itinerary from Heathrow to Darlington and I'll tag along."

"I'll do that as soon as I hang up," said Jarrod, who had pulled the printed itinerary from his travel bag and had it in front of him. "Any thoughts about finding a club to play for in Australia? If shooting doesn't start until April, I'll be able to play a good chunk of the season."

"My knowledge of Australian football is zero," admitted Duddy. "Don't they kick it out of their hands over there?"

"Duddy ..." said Jarrod with a sigh.

"And they've got club names like Goolong and Murrabumbry? No, Jarrod, I'll not be able to help you there, but I can help you organise whatever it is at this end. A contract buy-out or a termination by mutual consent. Just let me know when you've got something, and I'll take care of it here."

"Fantastic, Duddy, and thank you as always for everything you do for me," said Jarrod, ending the call.

Jarrod was on a roll now, and D.I. Allison was his next call.

"Good morning, Jarrod. Lovely goal you scored the other night. What do you have in store in this one?"

"We shouldn't have any problems winning tonight," said Jarrod. "Say, I bumped into Dalton Piercey the other night at a game. Mentioned your name. Do you need to brief me?" Jarrod was sounding a little annoyed.

"My apologies, Jarrod," said D.I. Allison. "My fault. We tracked your man Yannick Lefevre leaving the country on a direct flight to Perth. We expect that his next stop was Melbourne."

"Yes, I've seen him. It's a little unnerving having seen him at a Darlington game and then again ten thousand miles away in Melbourne. What's he up to?"

"We're not sure. He's not out to get you, or he would have done that already. Perhaps he's working for someone?"

Jarrod was sceptical. It seemed like D.I. Allison wasn't telling him something, and there must be an obvious reason why he was stalking Jarrod around the world.

"Is there anything else I need to know?" asked Jarrod.

"Not yet," replied D.I. Allison, ominously. "We have Jens Lermann and Murtaka Chiya unable to travel at the moment as we're collating evidence to charge them. We'll be needing you here to testify when that time comes."

Jarrod had expected this all along but had chosen to forget about it. Of course he would be expected to be involved in court proceedings. Jarrod was the number one witness.

"Well, give me a bit of notice if you could," said Jarrod. "And can you assure me that me and my family are in no danger?"

"I can assure you," said D.I. Allison, "that you are in no danger. You would be much more valuable alive. I mean, you've got nothing to worry about."

This was the first time that Jarrod had felt any doubt about D.I. Allison. They had a great working relationship, they were both football men, and the detective inspector had been nothing but open with him. But now, something felt wrong.

"Now, how good was Darlington's win on the weekend?" said the D.I.

They finished off their call with football talk, as they usually did. Darlington had moved into second place with a home win over Rotherham United and were up against Blackpool tonight with the chance of going top. Peter Van Vloten had played a blinder, and Benson Gadriga had grabbed two goals. Darlington were purring. And Jarrod wasn't there.

24

Mood

The players belted out the national anthem, this time Jarrod getting the words right, and the fifty thousand people in the stadium roared along with local singer and poet Derry Tinkler. This game meant something. The memories of their previous encounter with today's visitors were ready to be banished.

Jarrod had organised for Seb and Aneka to sit with Caleb in the commentary box pre-game to see how it all worked, and he made a point of waving up in the vague direction of the media area. The scene was set for a big game. The final adverts were playing on the big screen. Up came an advert that Jarrod hadn't seen for a while, an Aussie twist on the BetShed advert he had shot a few weeks back. Jarrod stood for a moment with his hands on his hips and took it in. It was very clever, showing him running across the sand and then through the rainforest before entering what looked like Townsville stadium and scoring the winning goal. Up went the arms to the sky and his head went back. There were chuckles around him as the advert finished. He was international now.

The referee sounded the opening whistle and the game started with Kyrgyzstan knocking the ball back to their goalkeeper and toying with it in defence while the home team worked out whether or not to pursue the ball. The visitors were here to frustrate. And frustrate they did, not giving Australia any time with the ball, and when they did finally get possession, there were some clumsy challenges.

With Melbourne Victory player Marty Clarkson finding time down the right flank from his defensive position, the game opened up. Jarrod was caught in possession as he tried to create some space in midfield and that gave the Kyrgyzstan team their first chance of the game. The long ball gave the small section of away fans hope as it was brought down and the shot fired just past the post. Jarrod gave out a frustrated instruction to his teammates to let him know when he had a man on. The half came to a close with some heavyweight time-wasting from their less-physical opponents, and a chorus of whistles.

This was where coach Mike Jerszek had to earn his corn. With captain Nikos collared for a half time interview, he was conspicuous in his absence in the dressing room. Without the captain to back up the players, Mike ripped into the team in a momentous dressing down. Jarrod was taking this in as an interested future coach as well as a frustrated current player. Nikos finally arrived and slammed the door after him. Mike stopped and Nikos started, repeating almost everything that had been said already, but in a tone and a language that was more upfront and much more damning. This was a dressing room that needed an injection of belief. Jarrod wasn't game to throw in anything positive, though, and left it to Jan to remind his teammates that he would "make them look good" if they passed it to him. That broke the ice and the players started to gee each other up. More like it.

The wind had been taken out of the crowd, who had been lively early on, but they had lost that edge and had been rather subdued as half time approached. That was reignited though in the first exchanges of the second half. Defender Rusty Ibrahim was pole-axed from behind, and a few players rushed in to remonstrate with the aggressor. Rusty got to his feet, showing the blood that was forming in his sock. He then walked across to the player who had chopped him and shook his hand firmly. This was like the kiss of death from the wiry left back, and the fans and commentators all picked up on it. The crowd sparked back into life, hoping and expecting some Roy Keane-style retribution.

Jarrod exchanged passes with Miles Carter on the right and chose to turn in-field and ignore Miles' great run past his defender. The space had been made and Jarrod advanced, drawing in two defenders before slipping the ball left to Ed Charrah. His first touch was heavy, but with the defence slow to react, he stretched out his leg and poked the ball under the advancing keeper and into the net for a quality opening goal. That was it, the seal was broken. The stadium was awake and alert now. Australia rattled home a further three goals, Jan scoring two and Dane the other as the home side over-ran their opponents. The crowd was lapping it up. There was even time for Rusty to execute the perfect sliding tackle to thwart a potential breakaway in the final minutes, leaving his player on the ground in a heap. Rusty stood over him with his hands on his hips watching him peel his face off the turf, the crowd roaring with approval.

This had been a great turnaround. Jarrod made way for Marley South in the latter stages to great applause, and enjoyed giving out high fives and fist pumps to the bench as he took his place. Jarrod was collared for an interview at the end, but felt he needed to decline it as he wasn't on the field at the end, leaving Caleb to frantically organise one of the other players to share their insight into what had been a thoroughly professional second half. Jarrod wanted to soak up the atmosphere. Every game with the national team felt like his last, and he knew he had to savour these moments that he had been blessed with so late in his career.

Caleb did catch up with Jarrod after the game as the players assembled in the mixed zone with the press conference having been wrapped up quickly. He had his cameraman in tow and a sound engineer, and they set up quickly.

"I'm here with Socceroos midfield man Jarrod Black," said Caleb by way of an introduction. "I understand that time is pressing as you start the journey back to England, but how did you enjoy tonight's game?"

"The second half was an absolute joy to be involved in," said Jarrod, not disguising the fact that the first half was as tough a grind as he had experienced. "We have to tip our hats to the visitors Kyrgyzstan though.

They came with a game plan and looked to be executing it perfectly."

"What was said at half time to change things around?" asked Caleb with a glint in his eye.

"You can imagine the mood in the dressing room," said Jarrod. "We all want to give as much entertainment to the football fans of Australia, and when it's not clicking, it's very frustrating. We did some soul searching at the break and found our rhythm straight away in the second forty-five."

"Jan Haratounan with another two goals, are you enjoying playing in this system?" asked Caleb. That was a bit of a nothing question.

"The system is close to what I'm used to at club level," said Jarrod. "The quality and tempo are a lot more intense though. Jan is one of the best strikers I've played with in my career."

"And so, your career will continue into the next round of qualification," said Caleb. "Congratulations on the win, and we'll see you again soon in the green and gold of Australia."

The cameraman lowered his camera and the sound engineer stepped away to get his boom arm out of the way.

Caleb sighed. "Sorry, Jarrod."

"Sorry?"

"Yes, I have a lot of questions that I was so tempted to ask you there; I think it might have come across in the interview there."

"I don't think so."

Caleb raised his eyebrows and smiled. He held out his hand to shake Jarrod's. "See you back in the UK."

25

Ripped

After a late, late supper, a team debrief and a short sleep, the players who were heading back overseas were all up early for breakfast. It was still dark and there were some bleary eyes over a light continental buffet. Marianne, Seb and Aneka walked in through the open doorway to the club lounge, followed by Mum and Dad. Aneka raced across to give Jarrod a hug. Mum and Dad had their bags, and they were obviously leaving for the airport first. Jarrod accompanied them down to the foyer and the goodbyes started. There were tears all round as the airport shuttle pulled up and the kids clung to their grandparents as they made their way to the door of the bus. The mixed emotions, smiles through moist eyes, and eager waves farewelled Jarrod's mum and dad as the bus disappeared around the corner. Jarrod always felt very empty when leaving his parents, and he knew how his kids would be feeling too; all that love and attention, fun and laughter, and hugs and cuddles just ripped away once again.

Marianne and the kids had a few hours before they needed to be at the airport for their flight to Noumea, but Jarrod was the next to have to leave. He hugged his kids, and they watched on as Jarrod embraced his wife to giggly "oohs" from Seb and Aneka. Jarrod grappled with them both before running off back into the hotel. He was not blessed with a great deal of time to pack up and be ready. He had seen the bus arrive outside by the time the lift arrived to take him back up to his room, and some of the players came out of the lift ready to go. Twenty minutes later, the team was invited to board the bus. Jarrod took his place next to the window and looked longingly at the hotel, and the surrounding buildings. He was definitely affected by his time in Melbourne and could feel he was attracted to it. The bus pulled away towards the road and he saw Seb and Aneka running beside the bus, laughing and goofing around. That put a big smile on his face. He'd see them in less than a week back home in Darlington, but he also knew they would be back in Australia soon.

26

Volume

The journey back from Australia was smooth but ultimately very draining. An extended wait in the lounge at Melbourne Airport where the players indulged in a rare champagne, and an alteration to the connecting flight at Dubai saw them fly into London City Airport via Zurich. The original overnight stay at Heathrow was jettisoned, and Jarrod alerted Duddy while passing through Dubai that he would instead be arriving early into London the following morning and catching an early train from Kings Cross. Duddy was more than happy to accommodate the change and Jarrod passed through the journey details once he had received an amended itinerary on his phone. He would be catching the train with Jan and James, so this might be a little tricky.

Duddy was already on the train when Jarrod and his travelling companions boarded. Duddy was in the next carriage and had a seat next to him that was only booked to Peterborough, and he alerted Jarrod to the fact. James was the first to leave the train, and Jarrod let Jan know that he had some business to attend to in the next carriage, giving an ambiguous wink as he left. Who knows what Jan thought he was up to.

"Duddy, my friend," said Jarrod, putting his hand on Duddy's shoulder. The huge frame of the Scotsman jolted, and he scrambled to move to the window seat to let Jarrod sit down.

Duddy had the most booming voice, and with the carriage not entirely empty, he tried his best to turn down the volume. "Right," he said, clearing his throat. He'd been snoozing and his eyes were a little bloodshot. "Here's the deal …"

The deal that Duddy went through started with the basics. Jarrod would receive an advance payment of 700,000 US dollars, as well as full accommodation and relocation expenses to get set up in Melbourne. Jarrod didn't work in US dollars, but could get a feel for the magnitude. He would have another three grand per week budget for a house for the family, cars, food, cleaner, everything. There was provision for private schooling for the kids if he chose to take it. The remainder of the eighteen million dollars would be paid in instalments, one at the conclusion of filming, and one when the movie was released. It was all taxable, so Jarrod would need some good tax advice.

Jarrod would be expected to be available every day from April when shooting started, even if not working, given the nature of the job. Shooting and re-shooting could be done at any time at the behest of the directors and the production company. Duddy assured Jarrod that this was thoroughly normal, and that when on location, there would be little down time in order to maximise efficiency. It sounded like Jarrod was going to work hard for this ultimate pay day but he wasn't fazed one bit.

Duddy went right down into the tiniest details; Jarrod asked questions and Duddy had an answer for everything, or at least took a note of which questions to take back to the production company. The timeframe pointed to a late November arrival in Australia, with preparation, acting lessons, stunt work training, personal training and media work to get him ready for a start just after Easter.

"So, I can play football until April?" asked Jarrod. It was more of a request for confirmation than a question.

"I have mentioned your position on that," said Duddy. He paused. He was thinking of the best wording for his next sentence. "It may not be a good idea to play full-time though," he continued. "You are going to have way too much on your plate to be able to play at the top level. Having said that, I have no idea what the top level is like in Australia. You call it soccer, don't you? It's the A-League, right?"

"It is the A-League," said Jarrod, impressed that Duddy had at least some knowledge. "And we call it football."

Duddy acknowledged the aggression in Jarrod's tone and laughed.

"Okay, it's football," said Duddy. "But see if you can play at a standard that will only take up a small amount of your week. I'm warning you, being the star of a blockbuster movie is demanding and exhausting."

Jarrod and Duddy sat looking at the notes that Duddy had made in his doctor-like handwriting.

"You do realise how amazing this opportunity is?" asked Duddy.

"I do."

"Don't risk it all just to play footy."

"I understand that," said Jarrod. "But I'd really like to play, and I'd like that to be part of the negotiation."

"About that," said Duddy, glancing sideways at Jarrod. "You've not appointed me as your talent agent yet."

"You're already my agent."

"Your football agent. If I'm going to go into bat for you in the movie business, well, that comes at a different price point. I know this business as well as football."

"Duddy, I trust that you will look after me and make this a fair deal for both you and me," said Jarrod. "Please can you be my agent?"

Duddy held out his hand and Jarrod took it. The enormous fingers of Duddy's hand completely covered Jarrod's hand and he squeezed gently to secure the deal. Jarrod sat back in his seat and looked up for a moment and breathed a long sigh.

"Are you going to be right for the weekend?" asked Duddy.

"I'm not sure, to be honest," said Jarrod. "Jet lag never used to bother me, but my body's got no idea what time this should be. I might need a good sleep when I get home."

"Now, I suggest you discuss with your manager about this," said

Duddy, as if to suggest that there should be no sleeping while there were things to sort out. "And set people talking back in Australia."

"They already are," said Jarrod. "But I might need to set some expectations of the level I should play at."

"Do that," said Duddy. "And when you've found something, let me know and we'll make this a football move as opposed to a movie star move."

Jarrod put his hand on Duddy's shoulder again as he stood up and gave him a little pat. They would see each other again very soon.

When he got back, Jan looked at Jarrod quizzically. He'd been gone since Peterborough, and they were past Doncaster now.

"Who was that you were talking with?" asked Jan. He'd obviously gone past them on the way to the toilet or to have a snoop.

"That was Duddy Freiberg," replied Jarrod. "He's an agent. Good person to know. If you ever need to find a new club to score thirty goals a season for, he can help."

"Interesting," said Jan. And that was thankfully where he left it.

27

Mainstream

Jarrod and Jan embraced as the train approached Darlington. They had spent a lot of time together today and for the last week, which had seen them travel around the world and back again. Jarrod made his way further up the train to catch Duddy, but he wasn't at his seat. Fifteen minutes later, after remembering where he'd parked the car last week, Jarrod was driving through the front gate of the Arena car park.

He parked and could see the cars of his teammates. They would be in training this morning on the adjacent training academy field, and he could see a lot of bodies going through drills through the fence. The radio was playing the news on the hour and just before they got to the sport, attention turned to the big news story of the day. Murtaka Chiya and Jens Lermann had been in custody for further questioning over the match-fixing scandal. The name Yannick Lefevre was tossed in there too, as if to give it some extra spice and make Jarrod sit up and take notice. The name Jarrod Black was mentioned, and Jarrod started feeling a paranoia that he hadn't felt since he had been at Newcastle at the height of the scandal. He felt as though his name was being thrown around to construct a story of a potential conflict or grudge between himself and the perpetrators of the crime, painting an unnecessary target on his back. D.I. Allison had said that he was in no danger, and he was inclined to believe him.

That confirmed to Jarrod that the story had broken officially into mainstream media after being protected for so long by a media embargo. He was now going to be subject to a lot of scrutiny in the press and a lot of requests for more information about how the whole story unfolded.

Jarrod turned off the engine, rubbed his face with his hands twice to stimulate his senses and got out of the car.

After saying hello to the reception staff and popping his head into Pauline's office with a wink while she was on the phone, Jarrod made his way along the long corridor to the training area. He walked through the changing rooms and out onto the field, breaking into a jog as he got closer.

"Welcome home, Jarrod," said Gary as he approached.

"Thanks, boss. What did I miss?"

"Oh, not much," said Gary with a smile. "Just top of the league, that's all."

Jarrod slapped Gary on the back. "Need a goal scoring international midfielder in the team for Saturday?"

"Yes, Jarrod. Yes, we do," said Gary. He placed his hand on Jarrod's back and beckoned him to start walking so they could be out of earshot.

"Would you like to join me as my assistant?" asked Gary.

Jarrod's standard response would be to stall and ask for more time, but he was in a decision-making mood and was a little hazy after the mammoth trip he had just endured.

"I would love to say yes," said Jarrod. "But I'm going to turn down your offer."

Gary stopped in his tracks and looked at him, half expecting this to be a wind-up. After all, Jarrod loved being at Darlington, they had a great working relationship, his playing career was approaching its twilight and he was a few steps away from completing his A Licence. It all added up to a logical move.

"In fact," continued Jarrod, "I'm going to need to leave Darlington soon. At least for the short term."

The look of disbelief from Gary was tough to take in.

"Is everything okay?" asked Gary, unsure as to what was the source of Jarrod's change of direction, and genuinely concerned for his player's welfare. Perhaps it was Marianne.

"Yes, yes," said Jarrod. "Everything's going well. I just have a need to be in Australia by the end of November this year. Whilst I can't divulge why, let's just say it's not a footballing matter."

Gary couldn't understand what the situation could be and looked at Jarrod for more.

"I'll speak with June," said Jarrod. "I'm so sorry to have to do this. I do feel less guilty, though, now that we've hit the top spot in League One."

"So, it's non-negotiable?" asked Gary.

"I'm afraid so," said Jarrod. "Let's just say, you'll understand when you find out."

"Just tell me, Jarrod," said Gary, who was used to those close to him being upfront with him.

"Like I say, you'll understand."

Gary returned to training and bellowed some instructions, leaving Jarrod's side. It almost felt like Gary was deliberately ignoring him now and getting on with the day-to-day stuff. He could live without Jarrod, and if Jarrod knew Gary like he thought he did, he would accept this gracefully.

Jarrod waved at Ghali as he trotted back towards the changing rooms. He wasn't going to hang around as a distraction to training. He walked past Pauline's office and for once, she was between phone calls. He leaned through the door and smiled. Upon her insistence, he came in and sat in the seat in front of her desk.

"I don't suppose June is around today?" asked Jarrod.

"She's on her way back from York," said Pauline. "She had some business there in relation to Benson's contract."

"Oh?"

"But she's just off the train and she'll be back any time now," said Pauline without any inclination as to what the business was. "Is there anything I can help you with, perhaps?"

Their relationship was rock solid, Pauline the media officer at Darlington and Jarrod the club captain. They were a formidable team and played to each other's strengths when coming up against the press. He didn't feel ready to discuss anything with Pauline, but that changed when he heard June breeze through the front door into reception.

Pauline and Jarrod looked at each other as the footsteps clacked on the hardwood floor, getting louder. June appeared around the corner and walked in holding a lot of paperwork. Jarrod smiled and shot to his feet to offer his chair. In reality though, he wanted a captive audience, and walked over to the door and slowly closed it. Both women looked at him as he made his way over to the desk and perched himself on the corner. They were silent. Something was definitely up, and they knew it.

"Did I miss something?" asked June with a smile as she sat down and offloaded her paperwork onto the desk. The magazine with Craig Daniels on the cover was still there.

"Right," said Jarrod, clasping his hands together. "Here's the deal. I have a potential business opportunity that I am hoping very strongly to pursue that will involve moving to Australia for a year."

"A business opportunity?" asked June, as if to require more information.

"A business opportunity," reiterated Jarrod. "I would like to discuss how we go about it. I plan to play football still, but I can't play with Darlington."

June and Pauline looked at each other.

"You're moving to Australia?" asked June, incredulously. She was struggling with this one. She had just been involved in sorting out some contract wrangle with Benson and now all that good work was being rewarded with this?

"I'm so sorry to do this," said Jarrod slowly, putting his hand on the desk very close to the magazine. "Especially after everything you've done for me. When you find out what it is, I hope that you can forgive me."

June crossed her arms. Pauline, on the other hand, sounded excited.

"Well, whatever it is, it must be quite important," she said. "So, what are your thoughts?"

June uncrossed her arms. Jarrod grabbed the spare seat and moved it next to June so they could all sit at the desk. The dialogue had opened. This was happening. They discussed whether Jarrod wanted to remain a Darlington player, they went through various different scenarios. June and Pauline were enthralled. They were in on a secret that no one else knew, even though they didn't know what the ultimate secret was. When they had come up with the best scenario, they agreed on a list of questions that they would need answered before they acted. When did he want to leave? Where was he going? Who would they deal with? They documented nothing. This was a conversation that would be considered off the record, and Jarrod gave both of them a hug as he walked out.

Jarrod's adrenaline was pumping. He didn't know which way to walk. He ended up jogging down to the medical rooms where he saw Sash and asked if he could get a massage to loosen his muscles that had been unused since leaving the field at the Docklands Stadium. Sash was more than happy to oblige. He asked one of his juniors, who looked young enough to be doing work experience at school, to set up the massage table. Sash watched on as the young physio kneaded Jarrod's calves. Jarrod could tell that this was someone very experienced in sports massage and was immediately in a trance-like state with thoughts and ideas whirling around his head.

28

Turned

"Marcus, how are you?" said Jarrod when D.I. Allison answered the phone. Jarrod was just outside reception in the car park.

"Hello, Jarrod," said D.I. Allison, not used to being addressed by his first name. "Things are going well, what can I do for you?"

"I just have a question for you," said Jarrod. "I'm not sure whether or not you can answer it."

There was a pause. Jarrod was compelled to continue.

"Do I need to be in the UK when the court cases come round?"

There was another pause. Before it got too awkward, D.I. Allison spoke. "By court cases, you're talking about Murtaka Chiya and Jens Lermann? Well, yes, we will be expecting you to give evidence in their trials if and when we get to that point. Why do you ask? Not planning on a long holiday, are you?"

"Well, yes, actually, I am," said Jarrod. "I'm heading to Australia in November, and I might be gone for some time."

"Interesting," said D.I. Allison. "Did your trip over there turn your head?"

"Yes and no," said Jarrod. "My head was already being turned. I have an opportunity to play football in my home country and I'm hoping to make it happen. A great lifestyle opportunity for the family and perhaps a new life for Marianne and the kids."

"Wow, your head has been turned," said D.I. Allison. "Rest assured, you'll not be more than a phone call away from us, but the worst that can happen is that we pull our trump card and issue a subpoena and get you on a plane back here."

"So, I will be needed then?" asked Jarrod.

"Most certainly," said D.I. Allison. "You're our star witness. You experienced the whole thing."

"I was afraid you'd say that."

"Don't worry though," said D.I. Allison. "If we can get enough evidence, and we do have a lot of it, then we might not need you in court, at least not straight away."

"Right …"

"I'm interested to know though," said D.I. Allison, changing to a more cheery tone. "What would Darlington think about losing you again?"

"Ha ha, yes, there is that," said Jarrod. "It's a little sensitive, and I've not discussed it with them yet. One step at a time."

"Well, if I had my time again, Jarrod, I would be heading off to Australia too. Taking the family and making the most of what your beautiful country offers."

Jarrod was silent. D.I. Allison was saying all the right things.

"I guess I'll just have to keep you up to date with my movements," said Jarrod. "Although if you're unofficially keeping tabs on Yannick Lefevre, I'll be on his radar just as he is on yours."

"No comment," said D.I. Allison. "But yes, please keep us informed of what your movements are. Say, you only have a few weeks then. Let's catch up for breakfast one morning. For old times' sake."

"Sure, Marcus, I'd like that," said Jarrod, before realising that he had another whole topic to discuss. "Wait, one last thing," he said excitedly. "What can you tell me about LF Sports?"

"LF Sports? You mean the TV company that has recently taken over the coverage of football in Australia?"

That was already enough to alert Jarrod to the fact that D.I. Allison knew LF Sports intimately.

"Yes, that's your friends Murtaka Chiya and Jens Lermann," the D.I. continued. "They have ploughed a lot of money into this company, an online betting venture, fully above board in theory. Now they're branching into television, and they're sinking millions into content. It does strike me as an enormous conflict of interest, having your major broadcaster also being an institution where you can bet on games. Chiya and Lermann are here though, they won't be going anywhere soon."

Jarrod had heard enough to know that D.I. Allison and the Met Police, in fact the police in Australia too, were watching on with interest at the developments on the media landscape in the A-League. They finished their conversation and Jarrod stood for a moment, holding his phone. It was hot to the touch and his ear was hurting from having the damned thing pressed so hard against it, and he could feel sweat accumulating in his earlobe. He felt a wave of tiredness all of a sudden, a wooziness that made him feel light-headed. Perhaps it was time to head home. He'd need to stop by the shops on the way though. The house had been empty for a week, and there would be little food to keep him going for the next week until Marianne and the kids returned.

29

Cutting

Jarrod hadn't quite made it to the entrance of Sainsbury's when his phone rang. The phone was buzzing all the time today and he couldn't keep up with all the calls, messages and social media notifications, but this was Duddy, so Jarrod answered it.

"You made it home okay?" asked Jarrod.

"Oh, aye," said Duddy. "Not long ago, to be honest. Now, I received an email just before I got in—Zion Films with the terms of engagement. A document showing how you will be remunerated and when, as well as an actor release form, non-disclosure agreement, all standard stuff. It's definitely in Melbourne. I just wanted to let you know. You'll find it in your inbox. Have a read and let me know if you have any questions."

"Do I have to read it?" asked Jarrod, semi-serious but not in the mood to be scouring complex paperwork.

"I can give you a brief summary," said Duddy, sensing the fatigue in Jarrod's voice. "But you'd have to listen."

"I'll have a look, Duddy," said Jarrod. "Tomorrow. But thanks for letting me know. Is it 100% locked in then?"

"It's as 100% as it can be at this stage," said Duddy. "It's not a contract, it's simply stating what will be in the contract. If we need to negotiate anything, you'll need to let me know as soon as you can."

"Tomorrow," said Jarrod. "I'll call you in the morning."

Jarrod walked into the shopping centre and grabbed a basket before turning and dropping the basket back in the pile and commandeering a trolley instead. He wasn't planning on getting much, but just couldn't bear the thought of carrying an overloaded basket around when temptation took over. He could sense himself descending into a trance, and with it, all patience and happiness seemed to be draining out of him. The last thing he needed was to bump into someone in the shops.

"Oh, hello, Jarrod," said the cheery voice. Jarrod turned to see who it was. He was shaken out of his trance and smiled when he saw it was Pippa Robson, the school mum who constantly helped them out when Jarrod and Marianne were both away. The kids had been at the Robsons' house many times after school while Jarrod or Marianne were running late. She was a lovely lady, relaxed but efficient with her parenting and always quick to cleverly throw a cutting remark into a conversation.

"Say, what are you doing tomorrow morning after drop-off?" asked Jarrod. "Can we grab a coffee? I have something to run past you."

"Your kids are away though," said Pippa, puzzled.

"Yes, but I just need to talk something through, and I'd like to talk it through with you," said Jarrod.

"Okay," said Pippa. "Take me somewhere nice. Ooh, a date. I'll tell Richard I'm at my mum's. I don't start work till midday."

"Ha ha, see you in the morning," laughed Jarrod.

The exchange put Jarrod in a livelier mood, something he really needed to get through the next twenty minutes at Sainsbury's.

30

Kick-start

Jarrod had made it home. There was a pile of letters on the floor next to the letterbox, which he brushed aside with the door. It was cold and stark. Nothing a fire wouldn't fix. The longest of long days was coming to an end and he was secretly congratulating himself for making it this far without crashing out. It was the only way to reset the sleep patterns—make it to the next night-time regardless of how tired you were. He packed away the shopping, put on a load of washing and cranked up the gas fire. He was tucking into a piping hot single-serve soup like a true bachelor when his phone buzzed. It was Des Davis.

"Wow, Des," said Jarrod, straining to put his hot bowl on the floor before readjusting himself in the sofa. "How is Hartlepool treating you?"

"Hello, Jarrod," said Des. "Hartlepool humming along just fine, thanks. Just checking in to see how things were tracking. I was half expecting to see you announced as Gary's number two by now."

"Ah, yes," said Jarrod. "Gary has been in touch about that."

"So, are you going to take it?"

"It's up there at the top of the options," said Jarrod, without giving too much away.

"Gary's a great guy to work with," said Des. It was now sounding like Gary had put Des up to this phone call and he was using him to try and coax Jarrod into the job.

"I know he is," said Jarrod. "The timing might be just off though."

"You've got a better offer?"

"No, no. Well, let's say I've got some different projects coming up and it might not tie in with those projects."

"I'm all ears," said Des.

"All in good time, Des, I can't give too much away at the moment, but there's an itch that needs to be scratched."

That was a massive understatement.

"Well, if you're after something that will open doors for you in the future, I can only recommend working with Gary," said Des. "It's kick-started my career, that's for sure."

"You're in a good place," said Jarrod, throwing the subject of the conversation back on Des, without having any knowledge of how he was tracking at Hartlepool. "You're a top coach, and a good man. You've got my recommendation, now and into the future."

"Thanks, Jarrod," said Des. "I'd love to work with you again in the future too. If you're looking for a challenge, there's always a spot here for an experienced central midfield kingpin to guide us to promotion."

"Ha ha," said Jarrod. "Don't tempt me. Hey, I'll come up and see a game soon."

"I'll look forward to that."

That was an odd conversation, thought Jarrod. Gary and Des were tight. That was definitely a call designed to work out the lay of the land for Gary and for his plans.

31

Scones

Jarrod felt weird going to the school drop-off with no kids in tow. He parked up away from the school and walked the few hundred metres to the school gate. Pippa was there when he turned the corner, peering through the railings. She had just dropped her girls and was waiting for the moment where one of them had forgotten something. Pippa turned and smiled as Jarrod walked up. Jarrod noticed her eyes and could tell that she had mascara on, something he had never noticed in the past. She reached in for a kiss on the cheek, something they had never done either. This was maybe crossing the line from being school friends to being genuine friends, and it seemed right.

They walked back to Jarrod's car, saying hello to a few other school parents on the way. Jarrod drove them to the town centre and parked up. They walked down Skinnergate and into a side alley to the café he'd been a few times with Marianne when they'd been out and about in Darlington. The town wasn't renowned for being a tourist destination, but he was in a truly British town with centuries-old buildings, and it still felt like a holiday destination for an Aussie overseas. They settled in and ordered a pot of tea and Jarrod ordered a round of scones, one of his English food vices.

"Thanks for coming along," said Jarrod. He'd been saving the talk and they had only talked school news since they met at the gate.

"There's something on your mind, Jarrod," said Pippa, looking him in the eyes. "Tell me what it is."

"I'll tell you, but I need your strictest confidence," said Jarrod. He'd never used those words, and it sounded a little pompous. Pippa was not one to get involved in the schoolyard gossip and liked to keep herself a little removed from the tittle-tattle that went on in school. It could have been a line that put her on the defensive.

"I'd better turn off my recording device then," said Pippa, pressing an imaginary button on the lapel of her denim jacket.

Jarrod smiled. "So, we've only been in Darlington for a year, right?" said Jarrod.

"Right," said Pippa, opening her hands to him. "And a hell of a lot has happened in that time."

"Yes, that is true," said Jarrod. "And we love it here. Everyone is so welcoming; there's a true sense of community and the fact that I play for the local football club is usually never mentioned in conversation. I feel like we've been accepted into Darlington because we're decent people, not because I'm a footballer."

Pippa looked at him a little puzzled, tilting her head to one side. Her hands were still open.

"This sounds like a goodbye," she said, skipping ahead five minutes, almost asking for Jarrod to cut to the chase.

Jarrod recognised it and readjusted the conversation that he had rehearsed in his head all morning.

"I've been in discussion with a movie production company," said Jarrod eventually. Pippa instantly closed her hands and sat forward. Jarrod's voice had gone quieter, and she had to move closer to hear. "There's a role in a new movie and I have an opportunity to move to Australia and be the lead actor."

Jarrod could see Pippa's eyes widen. Her eyebrows weren't able to go any higher.

"Filming starts next year," continued Jarrod. "But I'd have to be there middle to late November. Apparently, it takes a few months to prepare beforehand. Or at least they may have recognised that there's a bit more preparation required with a novice like me."

Pippa wasn't responding. She seemed a little dazed.

"I just needed to get this off my chest," said Jarrod. "You and Richard have been so good to us. Our kids are good friends …"

"I think our Michaela might be thinking it's a bit more than that."

Jarrod sat back in his chair.

"Do you think they're a bit more than friends?" asked Jarrod. "I know that Seb seems to go quiet whenever he's around Michaela, and he's always super keen when we say you're coming over or we're going to yours."

"She'll be heartbroken," said Pippa, with a sly grin.

"Ha ha, you bugger. You can't say that!"

"Don't worry about that, tell me more," pressed Pippa. "What's the movie? Will you be coming back? Who else is in it? What's Marianne going to do?"

"Can't tell you," said Jarrod, holding out the four fingers of his left hand and pointing to each one as he replied. "Don't know. Couldn't tell you. Don't know."

"Right," said Pippa with a comedic slump of the shoulders. "You're not prepared for this at all, are you?"

"It's still pretty fresh, to be honest," admitted Jarrod. "As you know, Marianne and the kids are over there now, and it just seems so right."

"Are you still going to play football?" asked Pippa.

"I certainly hope so," said Jarrod. "But it might mean an abrupt end to my Darlington career."

"Maybe a pause," said Pippa hopefully. "I don't think you'll want to come back here once you've been in Australia though. Surely it's been on your mind all along. Who would want to live here when you could live in Australia?"

They talked for a good hour. Pippa was intrigued. She was also very practised at speaking with people on a daily basis—she was, after all, a physiotherapist. She told him the BetShed advert was good, and that she thought he spoke really well whenever he was on TV. Everything she said, in fact, was so positive that he was more and more convinced that it was the right thing to do. She invited herself over for a holiday at Christmas with the family. This conversation could not have gone any better. She assured him that the kids would adapt easily, that Marianne would enjoy the change of environment after everything she had gone through in recent times.

They shared the scones and ordered more with a fresh pot of tea. This was good, cathartic even. Pippa was not the person he would have reached out to if it wasn't for seeing her by chance last night in the supermarket. He was thankful for her input and knew that they had the makings of an enduring friendship. When they checked the time, Jarrod knew that they would both be in a rush. He'd already paid earlier when Pippa disappeared to the bathroom for a minute, and they quickly left and retraced their steps to the car. Jarrod dropped Pippa to where her car was parked and left her with a hug. She was delighted to have been able to help out and was now a party to some very big news. Jarrod knew that he could trust her to keep it to herself.

Before he drove off, he checked his phone. The hundreds of notifications were punctuated by missed calls from Manny Leonard. He needed to return the calls before it got too late in Australia.

32

Moscow

"Mr Leonard, how are you?" said Jarrod as the line clicked in after an extended delay.

"Ah, my good friend Jarrod. Just the man."

Mr Leonard had some news for Jarrod. The possibility of bringing Jarrod back to Australia was already well and truly viral, in the football world at least. Melbourne Victory, Perth Glory and Macarthur FC had all been in touch to declare their interest, as had a number of other clubs in the new second tier A-League 2. There were two teams in particular who had already got to the stage of talking money, both of them in Tasmania— South Hobart FC and Launceston City. It sounded tempting. Jarrod and Anna had been to Tasmania on holiday as kids and had great memories of the place, and Jarrod made a mental note to check in with Anna who had been there recently during the Women's World Cup. The practicalities of being in Tasmania while movie production was in Melbourne was the obvious hurdle and Jarrod made the decision on the spot that it had to be a Melbourne club.

"You're telling me that now?" asked Mr Leonard, with a chuckle in his voice.

"I just found out a few hours ago," said Jarrod, stretching the truth. "I'll be based in Melbourne from the end of this year."

"So, we've got Victory, City and Western United," said Mr Leonard. "Plus, we have South Melbourne and Bentleigh Greens in AL2."

Jarrod had to think for a minute to work out what AL2 was and felt like slapping his forehead when he realised Mr Leonard was referring to the second division.

"I was just at the Lakeside Stadium," said Jarrod. "Good facilities there, and I can imagine a good atmosphere. Can you look into it?"

"Athletics track around the field though," said Mr Leonard. "It's a bit 1980s Moscow."

"It's a bit twenty-first-century Gateshead," said Jarrod, reminding his agent of where he had spent the majority of his career.

"I'll get in touch. I know a few people there," said Mr Leonard.

"And Danny Zorbas is still there, I think," said Jarrod. "He was one of your players, wasn't he?"

"Ah yes, young Danny. Leave it with me."

Jarrod was happy to have put the idea out there that Division 2 was a possibility, and he left the call with a lot of hope and a little excitement too. He sat in his car and looked up the structure of the A-League on his phone.

The second division had been running for two years already with no relegation from the A-League, or from the second division, only promotion in a move that would bring both divisions up to sixteen teams. Now that they had proven the pyramid could work, the two divisions were joining together this year as A-League and A-League 2. For the next two years, one team would be relegated from the A-League at the end of the season. In the usual convoluted Australian way, the promoted teams from A-League 2 would be the first past the post and then the champions from the end of season Championship finals. Jarrod couldn't work out why they wouldn't make it like play-offs in England with teams two to five playing each other and the ultimate winner going up. No, they had to have a Premier and a Champion, and if the Premiers were also Grand Final winners, then the loser would be the second team promoted. Jarrod sat shaking his head, but he was intrigued, and he wanted to know more.

33

Turbulence

Jarrod was sitting in a bar in Terminal 3 at Heathrow, up on a high stool, watching a re-run of a Japanese J2-League game on his iPad. He was engrossed. The players were all so technically gifted, but the two non-Japanese players in the green shirts were clearly part of the team for their physicality as well as their undeniable skill. Mr Leonard had been in touch a few weeks prior to propose a one-off two-week sojourn in deepest Japan en route to Australia. Jarrod had run it past Marianne and she was okay with it, if not entirely delighted. Jarrod would, after all, be away for some time before Marianne and the kids made the move over, prior to Christmas.

Gary had already come to terms with losing Jarrod and had extended two of the loan deals they had in place to help fill the gap. June had been very accommodating to the changing situation and had struck deals with both J2-League Matsumoto Yamaga, where he was spending the next fifteen days, and with NPL club South Melbourne FC, where he was due to join up towards the end of November. Jarrod was still a Darlington player on paper, and at the conclusion of his season in Victoria, would technically be expected back on Teesside. He had fast-tracked his qualification at St George's Park in the interim and was awaiting results of the video session that formed the final assessment before being able to say he was a UEFA A Licenced coach. This had been an intense six weeks, and all the time, he kept a level head, continuing to push Darlington to stay in the top two of the division.

The turbulence and perfume of a passing lady, who had bumped his stool slightly, stirred him from the screen. The lady didn't stop. He looked down. He could see that his bag had been moved, and that the long shoulder strap was caught under the leg of the stool, preventing it from going any further. He sat upright. Perhaps he had just been kicking it unknowingly while he stared at the action on the screen. He stood up and looked around. The lady had already disappeared from view, but her perfume still lingered in the air. There were not many people in the open bar area, and no one was looking his way as if something suspicious had happened. There were people of all shapes and fashions in there, Heathrow being the crossroads of the world. Jarrod sat down again, edging his bag closer, but making sure the strap was still trapped under the leg of the stool. The words of a Nirvana song played through his mind: *Just because you're paranoid, don't mean they're not after you ...*

34

Sensation

A two-week, three-game stint in the town of Matsumoto, a five-hour drive from Tokyo, was meant to give Jarrod a taste of Japanese football and fulfil a desire that had been brewing since his first overseas trial in his teens. What he hadn't counted on was becoming an instant sensation, propelling the club into the play-off spots at the top of the second tier and achieving cult-hero status within a fortnight. He had scored in each game, and they had won them all. It was with a heavy heart that he left his lodgings in the town to head back to Tokyo for a meeting with a local journalist, and an appearance on live TV for the English Premier League coverage, before flying out for Australia later that night. He was turning his back on a chance to make history—he was still looking through the back window as the car entered onto the motorway, and he had mixed feelings about leaving such an opportunity behind.

Jarrod was dropped at the Park Hyatt in Shinjuku. The reception staff had been briefed and his luggage was checked in. He was showing blind faith in this process, having never met the journalist who had organised this meeting. He was two hours early and knew exactly what to do, commandeering a locker in the fancy forty-fifth-floor day spa and swapping his clothes for swim shorts. He took time to relax in the spa, took a refreshing cold-water dip in one of the small circular plunge pools and then knocked out a kilometre in the pool. He'd never been much of a swimmer, but Marianne had taken him along to her swimming a few times where he'd benefited from some expert tuition from an ex-Olympian. He at least knew how to conserve as much energy as possible to keep moving over a decent distance. There was also a high chance that he would be doing some water-based shooting as part of the upcoming movie role, so he was keen to get back into the groove.

As he climbed the steps from the pool, a gentleman was there holding the towel. It was Mr Barnes. Jarrod had met Adrian Barnes, a very eloquent and charming fellow, on two occasions in the past back in Newcastle. He was part of the entourage for the Indian businesswoman Murtaka Chiya, and Jarrod had him down as Murtaka's personal assistant. He was as immaculately dressed as he remembered, this time looking like a member of the royal family with his beige slacks and pristine white shirt with his sleeves rolled up.

"Mr Barnes," said Jarrod with little emotion, almost resigned to what was surely going to be a twist in his Tokyo experience, accepting the towel as if this was totally normal.

"Good day, Jarrod," said Mr Barnes, not offering to be addressed by anything other than Mr Barnes. "Good to see you."

Jarrod had only ever had a pleasant experience with Mr Barnes, but he definitely associated him with stressful times.

"Should I be happy to see you?" asked Jarrod.

"Oh, I'd say so," said Mr Barnes. "There's someone who would like to meet with you. Please come this way."

Again, Jarrod felt no inclination to decline the offer, and he knew there would be no choice anyway.

They walked together around the corner towards where the lockers were and then Mr Barnes walked ahead and checked through a small window in a big wooden door. He opened the door and beckoned Jarrod inside. He walked inside and was immediately stopped by the heat. This was a dry sauna, but it was almost unbearably hot. Jarrod could feel his eyes drying out immediately. After the initial shock he took a step back and removed the towel and hung it on the nearest hook by the door. The door closed after him. He crept around the corner, the floor at least not as hot as the air around him. Murtaka was there, sitting on the big wooden step, her long legs reaching up to the small towel she had to protect her modesty. The rest of her body was on show, and Jarrod noticed straight away that, other than the tiny towel, she was totally naked.

Jarrod didn't know where to look. Her long hair was covering her breasts, but there was nothing shy about her posture. One leg was straight ahead of her, the other bent at the knee and she was the picture of calm, eyes closed, and face pointed slightly upwards, perhaps to avoid the sweat running into her eyes. She slowly opened her eyes as Jarrod walked towards her and she stared into his.

"My friend, Jarrod. Come and sit."

She put her hand on the bench where she wanted him to sit. Jarrod's heart was now racing, and he couldn't tell if it was due to the heat or whether it was because he was flustered at seeing such a beautiful woman in such circumstances. Whatever the case, the heat would hide his blushing face.

"Murtaka, why are you here?" asked Jarrod.

"I'm here to see you," she said, moving her hand on to his thigh.

Jarrod didn't flinch but wanted to get up and run as fast as he could out of the sauna. He was spooked.

"I would like to know if you would like to help me and my company make football in Australia the richest sport in the country," she continued. "Is that something that interests you?"

"I don't follow," said Jarrod.

"We have captured the football market in Australia," Murtaka continued. "Now we have to make football the biggest sport and get a return on our investment."

Jarrod thought for a moment.

"If there's anything underhand involved, I'd like to know upfront," he said.

"We just need some of that special knowledge of yours," she said, placing her finger at the top of his chest and running it down between his pectoral muscles. "Can I count on you to give that to me?"

"As long as you're not asking me to cheat," said Jarrod. "Then I don't see why not."

Murtaka took her finger away.

"I promise," she said. "You're not coming back to Japan, I take it."

Jarrod had to think fast. "The offer is there," he said. "They want me in Matsumoto. It's very tempting."

"I'm very tempting too, Jarrod. You'll hear from me when you're in Melbourne. Look after yourself, and we'll see each other very soon."

She reached in and kissed him on the cheek, her face lingering very close to his, her breast touching up against his arm. He was frozen to the spot. He could almost feel Marianne's nails digging into his arm. Murtaka got up, holding the towel nonchalantly in her hand, and walked confidently over to the door and out of view. A whoosh signalled the door opening and a second whoosh meant she had gone. Jarrod's eyes felt as though they were burning. He quickly walked over to the door and grabbed the towel and left. There was no sign of Murtaka or Mr Barnes. In fact, there was no one there at all. He walked back through the corridor and into the spa area and eased himself back into the warm spa. It felt freezing cold, although he knew it would be the temperature of a hot bath. It must have been very hot in the sauna.

"Fuuuck," he said, resting his neck on the side of the spa. What had he got himself into now? How on earth was Murtaka here in Tokyo? How could he be such a creature of habit and end up in the spa? And why would she trust him ever again? How had he kept it together in there? He was almost melting into the spa now and had his ears under the water as if to hide from the outside world.

35

Lewinsky

The clock on the wall suggested that he should get out and get ready to meet the journalist. He had notions of there being no journalist and that Murtaka had used that as a ruse to get him here, but he had checked, and this was a real media person that he was meeting.

"Thank you for meeting with me," said the young reporter, with perfect English. Jarrod had met him as planned at the reception and they had settled into a booth in the lobby bar, cocooned in a cane orb, one luxurious seat each side of a beautiful wooden table.

"What can I do for you, Akio?" asked Jarrod, expecting this to be a football interview to cover his short spell in Japan. They had never met, and Jarrod didn't recognise the name of the publication, nor had taken the time to look it up.

"I would like to run through your relationship with Jens Lermann," said Akio, placing his mobile phone on the table and showing Jarrod that he was pressing record on a dictation app.

Jarrod raised his eyebrows. He had been formulating sentences in his head earlier in the day about how he had loved his time in the country and how he loved the Japanese way of life, the usual fluff. That certainly wasn't the theme here.

"Jens Lermann. The businessman?" asked Jarrod as if to clarify that this wasn't in fact the former Arsenal goalkeeper.

"Yes, Jens Lermann of LF Sports, the new media partner of the A-League in Australia," said Akio. "I believe you have had a relationship with him in the past?"

Jarrod didn't know what he should be divulging about his past dealings with a person who he had last seen under police custody at St James' Park when he left the field proudly wearing the famous black and white stripes after a dramatic pre-season victory against Barcelona. Mr Lermann had been part of a nefarious but well-intentioned plan to take over Newcastle United, his arm's-length relationship with the main protagonists in the plot allowing him to evade any criminal prosecution. Any journalist who had broached the subject with Jarrod since it had taken place had been responded to with the number of New Scotland Yard and an official email with police letterhead. Thousands of miles away from that madness, he didn't feel as constrained, and made a decision to at least give this young up-and-coming journalist something for his troubles.

"Yes, I met with Mr Lermann in Darlington," said Jarrod. "And then I saw him in Newcastle. I've not had any relationship with the man though. I'm listening."

"I would like you to respond to rumours that you are part of the LF Sports group, and that you are moving to Australia to assist in the growth of the Australian league structure. Is that what is happening?" asked Akio.

"Oh, I think you might have some unreliable sources, Akio," replied Jarrod, making sure to use his name so it would stick in his memory. "Nothing could be further from the truth."

"So, you were involved in unearthing a multi-million-dollar illegal betting syndicate in Europe that implicated Mr Lermann and his associates," said Akio in a more accusatory tone. "But you say you have no relationship with them?"

"That's correct," replied Jarrod, feeling himself moving on the defensive.

"And now you are simply taking a sideways move," said Akio. "Or even a backwards move to Australia to finish your career? And it just so happens that LF Sports has purchased the rights to the A-League. Can you see why these rumours have come about?"

"I'm almost tempted to laugh," said Jarrod. He thought back to his 'chance' meeting with Murtaka Chiya barely an hour ago and felt himself reddening slightly in the face. Akio would love to know who he had been talking to earlier. His usual line of heading to Australia to follow up a business opportunity wouldn't sound too good at this point either, so he responded in the classic time-wasting way of answering the question with another question. "So, who is starting rumours?"

"No one is starting rumours, Jarrod," said Akio. He leaned over the table as if to whisper something to Jarrod and Jarrod obliged by leaning in. "You should give me some information before you get yourself into something that is way outside your comfort zone."

Jarrod sat back and pondered. That was a statement, and this young journalist was showing a ruthless side that was totally unexpected.

"I can honestly say that I am not in any business relationship with Jens Lermann," said Jarrod slowly. As he said the words, he felt like Bill Clinton talking about Monica Lewinsky, and that his meeting with Murtaka was just about to place himself into a business relationship by association with Jens Lermann.

Akio slumped his shoulders.

"I want you to take this card," said the reporter, handing over a slick business card. "And contact me if you come across anything that feels a little unusual or criminal involving Mr Lermann. This is an important story for me, and I am following many leads. I think we will need to speak again once you have been in Australia for a while."

Jarrod did the right thing, took the business card in two hands and studied it. It had a Signal 7 number on it, and Jarrod couldn't help thinking of D.I. Allison who swore by the secret nature of the heavily encrypted messaging app.

"What is your motivation to find a story in this?" asked Jarrod once Akio had stopped the dictation.

"I ask the questions, Jarrod," said Akio smiling. "Let's just say, this could be a massive story that you're walking into."

Akio caught the eye of the waiter and asked for the bill.

"You're heading to DAZN now?" asked Akio, changing the subject. "I can drive you there."

"That's very kind of you, but …"

He stopped himself and decided instead to follow his instinct that Akio was one of the good guys.

"… hey, that would be great."

Akio drove Jarrod through Tokyo in his tiny car, Jarrod's baggage taking up the back seat and the boot space, and tried his best to extract more information out of Jarrod. He asked if Jarrod knew Murtaka personally. Jarrod brushed it off, but Akio smiled and looked at him with knowing eyes. They had arrived at their destination and the low budget car looked out of place amongst the swish cars in front of what could have been a hotel but was in fact a TV studio. Akio wound his window down and talked with the concierge, and a luggage trolley appeared and the two of them got out of the car.

"Thank you, Jarrod," said Akio. "I hope to see you in Australia soon."

"Thanks, Akio," said Jarrod. "I want to help, but I can't think what it is you want me to tell you. Thanks for the ride."

36

Lifestyle

Jarrod was whisked away up a lift and into a chill-out room where he saw some familiar faces from the EPL coverage he'd been watching for the last two weeks. He shook some hands and exchanged smiles, before being shown into make-up. This was as busy a day as he could remember, but it felt so normal. It was still early, and the early game wasn't due to get underway for over an hour, but Jarrod needed to be briefed on what he was expected to do.

He knew he was going to take part in the English Premier League coverage, and that he was to be the expert on Newcastle United. After all, he'd spent some time there in pre-season and he knew all the players personally. He just wasn't sure how this was going to work with the language barrier. Jarrod had about twenty words in his Japanese vocab now, and it seemed that there was little English on offer from the people in the chill-out room. Luckily, Jarrod recognised the next person who walked in. Mino Takamuno was a household name in Japan after spending three seasons in the EPL, two of which playing for Liverpool. It was an obvious choice for a pundit for a game involving the Merseyside giants, and Jarrod was delighted to have someone to talk with.

They were taken through the running order for the show, half an hour of pre-game analysis, watch the first half, ten minutes of half time chat and then only a ten-minute window before the next game to dissect the action from the second half and wrap up the result. Jarrod would be fed questions in his earpiece and he would respond in English, obviously. Mino would translate the response, ask further questions in English and then translate back into Japanese. It all sounded confusing, especially for Mino, but he was very practised at it.

The pre-game ramble went very well; the first half action was exciting. Andros Szczepanski had given Newcastle a surprise lead, Jarrod off his seat to punch the air, but Bastian Christou had pulled it back to 1–1 at half time. Jarrod's mind was wandering to the flight he had to catch later, but he was engrossed in the second half as the Newcastle defence finally gave way and Angelo Tettoni scored late on to give Liverpool an important win. The wrap-up post game brought to an end a very smooth and professional experience, but the last line of the coverage would leave Jarrod wondering what had been said in Japanese. He definitely heard the words LF Sports, and looked around the studio for someone to translate, but talk moved on seamlessly to the next game of the night as Jarrod was ushered off set and thanked by the producer.

A quick bathroom trip, where he looked in the mirror and immediately washed his face, and thoughts turned to the 1:00 a.m. flight he had to catch in just over two hours. Jarrod was in the zone, managing to say a final thank you to the producer and was then escorted by a member of staff through the corridors and back to the lifts where he was reunited with his baggage, wheeled by another immaculately dressed member of staff. With army-like precision, a car was waiting as he exited the main doors, the baggage loaded in the boot and Jarrod was on his way to Haneda Airport, his head buried in his mobile phone as he found his itinerary and clicked the check-in link. The business class leg to Sydney allowed him a slightly later check-in time, and he was delighted to be able to skip the long queue at the economy desk. Thankfully the savvy lady from South Melbourne, who booked this part of the journey that her club were paying for, had booked the business class ticket, the price difference only a couple of hundred dollars, but the saving in stress and hassle priceless.

His phone rang as he waited at the gate. It was Sebastian.

"Dad!" exclaimed his son, his voice much lower than he remembered.

"Hey, Sebbo," said Jarrod cheerily. "Good to hear from you. How's it going?"

"Can I go to Michaela's after school?" he asked. Jarrod paused, processing the sentence, rewinding from this non-stop lifestyle to the real life he had left behind in Darlington. "Mum's not answering. Just say yes and I'll flick Mum a text."

Jarrod felt a million miles away. His son was growing up way too fast and this was Michaela he was talking about, surely his first big crush. The fact that Sebastian hadn't even asked anything about Japan or Australia meant that he really wasn't thinking about anything other than going to Michaela's after school.

"What's Aneka doing?" asked Jarrod, knowing that he couldn't make any decisions based on the limited information he had, and also sure that the question would elicit more discussion and debate.

"She's going to Gabby's already," said Sebastian. "My football's been cancelled tonight because of parent teacher night for the older years, and I'd like to go with Aneka."

"Sure, Seb," said Jarrod, now understanding the dynamics. "Go for it."

"Great," said Sebastian. "See ya."

"Okay …" said Jarrod as the phone cut out.

Jarrod was left holding the phone at his ear and staring into space. He realised he was missing his family, and missing them a lot. He would normally be ferrying the kids around and would have been the responsible driver in that situation, turning up when the mums were a bottle and a half into a great catch-up session, the girls having a scream, and Sebastian and Michaela being awkward somewhere else in the house. He missed it, just being around them. It would be less than a month before they would be reunited, and it would be a month of upheaval for them, more goodbyes as they moved home again, this time moving right to the other side of the world. But Jarrod knew it was a good move and it was time for them to understand what it meant to live in the best country in the world.

37

Stone

The final email that Jarrod sent on the complimentary business class Wi-Fi on the fancy new ANA plane was a reply to Duddy. He had been giving daily updates regarding his contract with Zion Films and Robert Biscotti, but Jarrod had stopped replying to them as nothing seemed to be changing. He still hadn't seen or signed any contract that mentioned the vast sums of money being peddled by Duddy. The email was a one-liner, that he was on approach to Sydney, and he would be in touch very soon, but he wanted his agent to know that he was very close to starting the project and still hadn't put pen to paper.

The mid-morning arrival into Kingsford Smith Airport was ideal, and Jarrod felt fresh after the five hours' sleep following dinner. The usual trick of declaring food items and then answering 'chocolate' when prompted to get through the long queues after the baggage claim got him straight through, and there were Mum and Dad waiting for him as he turned the corner. He left his trolley behind and raced up to hug them. It hadn't been that long since he saw them, but he held them both tight in a group hug.

"Welcome home, Jarrod," said Dad, his eyes welling up with happy tears.

The journey out to the suburbs and to Jarrod's family home was incredibly quick, with a new tunnel taking them a good stretch of the way before they popped out near Olympic Park. The distant suburbs were now closer than he remembered to the city and the Eastern Suburbs, and the number of new houses in the street was testament to the area's emergence as one of the most sought-after suburbs in Sydney. There were now high-rise buildings behind their house and a light rail line running along the adjoining street. Things had changed and Mum and Dad were quick to point out the changes, very proud residents of their neighbourhood.

The house was just the way he remembered though, the front door more modern than the rest of the exterior and the clean and crisp décor still resisting the trinket clutter of old age. After meeting the new dog, almost a replica of their last two beige dogs, and Dad opening the back doors to let in the warmth from the sunny late November morning, Jarrod was already feeling at home. Even more so when he went up to his old room and found it just as he remembered from last time. Jarrod looked at himself in the mirrored wardrobes and smiled. He was home. His mind was back in his youth, and he was happy.

A long dog walk to the nearby Meadowbank Park and a home-cooked dinner rounded off the most relaxing day in Jarrod's memory. As he readied himself for bed, he had a text from Duddy that prompted him to check his emails. He had done well to make it this late and the last thing he felt like doing was logging on. Sure enough, an email was there, a short paragraph from Zion Films forwarded from Duddy. They wanted to meet in the morning and would send a car to pick him up. This one day of rest would definitely be a rarity. Jarrod went down to grab a glass of water, choosing the Gateshead FC glass that he had brought over years ago, and said goodnight to Dad, letting him know of his new plans in the morning. He hadn't told Mum about the movie, and Dad hadn't mentioned it since they'd talked a couple of months ago about it. Jarrod was conscious of not spreading the word until it was set in stone. As far as his parents were concerned, Jarrod was preparing for the rest of his life and coming to finish his career in Australia, riding the excitement of the A-League second division and the new TV deal.

38

Fox

Jarrod was up early, perhaps a by-product of travel weariness, but he felt switched on. He was ready, smartly dressed as if going to a business meeting, and waited, fidgeting, for the car to show up at the allotted time. The busy period was over, school zones were back to normal, and his driver found the route to Moore Park on his in-car navigation. Jarrod hadn't been told where they were meeting. His first guess was the new Sydney Football Stadium, but the obvious choice would be the movie production area formerly known as Fox Studios.

Jarrod was ignoring his buzzing phone as they joined on to Victoria Road at Gladesville and headed for the bridge. He was taking in the surroundings, remembering all the places he would go to play football when he was very young, and all the places he would hang out in his early teens. The car came to a halt at a set of traffic lights and another car pulled up slowly beside him. Jarrod glanced up as the black car edged forward. He could only see a silhouette of a driver through the lightly tinted windows, but the window started to lower, and he saw a wiry man with a shock of black hair. He pulled down his glasses. Jarrod froze. It was Yannick Lefevre, almost smirking, but looking quite menacing at the same time.

Jarrod did a double take and lowered his window too, almost against his good judgement. Jarrod's driver sensed that he was going to talk with the driver of the other car and didn't move, despite the lights changing to green.

"Hello, my friend," shouted Yannick, with a smile that revealed either a missing or a discoloured tooth. "We'll be talking with you soon."

Yannick patted the lapel of his jacket, similar to the threatening gesture he had made when they last spoke at St James' Park in Jarrod's last appearance for Newcastle. Surely he wouldn't have a gun. Jarrod was staring with his eyes wide open and realised it. He shook his head, showing no emotion, put up the window of the car and looked straight ahead as if to dismiss the threat. Both cars drove on and they stopped again at the next set of lights after the Gladesville Bridge, Jarrod having stared right past the resplendent Sydney Harbour Bridge in the distance. Again, the black car edged up slowly and the window pulled down. Yannick nodded his head with his eyebrows raised, acknowledgement of the shake of the head he had just received from Jarrod. There was no way Jarrod's window was going down this time, and the cars drove on. Jarrod glanced around at the right time to see Yannick turn right and disappear from view.

Jarrod's heart was racing, and the sweat on his brow was nothing to do with the warm day. He tossed around scenarios in his head for the rest of the journey, contemplating ringing D.I. Allison or even the contact he had from the Australian Federal Police. He even considered asking the driver who he was working for but kept quiet. The car stopped for a horse crossing the road before turning into a back street and into the backlot of what looked like production studios.

The driver pulled the car up to a doorway and a gentleman appeared. Jarrod thanked his driver and got out of the car, the man offering his hand to shake.

"Stevie Mosseman, Barrowful Productions."

This was the guy he'd initially spoken with when he'd dismissed the idea that this was something serious. "Absolute pleasure to meet you," he continued. "We have a lot to get through today. Come on through."

Jarrod went along with the flow, despite still being rattled by his earlier encounter and still being unsure where he stood with regards to a contract. They walked up a few steps into a demountable building, like the ones they would have at school back in the day.

"This is Barrowful Productions," said Stevie. "Just the two of us. This is J.B., who is organising the logistics of bringing everyone together from around the world to Australia."

Jarrod shook the young lady's hand.

"J.B. and I are the only ones out in Australia at the moment, and this is our temporary home. We'll have something a bit grander in scale when we get to Melbourne to start shooting. Think of us as the company that makes the movie happen. Our partners at Zion Films deal with the less glamourous side of things, funding, finance and all that. Thanks for coming in, Jarrod. Please, take a seat."

Stevie produced a document and went through a timeline of what was expected of Jarrod in the lead-up to Christmas. There were only five weeks, but it was a comprehensive document. He was due down in Melbourne in two days to meet his new teammates and get ready for his first match as a South Melbourne player. Jarrod had been assigned a personal trainer who he would meet with every weekday morning; he had acting lessons four times a week as well as stuntman training two mornings a week. He would check in with the production company three times a week and, from the second week, there were reading groups with fellow actors to learn scripts and rehearsals. Jarrod noticed that this wasn't only until Christmas, it was until the beginning of April. This was going to be punishing!

When Stevie asked if there were any questions, Jarrod took the opportunity.

"So, do I need to sign a contract before all of this happens? I mean, I'm giving you six months or more of my life here. I should be at least official by the time I start this process."

"Oh yes, of course," said Stevie. "The contracts are still with Robert.

We just need a couple more days to get that through the lawyers and accountants and we'll be ready to get you signed up and started. Don't worry. It's the way it works. You have my word. It's as your agent Duddy would have explained. Now, excuse me for a moment, I need to make a few calls."

The young J.B. pounced as Stevie left the room.

"Right, I need to get some basic information from you," she said. They sat for another half an hour, J.B. peppering Jarrod with questions such as address, emergency contacts, phone numbers, email addresses. He didn't have an answer for some of them. He would be in a hotel in Melbourne for at least a week, and he figured his dad would be the closest person as an emergency contact.

"What's the J.B. stand for?" asked Jarrod when it was clear that there were no further questions.

"Jacqui Brown," said J.B., smiling. "Bit of a movie character name, and there were three Jacquis when I first started working for the company, so I was known immediately as J.B."

"It suits you," said Jarrod, almost blushing when he said it. It sounded like he was being flirty.

"I might have to drop it soon though," she said. "Your initials will be all over the place, in run sheets, scripts, memos. Can't get confused between us two, eh?"

Jarrod smiled. Fair point.

"Say, do you know where filming will take place?" asked Jarrod.

"Well, I know it's in Melbourne," she said with a laugh. "It was meant to be in Coffs Harbour, but that wasn't going to be ready for another twelve months."

"So, where in Melbourne?" pressed Jarrod.

"It's pretty central, a bit like here," said J.B. "Docklands Studios. Next to the big wheel. Oh, and the Docklands Stadium of course. You'd know that."

"Sure, although I don't know Melbourne that well."

Jarrod could picture where it was in relation to the Lakeside Stadium, where he'd be playing home games with South Melbourne. It was very close.

"There'll be a lot of time on location though," said J.B. "Out East, I'm told. I've never been there myself."

Stevie burst back through the door.

"Looks like you've been through everything with J.B.," he said. "Your car is here to take you back out West. Before that though I'll give you some telephone numbers. I'll just send them through now—save them to your phone."

Stevie fiddled with his phone and Jarrod's pinged three times as the contact cards came through.

"You should have three there," he continued. "First one is Malik, your personal trainer. Yes, you need to be in shape, not just fit."

Jarrod looked at J.B. with one eyebrow raised.

"Second one is Alex, from the Stunt Studio. He'll be expecting you next week. It's all in the document I gave you earlier."

"What sort of stunts are we talking here?" asked Jarrod.

"Look, most of it is generated using graphics these days, and we'll not be asking you to jump out of a gyrocopter with a jet pack or anything," said Stevie. "But there'll be a lot of jumping, falling and fighting, on land and in the water."

Jarrod glanced at his growing pile of paperwork and the document was indeed there.

"And the third is the main number for our Docklands Studios. You should check in every couple of days if you haven't heard from us. J.B. will be your contact. In fact, you'll probably not need to as we'll be in touch every day anyway. There's so much to get through. You've got acting lessons most days, and there's a whole script you'll need to work through. You're not going to be bored in Melbourne, that's for sure. We'll be down there from Friday setting up our base there. God, there's so much to do."

Jarrod stood up. He shook J.B.'s hand and Stevie showed Jarrod the way back out through the door and to the car. It was the same driver. This was no Uber.

"Thanks for coming at such short notice," said Stevie. "We'll be in touch via Duddy with the details of the contract, and we'll see each other later in the week down in Victoria."

Jarrod was almost bundled into the car, the door closed quickly, and they drove off. Stevie scurried back inside, his ear pressed to his phone. This was a high-stress environment Jarrod was walking into and he was a little alarmed. But very excited. The small screen in the back of the car played a welcome message and then cut to an ad. It was BetShed. Jarrod had no idea the company was mainstream in Australia. He smiled as his almost animated character on the screen turned his head up to the sky with his fists clenched and roared.

39

Banking

Jarrod pottered around at his parents' house the following day and took a train up to a shopping centre to try on some clothes. Stevie had said that he would be getting a personal trainer, so getting new clothes at this point might not be the best idea. His shape might change soon. Approaching the twilight of his career, he had already noticed his legs and his backside were getting slightly bigger, but he maintained the same weight that he had done for many years, at the top end of the normal height to weight ratio without being classified as overweight. This truly was a day where nothing would happen. He was due down in Melbourne the following day and everything was organised. His phone was strangely quiet too, but he did get a text from his bank in the UK, who were querying why there was such a large transaction on his account.

Jarrod logged in to his internet banking and saw that he had a deposit of nearly half a million pounds in his everyday account. His eyes widened. He found a bench in the main shopping centre thoroughfare and sat down. The description was pending, so he couldn't tell where the money had been deposited from. He called the number that came up in his messages in the banking app.

"No, I think that's all normal," said Jarrod. "It's an initial deposit for some work I'm doing in Australia."

The banking representative on the other end of the line was excited but Jarrod was keen to end the call there and then. He flicked a text to Duddy to ask whether the contract had been finalised, saying that there was half a million pounds in his bank account all of a sudden.

It was probably too early for even Duddy to reply so Jarrod just got on with his day. There was a nagging feeling that the money could be something else.

40

Mediterranean

The passengers filed off the plane, along the air bridge and into Tullamarine Airport. He would have a representative of South Melbourne to meet him. Sure enough, there was a stout man holding a sign with the blue and white logo and the acronym SMFC. He recognised Jarrod immediately as he almost walked past and stuck out a hand to stop him. They shook hands and made their way to the baggage reclaim. Jarrod had gone over a little with the baggage limit but didn't get hit with any fees after flashing his Qantas membership card from his time with the Socceroos. They waited a good twenty minutes, Jarrod using the time to find out more about the man he had never met and to whom he was trusting his life.

Turned out his name was Johnny, he was part of the supporters' club, but was an Uber driver and was always happy to do a special job for his beloved South Melbourne.

"You're going to love it here," said Johnny. "I'm guessing you've not spent much time in Melbourne. There's so much going on."

"My sister kept banging on how good it was," said Jarrod, "I thought I'd better come and see what all the fuss was about. The team's going pretty well, I see."

"Sure thing," said Johnny. "Third in the table in our first season in the A-League. That's pretty special."

Jarrod was tickled by how he called the league the A-League. Whilst it was technically the A-League, it was more commonly referred to as the Second Division but was officially known as the A-League Division 2. The Championship may have been a more commonly used term to keep it in line with other second divisions, especially in the UK, but Jarrod found it refreshing that it was Division 2.

"Who do we have on the weekend?" asked Jarrod, knowing very well that they had a home game with Sydney powerhouse APIA Leichhardt, but he was unsure of the kick-off time on Saturday.

"We've got APIA, always a good Mediterranean derby," said Johnny, smiling.

Jarrod was aware that the ethnicity of clubs was important in Australia but had figured it would have been tempered somewhat by the A-League and Football Australia to try and make clubs more open to everyone.

"They're well behind us but have a game in hand," continued Johnny. "It's a six-pointer. Massive game. Plus, we owe them a touch-up."

Jarrod's bags finally arrived, and he got them off the carousel and onto his trolley. It was quite a stash.

They found the car in the multi-storey car park across the road and set off for Melbourne. It wasn't long before they arrived at Jarrod's home for the short term, a serviced apartment near the stadium and tantalisingly close to the Pullman Hotel he'd been staying in with the Socceroos earlier in the year. Johnny was keen to take Jarrod to training, and they were only in the apartment long enough to listen to the basics from the concierge before they headed back to the car and drove the short distance to the stadium.

It was clear that Johnny was some sort of celebrity around here. He had a reserved car space, he knew everyone by first name as he walked through the front gate, and the players all stopped to greet him as he walked around the edge of the training field towards the group of coaches who were convening for a chat. The manager, Aurelio Kantaris, looked up and cheered loudly when he saw the two approaching.

"Johnny!" he cried. "You've brought our new star man!"

Aurelio and Johnny greeted each other warmly. Aurelio offered his hand to Jarrod, and he shook it, as well as all the hands of the coaches.

"Welcome to South Melbourne," said Aurelio. "Have you got your boots with you?"

Jarrod smiled. Little did Johnny know that he did have his boots in his bag. He took off his tracksuit to reveal shorts and a training shirt, sat on the grass and pulled on some socks and put on his boots. For all Jarrod knew, Aurelio was joking, but he'd called his bluff. He was ready in a minute, and went to shake hands with his new teammates, leaving a pile of belongings in a heap where the coaches stood. One of the coaches came across and ushered Jarrod over for a warm-up while the rest of the players did a passing drill. Jarrod was so raring to go. It had been five days since he had touched a ball and, aside from some stiffness from sitting in cars and planes, he was totally niggle-free. He joined his teammates again once they were organised for a game.

The next thirty minutes was a baptism of fire for Jarrod. He had mistakenly considered this level of football to be lower than Darlington. Whilst it was definitely not as intense, the skill level was as good if not better, and the direct forward play that he was used to in England was a contrast to the keep-ball that was on show here at his first training session. He was almost frustrated to have to go backwards and sideways so often, as the option for the through ball and the athletic overlap was never given. What it did show him though was that physically he was going to be one step above all of these players. He could run for hours, and even in this half-hour practice game, he found himself in attack and then in defence, able to keep up with everyone.

The sweat was dripping off him at the end. He felt great. He noticed his bib was drenched, surely something to do with the humidity, and he joined the rest of the players in the dressing room after gathering his clothes from the side of the field. What a great introduction to his new team, and it had given him a short sharp lesson as to what to expect in his new footballing venture.

That evening he caught up with his old friend Danny. They had played together at Parramatta, and they had stayed in touch ever since. Danny had been with South Melbourne for a few years but had recently retired following a recurrence of a long-standing hamstring injury. He was part of the coaching set-up for the women's game now and would be a great person to help him get to know Melbourne better. They enjoyed a drink and a pizza at a fancy Italian restaurant nearby and swapped stories after many years apart. Settling into Melbourne would be great, but he knew that as soon as word got out about the real reason for his move to Melbourne, he would be unable to head off out for dinner on a whim. He was determined to make the most of it. Danny would be a good person to know.

41

Angst

The Friday night game was now a big thing in Australia. Since LF Sports had taken over coverage of pretty much all football in the country, they had muscled in on the NRL and AFL and gone head-to-head with the traditional Friday night footy, making this one a free-to-air game on TV every week, and it was a massive hit. The pre-game and post-game shows were fantastic viewing, and a full preview of the weekend's fixtures made it a very popular show. Jarrod had a call from Mr Leonard to let him know of LF Sports' offer to be involved in this Friday's show. Sure enough, just as he was heading back to the apartment from dinner, he traded texts with the producers and received a call to ask him to come in tomorrow at 5:00 p.m. for the evening. Their studios were next to the Docklands Stadium, and it would be a great opportunity to have a quick look around the area.

First though, Jarrod had to get himself settled in his apartment and get some sleep. This was quite a homely space, a few years old, with a full kitchen, just missing the food. The kitchen was sparkling clean as if it was never used for cooking. Jarrod had been in the apartment all of thirty minutes since he arrived and his well-practised routine of unpacking toiletries and clothes from years of travelling through England meant he was in bed and ready for sleep in half an hour. Time to check in at home first though and he rang Marianne. She sounded frazzled.

"Are you sure we're doing the right thing here?" asked Marianne.

"What makes you ask?" queried Jarrod.

"It's just ..." she started, and then she went silent.

"Are you okay?" asked Jarrod with concern in his voice.

"The kids," she said. "They love it here so much. I love it here. Why are we giving this all up?"

Jarrod was puzzled. They'd been through this before, and they were as strong a family unit as they had ever been. Their decision had been made and everyone was clear on what was going to happen. They had all been excited when he had left for Japan. It was an exciting time of life for all of them, if a little daunting.

"Oh, Marianne," said Jarrod. "This is such a big thing. We just have to get through the next few weeks, and you'll be over here, and we'll be making the best moves of our lives. We're going to have the best life ever in Australia."

Jarrod could sense some angst from his wife. She put Sebastian on for a few words, Jarrod grilling him about his time at Michaela's, which lightened the mood. Then Aneka chimed in with a long announcement of what she had been doing at school recently. School was off today for a teacher training day, and it was hammering with rain in Darlington, another wintry, cold day in the North East of England. Jarrod could understand the lack of desire to get prepared for relocation when the weather gods were at play, but he hoped Marianne hadn't lost touch of the big picture. It was coming into summer in Melbourne and the city was alive.

"Can't wait to see you, Jarrod," said Marianne. "Promise me this will be all worth it in the end."

"Oh, I promise all right!"

Jarrod left that conversation a little concerned. There appeared to be a chink in the family's armour, and he felt that he should be there, especially to help with the relocation. He lay awake for quite some time, mulling over that conversation and trying to make sense of his own thoughts.

42

Studios

After an unsettled night's sleep, Jarrod was slow to wake. His body clock was all over the place, but he was up and dressed in time to head out to training. Johnny was waiting at the entrance to the apartment block, and they made their way to the Lakeside for a morning session ahead of the big 'derby' game on Saturday. The professional set-up at South Melbourne gave Jarrod a sense of belonging. He was given a full training kit, embroidered already with his initials, and slotted straight into training as he had done the previous day. After the session, quite a physical workout followed by a good session on set pieces, Jarrod was welcomed into Aurelio's office. He was taken through some contract paperwork with another man, who was introduced as Mike, and was then asked to head outside for photographs with the waiting media.

Jarrod was taken aback by the interest his arrival had generated. There were TV cameras as well as a pack of journalists and photographers. He was handed his new playing shirt and instructed to stand in various poses to highlight all of the sponsorship patches. The sleeve sponsor caught his eye as he was turned sideways to get a close-up shot. The patch read Chiya Inc—Jarrod tried his best to avoid looking startled and simply smiled at the cameras. He just couldn't get away from Murtaka Chiya and the memories of his summer sojourn in Newcastle-Upon-Tyne, embroiled in the takedown of a major crime syndicate that seemed to have had mixed results.

Jarrod surveyed the faces behind the cameras and Akio, the reporter he had met in Tokyo, caught his eye and they nodded heads in acknowledgement. What the hell was he doing here?

Jarrod then treated the waiting media to a few keep-ups for the cameras before answering a few basic questions about what he was looking forward to with his new club, the LF Sports banner used as a backdrop. Time was ticking on, and Jarrod was conscious that he had to be at the television studios at 5:00 p.m., and he also wanted to have a look around the Docklands to see the studio where he'd be based initially for the shooting of *From the Gallows*, the Harlowe Croft movie that had brought him to Australia in the first place. The media scrum dispersed, and Jarrod checked a few basics about the running order of the game the next day before Johnny dropped him back at the apartment. Jarrod could have been driven straight to the TV studios but decided to keep Johnny out of the picture so he could go sightseeing first.

The Uber dropped him at the LF Sports studios and Jarrod made his way around the block and along a street dominated by soulless warehouses and high metal fences. A boom gate signalled the main entrance and on a small sign containing the tenants there was a handwritten Barrowful Productions. Jarrod glanced at his phone and decided that he had enough time to say hello. The security guard phoned ahead for him, and he was directed to a door in the first warehouse. As he approached, J.B. burst out of it and held it open for him to come through. She welcomed him with a kiss on the cheek that brought back memories of his sauna encounter with Murtaka. J.B. did look hot and had the air of someone who was rushed off her feet.

"What a surprise," she said. "Come and meet the team."

Surprisingly, for a Friday night approaching 5:00 p.m., every desk in the big open-plan office was taken and there was a lot of energy.

"Wow. Are all these people working on the movie?"

"That's right," said J.B. "We've also got another ten or so people in Sydney organising the logistics for the shoots."

Jarrod shook a few hands. They all referred to J.B. as Jacqui, so Jarrod quickly adopted her normal first name. There was only room for one J.B. in here. There were scriptwriters, product designers, art directors, and they were all keen to meet the star of the movie. Jarrod took Jacqui to one side for a moment.

"Say, Jacqui," he started, still trying to formulate his question. "Is the contract in place? Did I get the advance?"

Jacqui took a step back. "Yes, why do you ask?" she asked, looking surprised.

"Oh, I just haven't had confirmation yet," said Jarrod.

"We let Duddy know yesterday that the advance had been paid and the contract is with him ready to sign," said Jacqui, not quite sure as to why Jarrod wouldn't be aware of all this.

"Yes, yes," said Jarrod. "The money is there. I just didn't get any notice."

Jacqui looked relieved. Jarrod was relieved that he had discovered where the money in his account had come from and that it was indeed for the movie.

"Listen," said Jarrod. "I'm due next door at LF Sports in eight minutes. I'd better get a move on."

"Okay," said Jacqui. "Thanks for dropping in unexpectedly. As you can see, it's full steam ahead here. Busy week coming up for you."

Jarrod left with a few quick smiles and goodbyes as he retraced his steps and broke into a jog as he passed the security guard with a wave.

43

Buzz

"Jarrod, great to see you," said the svelte presenter as Jarrod was shown into the production area. "Tom Archison. I've followed your career all the way from Gateshead. Great to finally meet you."

Jarrod had seen Tom many times on TV and knew of him as a record-breaking player with the Socceroos after equalling scoring in the most games in a row with the national team back when Jarrod was a youngster. They'd been connected on social media, but Jarrod was quite removed from his online presence these days.

"Thanks for having me," said Jarrod. He was experiencing an overload of new faces and names already since being in Melbourne, but his mind was sharp, and he felt ready to be in front of the camera. He'd be doing it full time soon anyway, so why not get stuck in. "Really looking forward to this game."

Jarrod met the rest of the panel, one of them Marty Clarkson, full back for the Socceroos and Melbourne Victory player, and he offered a hug to Jarrod as soon as he saw him. The producer explained the running order of the evening, which included a discussion over dinner, a session in make-up and then the pre-match show. They would then watch the first half and come back during half time and at full time to offer some analysis. This was pretty standard and was similar to the experience in Tokyo. The only problem was that Jarrod was way behind the rest of the panel with his A-League knowledge. He was told not to worry, and to give his own insight into what he saw on the field. The two teams in action were Floreat Athena of Perth and Sydney Olympic. This was a big game for the Greek communities in both cities, and Jarrod would be asked to contribute a few words about what it meant playing for a club with Greek origins.

Over the early dinner, Jarrod took the opportunity to ask the third panellist, South Hobart's Welsh import Grant Howett, what he knew about LF Sports. Grant had been lured from the lower leagues of English football too, his Newport County team finding success in the same division as Jarrod's Darlington.

"They seem to have unlimited money," he said. "They're ploughing so much into the game here, and it doesn't look like it's going to end soon. Fair play though, we're getting good crowds, the football is fantastic and there's a lot of opportunities for overseas players to come and have a go. Good to see you join the revolution, Jarrod."

"Does South Hobart get money directly from LF Sports?" asked Jarrod.

"I think they do," said Grant. "It's all linked anyway. It's as though I'm an LF Sports employee. I didn't get a choice of whether or not I was coming on the show tonight. Good thing I enjoy it."

That was interesting insight. They both rejoined the group conversation and went through the team lists. There were some familiar names, former Socceroos, ex-EFL players and a couple of South Americans with good pedigrees. The late stages of the Wellington Phoenix vs Brisbane Roar game were showing on the monitors with the sound turned off, the footage coming from a live feed via the NZ studio. This was a football lover's playground and Jarrod felt at home.

The game was a cracker, played in front of a packed house in Perth, despite it being a 5:00 p.m. kick-off there. The football was high quality without being as frantic as Jarrod had remembered. The half time analysis was spent deliberating a VAR call. The new rule introduced this season where both teams were given two opportunities in a game to call a VAR challenge was refreshing. The angle of the footage of the offside was a little off-centre so it was difficult to gauge, but the technology was right, and the home team were denied a goal. The debate about the validity of the new VAR rule continued for the rest of the half time chat. Jarrod found himself defending the new ruling, claiming that the risk of using up the VAR challenges could create fascinating sub-plots to the game, and that the reduction in VAR interruptions would only help the enjoyment of the fans in the stadium itself.

The post-match discussion was a celebration of what was a fabulous game, Sydney Olympic holding on for a 2–1 win despite a real fightback by the home side. That put Olympic in a good position, alongside APIA Leichhardt and in striking distance of the top four. Jarrod was asked a couple of questions about the game tomorrow night and answered expertly without having to know anything about the opponents. The buzz that he felt as the final credits rolled was palpable. This could be a regular gig, and he hoped he came across as confidently as he felt on screen.

The production crew were heading around the corner to the Docklands to have a nightcap as the rest of the program moved to a pre-recorded preview show. Jarrod joined them but had made his excuses and left the bar before the first round of drinks materialised. There was no point in jeopardising his condition and performance for his debut in Australia, and half an hour later he was climbing into bed, a cursory flick of his Twitter revealing that his appearance on TV had been well received. He texted an "I love you" to Marianne and the kids, Marianne firing back with "George Clooney, they're calling you. Silver fox" in reference to the social media interest in his punditry appearance. Jarrod sat up and looked in the mirror on the other side of the room. Not that many greys, surely!

44

Specialist

Match day had arrived, a Saturday 5:00 p.m. kick-off at the Lakeside. The squad was due at the stadium at 1:00 p.m. Jarrod had organised a coffee meet with his sister's friends, Dana and Milena, Anna having insisted on it and set up the meet herself from her new home in the US. She warned Jarrod that he would need tickets for the day's game as they were big football fans. She also bet him that he would find Milena attractive. Jarrod had already met them when he was last over, and Anna was right about Milena. He grabbed a newspaper and found a seat at the café, but before he could open it, the girls appeared, both planting a big kiss on his cheek before he could even stand up to greet them.

This was such a tonic. Jarrod felt so far away from his sister. She had just completed her first half-season with Portland Thorns in the NWSL, culminating in a Grand Final appearance and a lot of love from the fans and media. The way these two ladies ripped into conversation, it was clear that they were great friends of hers and they also knew quite a bit more about him than he had anticipated. Milena made out that she was engaged to Taj Hamadi, the former Socceroos wonderkid. Jarrod could see right through that ruse though and they all burst out laughing. Jarrod didn't want to leave, but his agenda and his eagerness to be at the Lakeside in good time meant that he had to curtail a fabulous morning. He handed over his two free tickets to the game, apologising that they weren't in a catered box, and they left with big hugs and promises to catch up when Anna was back from the States in the next week or so.

Jarrod made his way back to his apartment. He cut his toenails in the bathroom, something he would never do inside at home, and while he was sitting on the closed toilet, he checked his phone. There was a barrage of messages from Duddy regarding his contract. It looked like Duddy's phone had not been sending texts for a couple of days and they were all coming through at once. That put his mind at ease about the money sitting in his bank account and about the existence of an actual contract for the movie deal. In his current mindset though, the movie was the last thing on his mind and all he wanted to do was make a good first impression in his debut for South Melbourne.

He was downstairs in the reception area soon after, decked out in his SMFC training gear. The club had ordered a car to come and collect him, Johnny not available on match days as he would be at one of the local pubs selling merchandise and organising tickets for the supporters' club. A white Mercedes pulled up at the front door and the smartly dressed driver got out and signalled to Jarrod. They drove off at speed.

"Good afternoon, Jarrod, my name is Temuri," said the driver. He was bald and could have easily been the Newcastle United legend of the same name. "If you don't mind, I have a few questions for you."

Jarrod was in a good mood and was happy to hear any questions.

"Who is the set-piece specialist in your team today?" he asked.

Jarrod knew what this was about. The conversation took him back a few months to when he was embroiled in the illegal betting scandal that took him to St James' Park.

"Who's asking?" asked Jarrod with a smile. "You're not looking for inside information, are you?"

"Of course I am!" came the honest response. "I like to make a bet on each game, and I don't know if it is you or Jon Kosmidis who is going to be taking the free kicks and penalties."

"Ha ha," said Jarrod, reassured that this was a genuine supporter who was having a little flutter on the game. "I'll be taking corners from the left and free kicks around the box. Jon hasn't missed a penalty in two years.

If he's not on the field, I'll happily take one."

"Thank you, Jarrod," said Temuri. "Do you know if you'll be playing the whole game?"

"I expect so," said Jarrod. "Although I've had limited training this week and a lot of travel. Don't be surprised if I run out of steam."

"One final question," asked the driver after a long pause as they turned into the entrance to the stadium. "A player is racing through on goal. You are the last man. Do you take him down and get sent off to save the goal?"

"Woah," said Jarrod, reaching for his bag and ready to get out of the car. "I'll do whatever it takes at the right time to make sure we win."

"Thank you, Jarrod," said Temuri, and Jarrod was already out of the car shaking his head. It was an interesting question though. He was rarely in that situation on the field, but it had happened a few times. He had often won the ball cleanly but had always waited for the player to get in the box before trying a tackle and had only received a yellow card if it resulted in a foul. The seed had been sown in his mind.

45

Number

The teams were coming in from their warm-up. Jarrod noticed Temuri, at least he thought it was him, having only spoken to the back of his shiny head earlier in the day. He gave a wave which Jarrod returned. Jarrod then watched as he walked over to a tall, thin character and knew exactly who it was. That fucking Yannick Lefevre. Yannick was engrossed in his phone for a moment and looked as though he was hurriedly completing something before looking up with an air of satisfaction at having completed his task and patting Temuri on the back with a smile. Jarrod winced. What was that lowlife doing here? He just couldn't shake him.

The referee for today, a stern-looking but attractive lady, caught up with Jarrod as they walked into the tunnel area.

"G'day, Jarrod," she said, softening her features as if she had just been cured of white line fever. "Pleased to meet you." She held out her hand to shake. "I'm Isabella," she continued, "You can call me Bella. I'm a big fan of yours."

"Wow, pleased to meet you too," said Jarrod. "A big fan? Of mine? What …?"

Bella had quite a strong English accent, probably Yorkshire, Jarrod had decided, drawing on his many years of being in and around English accents.

"My dad's from Gateshead," said Bella. "We used to go to the games whenever he wasn't refereeing."

"Oh, your dad was a referee in England?"

"Steve Alves," she said. "You might know him?"

"Ah, yes," said Jarrod, surprised. "I recognise the name. I think he used to do a lot of the pre-season games for the reserves and juniors."

"That's him," said Bella. "Good-looking fella, just like his daughter."

"Say hi from me," said Jarrod. "I'll see you back out on the field in ten minutes."

Bella retreated to her referee room with a cheeky smile.

The crowd had swollen when the players arrived back onto the field, led by the referees, and with their mini mascots by their sides. There was a huge roar and it felt as though there were more people here than there would have been at a regular Darlington fixture at the Arena. Jarrod had been named in central midfield. Regular captain and fellow midfielder Jason Zalalas was serving the last of a three-match suspension for a fracas in a fiery game last month, so manager Aurelio had an easy choice to slot Jarrod into his spot. He was alongside Harry De Fonte, who had previously been dropped to the bench after two lacklustre displays, according to accounts of the two games before Jarrod had arrived.

Jarrod was keen to get involved and was sucked out of midfield trying to chase a ball that bounced slowly through to the keeper. Aurelio was shouting to leave it, and Jarrod knew straight away that he had to think differently and resist the temptation to go gung-ho, looking to attack whenever they won possession. He was in Australia now. He would probably be affected by the conditions that were warm with an equally warm wind, and he could feel the sweat building up already above his eyebrows. APIA were a capable-looking team, and they had some quality players, especially at the back. They had a good bank of fans too, clad in maroon and blue and making a real atmosphere.

Jarrod was finding the game hard to get into, and as he always did when he found himself in that situation, he started to do the simple things carefully and methodically, making sure passes stuck and that South Melbourne retained possession. APIA attacked with purpose and Jarrod found himself chasing the ball more than he should have. Just as the home team thought they had weathered the storm, a dreadful pass at the back saw the APIA attacker burst into the box. Jarrod was quick to react but had some ground to make up, and he went flying into a lunging tackle, catching the attacker and sending him to the floor just outside the area. This went against his judgement, but he had to make the tackle.

As the APIA fans shouted for his dismissal, the referee ushered Jarrod away from the rest of the players.

"What's your number?" asked Bella, looking unimpressed.

"Seventeen."

"Your phone number."

Jarrod looked at her incredulously.

She slowly pulled out the yellow card and placed it behind her notebook. "Or this might be a different colour."

The APIA fans were already baying for blood and were incensed to see the yellow card instead. Jarrod did what he was told and gave Bella his phone number. To the watching spectators and players, it would have looked as though he was getting a right telling off; her reputation was quite fierce. She noted it down and put her notepad away, brandishing the yellow card as the APIA players came in to question the decision. Jarrod held his hand up to apologise to the crowd. The free kick was duly blasted way over the bar and South Melbourne had survived. Jarrod was rattled and he was unusually quiet at half time, only perking up when Aurelio gave the team a collective rev up.

Dana and Milena were right against the fence by the tunnel as the teams emerged. He felt like he was making his debut again for Gateshead, two crazy girls going wild, shouting his name and twirling their scarves. Dana's was a Melbourne Victory scarf. Jarrod just put his hand over his eyes and shook his head.

The second half was much better from the home side, and they started to look like a team at the top of their game. Attacking midfielder Jon Kosmidis latched on to a through ball from Jarrod and gave them the lead with a delightful finish. The corner count was rising, and South Melbourne were turning the screw. Jarrod's corners had been ineffectual, but his last two in succession had found the spot. The third, relieving the pressure as APIA dominated possession, found the head of central defender Brendan Maley and the bullet header sealed the win. There was wild celebration, and that continued when, from the next attack, Kosmidis broke clean through and was upended by a mistimed last-ditch tackle. The referee reached for her book and pulled out the red card, before pulling out the yellow from behind it. It was a second booking though and the defender was shown the red card with no complaints.

The free kick was in range. Jarrod had come through the game still with quite a skip in his step, especially as his team were winning, and he placed the ball and watched as Bella counted her ten steps and sprayed the foam for the free kick. He could see why she was considered a bombshell of a referee, her long ponytail looking a little less taut than before. The fact that she took the game so seriously and made decisions quickly and confidently meant that the players would treat her with the utmost respect. Jarrod waited for the whistle. He started his run up as he saw the whistle reach her lips and he strode up and curled the most immaculate shot over the wall and into the corner of the post and bar, the keeper making the leap but unable to get anywhere near it. Jarrod raced over to the fans and saluted them. Oh, what a feeling!

The remaining moments of the game were played out to *olé*s from the crowd for every South Melbourne pass. The APIA fans were silent and still. The final whistle sounded, and the reporters made a beeline for the players. Jarrod was commandeered for his first post-match interview in Australia. He was pleased to see that it was with Caleb Powell.

"I'm with man of the moment, Jarrod Black."

"Caleb, no way!" said Jarrod. "I didn't realise you were with this mob!"

"Enough about me, Jarrod, how about that for a debut?" he asked. "Two assists, a goal, and all that after what could have been a night to forget in the first half. How did you see the potential red card?"

"The referee has obviously seen another player coming across to cover," said Jarrod. "I thought I was a goner too, though; he just nicked the ball away at the last moment."

"We all had that down as a straight red in the studio," said Caleb. "The VAR didn't overturn the decision on appeal, so I guess it wasn't clear and obvious. Your through ball for Kosmidis though—have you struck up a relationship with him already?"

"He's class, isn't he?"

This interview was going so well. Jarrod felt as Australian as he had ever felt in the last twenty years and was warming to this new adventure. They chatted a little more before Caleb passed back to the studio.

"Well done," said Caleb, once he knew they were off air.

"Thanks—I didn't think I'd see you behind the mic again for a while, with this new TV deal," said Jarrod. "Do you still think there's something fishy?"

Jarrod's adrenaline was pushing him to ask more than he normally would.

"The money is good," said Caleb. "That's all I can say about that. Anyway, the football is amazing, isn't it?"

"Much better than I expected," replied Jarrod. "Some quality players, that's for sure. Should we catch up for a chat, Caleb?"

"We should, we should," said Caleb, as he was urged over by the camera crew to catch Jon Kosmidis before he headed back into the tunnel.

Jarrod caught up with Dana and Milena, and they were joined by Temuri.

"Jarrod Black to score at any time and a win to zero," he said excitedly. "A couple of hundred bucks on that and I'm well up. Good work, Jarrod!"

He spied Johnny, who caught his eye and punched the air in triumph. The people were happy. Jarrod was happy. This had been a great start to his A-League career.

46

Browning

"Just move a little to the left, please," said the photographer curtly.

Jarrod did as he was told, and the bearded man snapped another barrage of shots. Jarrod was wearing his fourth suit of the shoot, and this time he had his hands bound in rope and a noose loosely draped around his neck. Two very attractive ladies straight from a Robert Palmer music video flanked him and he had the instruction to remain still and stare through the camera into the distance.

"Head up. Up further," said the photographer. "Now open your eyes wider …"

Jarrod resisted the temptation to tell the photographer where to go and used his dislike for the snapper to channel the ice cold look on his face in a scene of pure concentration.

"Next change, please," shouted the photographer, who was giving off no friendly vibes whatsoever, despite having been very jovial when they met earlier on in the day.

A gleaming gold Lamborghini had been sitting idle next to them, and he was keen to have a look inside, despite his apathy towards cars in general. This one looked sleek and sexy and was the signature car used in all the Harlowe Croft movies. Jarrod was handed what he hoped was a replica gun, the name Browning embossed on the side, and given instructions on how he should be holding it. He had held a gun before, but it was much bigger than this one. The Gateshead team had been taken for a bonding session to a shooting range and Jarrod remembered leaving with ringing in his ears and a sore wrist from holding a heavy gun that jolted violently with every shot. But he had enjoyed it. He resisted asking if it was real. Of course it wasn't real. He also resisted doing the cheesy poses that rappers tended to do with guns and placed the gun on a table and went to get his next costume change.

The graphic designer for the movie, Hugo Burton, who he had met briefly in the studio last Friday night, was waiting to chat with him as he got changed. Having any privacy was not an option.

"How are you finding it?" asked Hugo.

"It's quite straightforward," said Jarrod. "The nasty man with the beard keeps shouting at me, but I guess that's his job."

"That nasty man happens to be George Baillie," said Hugo. "And if you don't know who George Baillie is, just think of any iconic front page of a magazine in the last ten years and he was probably the man behind the lens. He's a bit of genius."

Jarrod felt immediately uncouth and unrefined. He'd never heard of George Baillie but had a feeling that Marianne would know of him well. He would casually drop his name into conversation when he spoke with her tonight.

"So, what's the timeline for these photographs hitting the screens or the billboards?" asked Jarrod.

"We've got a big release on the Saturday after New Year in the US," replied Hugo. "But we'll be releasing some on social media and online advertising in the week between Christmas and January 1st. So, be prepared for your public profile to change overnight and for you to become seriously hot property."

"On that, do I get any security yet?" asked Jarrod. He was freaked out by seeing Yannick Lefevre on Saturday and was sure that it wouldn't be the last time.

"You'll need to speak with J.B., er, Jacqui about that," said Hugo. "She's the one we all go to for the answers. I'm sure you've worked that out for yourself by now. She's around here somewhere. I've seen her this morning."

A colleague of Mr Baillie rushed over and let them know that Jarrod was needed again. He was dressed in a crisp white shirt and the sharpest suit he'd had on yet. He had been asked to go to the tailor's yesterday for a fitting and they had worked their magic overnight to get these suits looking immaculate. The tailor had remarked that his legs were a little over-muscly and suggested that he might be required to lose some of that muscle, which made Jarrod laugh.

Jacqui was with Mr Baillie when they returned to the set, and she greeted Jarrod with the now customary kiss on the cheek.

They were straight into the shoot again, and Jarrod was asked to open the car door and sit in the driver's seat before getting up and out of the car again, a big fan blowing his hair as if it was a windy day. They did this continuously until Mr Baillie tossed back his head and blew out his cheeks as if to suggest there was no hope of getting it right. Jarrod looked at Jacqui. Jacqui raised her eyebrows but didn't dare do or say anything else in the presence of this superstar of the photography world.

The two models were reintroduced into the set. Jarrod caught Jacqui smiling coyly as they were instructed to drape themselves around him. One of the models lingered just that little too long with her hand on his crotch and Jarrod could feel himself reacting to it. He recognised her perfume. He pretended to back up out of the shot for a sneeze, and the moment was gone. Mr Baillie threw his hands up in disgust as the make-up artist raced on set to fix up his nose and apply some more powdery substance. They resumed a good ten minutes later, the models told to change sides, Mr Baillie having sensed what was happening.

Jarrod was in this photo shoot for hours. He managed to get a drink and a sandwich but was told by the costume artist that she would break his nose if he spilled any food on the white shirt as that was the last that they had in his size. By the end, Jarrod had been on set for six hours and was feeling quite jaded. He expected it would be written across his face, but Mr Baillie was clicking the most ferociously he had all day just towards the end. Perhaps the moodiness in his face or the exhaustion and disinterest gave him a different perspective to work with.

The model who had given him cause to sneeze came up at the end as they were all preparing to leave. She asked if she could borrow Jarrod's phone in a strong Russian accent, which Jarrod unlocked and handed over before realising that it wasn't the usual way a selfie worked. She added her name and number to his phone and then rang her phone. She showed him her phone ringing and smiled and simply walked off without saying a word. Jarrod couldn't help but turn and watch as she left, a svelte figure in a tight dress, and turned his head to see Jacqui smiling at him. He was already feeling like hot property and wasn't sure how to react to it.

"Get used to it, Jarrod," said Jacqui with a knowing look. "She's going to be one of an ever-growing pack of wolves that will follow you incessantly. A chasing pack. Your unwanted entourage."

"I'm going to need some security, aren't I?"

"All in good time," said Jacqui. "You're a second division footballer at the moment. Make the most of your freedom."

47

Vegan

The days were crammed full. Jarrod had his first personal training session with his trainer Malik, part-man part-machine who had the tightest washboard stomach Jarrod had ever seen. The 6:00 a.m. start was no problem, and the gym was only a short jog from the apartment. It was definitely a walk back after a punishing session of abs, pecs and shoulders, but there was no chance of stopping for a rest. He was due at the studios at 9:30 a.m. for a script introduction and a chance to meet some of the co-stars of the movie for the first time. That went well, although he would have preferred a little more time to chat with his new colleagues instead of being whisked away again to stunt school for a first session in preparation for some exciting stunts in the movie. By the time he arrived at training at 6:00 p.m. at the stadium, he was fried. Thankfully his legs had not been worked too much and he got through the session of ball work and a low-key game without any issues. He had to turn down a drink with some of the players, knowing that he had to be up and about again in the morning to do it all again, the excuse being that he was in a business meeting with the UK during the night. That seemed to be a good excuse that he might have to use again.

Instead, he phoned home to Darlington when he got back to the apartment with a very healthy takeout in his hand from the vegan restaurant next door. They had always had a landline which seemed to only attract nuisance calls, and he rang that one first to see if anyone was home.

"Jarrod, my love, good timing. We were just moving out."

"Moving out?" asked Jarrod. "Where are you going?"

"We're in a hotel in Newcastle for the night and then we're on our way to London to stay with Nadine and Reggie," Marianne said excitedly. "They're over for a wedding and they've got a house for the week. It's a shame you're not here!"

"Ah, that's great," said Jarrod. "Give Reg a big kiss from me."

Reggie was Jarrod's soul mate and confidant from their time together early in their careers at Gateshead. He was also Marianne's distant cousin and was married to her best friend. They were always a tight-knit unit and the kids got on well. Jarrod and Reggie hadn't spoken for a few months and Jarrod got that feeling of guilt as they talked.

"I'm dropping the keys to the Arena today," said Marianne. "The house is looking good. I hope Peter likes it."

They had agreed for Peter Van Vloten, the Dutch import at Darlington, to take their house for the rest of the season while he looked for a place with his family. He had settled well at Darlington, and he was keen to get his family over to join him for Christmas in England.

"Have you seen any of the boys?" asked Jarrod.

"Oh yes, we were there on Saturday," said Marianne. "We were at the game, and we stayed around afterwards and had a drink with the guys. Roni says hi, and Mitch was also back from Scotland."

"Ah, that's great," said Jarrod. "Was it a good game?"

"Of course," said Marianne. "They won easily. Everyone was in such a good mood after the game. There was talk of promotion again!"

Jarrod was impressed to be getting the lowdown on the team he had guided to promotion last season. Despite knowing the score and having caught the goals on YouTube, he had no idea what else was going on at the club.

"That's three wins in a row," said Jarrod. "What a team. God, I miss it! Still, I don't miss the weather and the darkness. We're in summer here in Melbourne and it's lovely."

"Here he is again, the Australian tourist board," joked Marianne.

She seemed to be a lot more on board now that the house situation had been resolved and they were actually on the move. As usual, the kids had been ripped out of school and this time they were saying goodbye for potentially a long time.

"Can't wait to see you," said Jarrod. "It's been too long."

"Me too," said Marianne. "Gotta go. Love you!"

Jarrod was reassured that Marianne was now on team Australia. There had been doubts but the lure of a summer in Melbourne was quite a strong argument to tip the balance.

Jarrod sat and ate his noodles and meat substitute sauce in front of the TV. The news was coming up after the footy and he persisted through the adverts. Sure enough, just as it looked as if there couldn't possibly be any more adverts crammed into the commercial break, up came the BetShed ad, this time with a real Australian flavour. Jarrod was an AFL player, in a sleeveless top, and kicked a goal before tilting back his head and roaring to the sky. The ad ended in the usual way with him sitting back in his stool and smiling as if it had all been a dream. Jarrod sat with his full mouth slightly open, scarcely believing what he had just seen. That was some handy CGI to get him kicking a goal in Aussie Rules, but he was shocked at having seen himself on screen in that context.

Sure enough, his phone pinged and pinged again before he could pick it up. There was a text from South Melbourne teammate Nicky Stolic, who he had just passed up a beer with, with a video of the boys pointing at the screen in the pub, laughing and roaring as the advert played. Jarrod could see the funny side.

He made the mistake of scrolling down his messages and was caught in a vortex—there was a message from goalkeeper Harry Lowndes, his old Gateshead teammate. He'd heard Jarrod's name mentioned in a discussion about coaching roles at the International Stadium and wanted to know if there was any truth in the story. There was also a very risqué photo from an unknown number that turned out to be referee Bella—he didn't recognise her in the photo at first and felt guilty at having to study it closer to see that it really was her. That would remain unanswered. Moving further down the never-ending list of messages, there was a text from LF Sports presenter Tom Archison, mentioning the possibility of being a regular on the Friday night coverage for the rest of the season and into next season too. He also saw a message from Duddy sharing interest from other A-League clubs in securing his services permanently for next season, and there was a message from a +91 number purporting to be Murtaka asking him to call her. He was a man in demand.

48

Bastard

Jarrod knew that his life was going to be busy like this for the foreseeable future and didn't hesitate to climb into bed after making sure he had turned on the dryer to have some clothes ready for the morning session. Until he closed his eyes though, he was still 'on', and his phone vibrated with a call from his sister Anna.

"Hey, Jarrod," she said. "Have you got a house in Melbourne?"

"Oh, hello," said Jarrod cheekily. "I get the keys on Thursday. Oh, and I get a car on Thursday too. Shit, it's like my life starts on Thursday."

"Ah, great," said Anna, as if alluding to something.

"Why do you ask?" asked Jarrod as if being prompted.

"Does it have lots of rooms?" asked Anna.

"Lots of rooms?" asked Jarrod. It was his turn to prompt.

"Yes, how many rooms does it have?" asked Anna impatiently.

"Let me have a look at the brochure again," said Jarrod, reaching to the bedside table which had his whole life sitting on it. "Let's see, master bedroom, room for Sebastian, another for Aneka—oh, they have a bathroom they can share, and another room for Mum and Dad when they come down for Christmas."

"So, there's no ..." said Anna.

"And there's downstairs too, a couple of rooms, one each for the unmarried couple that will be joining us at Christmas."

"Ha ha, bastard," said Anna. "They're paying you well at South Melbourne, eh?"

"So, when are you coming?" asked Jarrod, ignoring that last statement.

"We'll be there on Saturday morning," said Anna. "You'll be able to pick us up at the airport, yeah?"

"If it's early, no problem," said Jarrod. "We've got a home game again, so I'll be here. Flick me the details. If anything comes up, I'll get someone to pick you up."

"You're a star, Jarrod," said Anna. "It's not true what they say about you."

"Whatever," said Jarrod. "Night night."

"Oh shit, what time is …?"

Jarrod hung up. That had been a typical call with his sister. Semi-serious but still full of love.

49

Fish

Jarrod's week had taken its toll. It was Thursday and Jarrod had been on the go since 5:30 a.m. The training session in the morning, followed by the script session late afternoon, had exhausted him mentally and physically. A big game lay ahead on Saturday, but there was a lot happening between now and then. Johnny had driven him over to the Lexus dealership and he had picked up his car. Johnny hung around to see what he was getting, and Jarrod hid his surprise when they brought out a top-of-the-range all-wheel-drive family wagon. He smiled as he sat in the car and quickly removed the welcome card from Zion Films who had bought the vehicle. The windows were tinted, and the seats were leather. There was even a sunroof. This was much fancier than any car Jarrod had ever had.

Johnny opened the passenger door and climbed in.

"You're joking, mate," he said. "Who's paying for this?"

Jarrod scanned the control panel, looking for the ejector seat and the heat-seeking missile launcher.

"Exchange rate is good at the moment, Johnny," was all Jarrod could think of.

"Let's have a spin," said Johnny.

Jarrod wound down the window and let the sales guy at the dealership know that he would be back in ten minutes. He drove out of the driveway carefully and slowly, remembering what his dad had told him about new cars—don't flog it straight away, give it a few weeks before you start pushing it hard. He couldn't help himself though, and quickly brought the car from 0 to 60 to test the acceleration. Jarrod was buzzing. Never liked cars, eh? Johnny was checking all the compartments, adjusting the seat. He managed to work out the radio and it burst to life with an old Regurgitator tune from way back at full volume. He was loving it more than Jarrod. They headed straight back to the dealership and Johnny jumped out and waved as he got back in his battered old Toyota. Jarrod finished the paperwork and posed for a few photos with the staff before carefully navigating the driveway for a second time and driving off slowly and steadily.

He now had wheels, and he had teed up a meeting at the new house with the real estate agent for 7:00 p.m. The late hour didn't seem to be an issue for the ever-positive agent, and Jarrod rolled up in his new car at the address in Toorak and was the first there. The neighbourhood was as exclusive as he could have imagined, every house with a high front wall that suggested privacy, security and wealth. This wasn't Jarrod's ideal neighbourhood, as he liked to get to know those around him. This looked like the suburb for the rich and famous, like something he'd seen in Beverly Hills when the family drove around Los Angeles while looking for their hotel some years ago in between seasons. Jarrod parked in front of the house, the front gate locked, and a car came up and parked behind him. If it was Yannick Lefevre he was going to drive off. He was surprised to see Jacqui getting out of the car with a smartly dressed gentleman. Jarrod turned off the car and got out.

"Jacqui?" said Jarrod in shock.

"You're going to need me for this one," she said. "I'm going to give you a female perspective."

"I thought this was a done deal?" said Jarrod.

"It is, Jarrod," said Jacqui. "But I need to be here. Let's say I'm your P.A. now. This is Anthony, the agent you were talking with today."

Jarrod smiled and shook Anthony's hand. He was a tall man, built like a rugby forward and had the ears to match.

"Thanks for meeting me so late in the day," said Jarrod, trying to take control of the conversation, although he had a feeling that Jacqui would very quickly take over.

Anthony pressed a button on the big bunch of keys. The front gate opened and the smaller gate that led to the path to the front door clicked open too. They walked in through the front door, which didn't seem to be locked, and into the house. Jarrod was straight away thrown by the luxury of the house. This was something special. It was like a beach house but in the suburbs, everything white with wooden touches; it was immaculately clean and freshly painted. It was fully furnished too, which Jarrod had requested so they didn't need to buy any furniture that would make the next move difficult. Jarrod had also requested a house with enough rooms for his whole family, but he had no idea of just how incredible the house would be.

As the brochure had shown, there were two big bedrooms on the ground floor, which had wide floorboards throughout, there was a bathroom between the two rooms, and then a corridor that took you through to the kitchen. This was like something out of a magazine. The kitchen was almost industrial, with a massive oven and a fridge that was bigger than anything he'd seen before. They went upstairs and Anthony showed him the bathrooms and the instructions for the spa, and they spent a good ten minutes in front of one of the control panels, running through the heating, cooling, security and lighting that was all controlled centrally. Jacqui made notes furiously and took photos on her phone as Anthony ran through it. They went out the back and ran through the barbecue instructions as well as the pool basics. Jarrod had never had a pool. This was amazing. He could see his kids loving this.

It was nearly 8:30 p.m. when Anthony had to make his excuses and leave. There was a bottle of red wine on the kitchen bench which Jacqui opened, and she poured two glasses before putting the bottle next to the stove, as if to suggest it would be good for cooking. A first taste and she knew she was mistaken. This was decadence!

"Jarrod, if you need anything, anything at all," said Jacqui, "you can phone me. If Marianne or the kids or anyone in your family need anything, I can help. I'm not that far away, and it is part of my job to make sure that the lead actor in the movie is left wanting for nothing."

"Thank you," said Jarrod, now realising that he would need Jacqui a great deal, even if it was to work out how to lock his front gate before he went to bed. He hadn't taken in any of the instructions and was still awestruck by his surrounds.

"You do realise what you're getting yourself into here, don't you?" asked Jacqui, taking a sip from the oversized wine glass.

"I honestly don't think I do," replied Jarrod to the slightly rhetorical question.

"You would have had some measure of fame in England, surely," stated Jacqui.

"Sure," said Jarrod. "I've had to dodge the cameras and keep my head down in cars. And I've had to make sure I'm professional at all times just in case the paparazzi are looking for a shot. I figured I was past that though."

"You're a small fish in a little pond at the moment," said Jacqui, without sounding condescending. "When those photos hit social media after Christmas, you are going to be a big fish in an absolutely gigantic ocean. Everyone is going to want a piece of you."

"I think they already do," said Jarrod. He wasn't sure if Jacqui's use of the big fish idiom was correct.

"What do you mean?" asked Jacqui.

"I feel like a wanted man," said Jarrod. "I don't know who to trust right now."

"You can trust me," said Jacqui. "And I'm the only person you really need to trust outside your family."

They sat and looked at each other. If this was a movie, Jacqui would be giving Jarrod an ultimatum and going in for a sexy kiss, but they were the consummate professionals and she sat and smiled until Jarrod spoke.

"My P.A., you say," said Jarrod.

"Your P.A.," repeated Jacqui.

50

Italian

Jarrod was running late to the airport on the Saturday morning but didn't ring ahead. He figured Anna would take ages anyway to get through customs. He was right and timed it to perfection. Within a minute she strode through arrivals with her girlfriend Elin, both pushing the trolley that contained a healthy amount of baggage.

Jarrod brushed off his strait-laced public persona to do the brotherly thing and he raced in for a hug. It was a lovely moment. Anna was so delighted to present Elin to her brother, and they also hugged. They both looked tired after sitting for half a day on the plane, but they had obviously freshened up and had a change of clothes as they both looked ready for summer.

They chatted non-stop for the whole journey from Tullamarine to Toorak and were sharing stories about their respective football seasons. Theirs had just finished and they had both played big roles in a successful season that ended with a second-place finish in the Shield and a Championship final defeat. They had both been retained for the following season, and both had signed up for a five-game spell in Melbourne albeit with different clubs. Anna was going back to City, while Elin had been snapped up by the newest W-League team Western United. Both clubs had come to an arrangement to house them together, but that wouldn't begin until the week between Christmas and New Year. Jarrod could feel himself swelling with pride at having his sister in the passenger seat and finally being able to talk to her face to face. Having missed her coming of age earlier in the year in the World Cup, he was ready to help her in any way he could.

Anna's face was a picture when they turned into the street and pulled up alongside the house.

"No way," she said. "You live here?"

"Since Thursday, yep," said Jarrod.

"You have to be joking," exclaimed Anna.

Jarrod had already forgotten how to open the front gate, but Jacqui had condensed the instructions into a text and he had it saved as his screen saver on his phone. He drove in and the big gate closed behind them. Jarrod emptied the car, and they moved all the baggage to the front door. Jarrod was making a big deal of it and opened the door and let the girls walk in first after telling them their rooms were just inside. Jarrod had hit the jackpot and Anna and Elin felt as though they had too.

"I'll see you at the Lakeside," said Jarrod as he left.

"If you have any problems closing up, just ring this number," he said, handing over a piece of paper with Jacqui's number, before taking it back and texting it through to Anna's phone. "You know the address, right?"

"Sure, see you there. Do we need a ticket?"

"Just go to the car park entrance and say you're with me, they'll let you in," said Jarrod. "I'll let them know that you're coming."

Jarrod was feeling strong. The upper body training over the week had left him feeling bigger, even if he didn't look it, and the football training had complemented it. There was a suggestion of fatigue, but Jarrod just brushed it off. He stood in the tunnel waiting to come out onto the field, the nervous feeling that he always had never failing to keep his mind focused on the game ahead.

Marconi were the visitors today, one of six Sydney teams across the two A-League divisions. They had a proud history in the top flight of Australian football in the National Soccer League before the A-League came to town. This season they were sitting in mid-table, poised for a run for the play-off places once they had negotiated this tricky game against high-flying South Melbourne. It was another big game in the second division; most games had either historical or ethnic meaning, and this one was no different. Both teams were proud of their heritage, Marconi founded by the Italians in Western Sydney and South Melbourne by the Greeks. These two teams had been the only two teams to have played in every season of the NSL before it was scrapped, and they had plenty of history in games between them.

The Italian community of Melbourne had come out in force for this one, and the visitors appeared to have a good following as a result of some astute advertising. The safe smokies in green, white and red were set off as the players walked onto the field and the atmosphere was quite hostile. Jarrod had played in plenty of derby games over the years, but ethnically charged games were something new to him.

The first half was a great advert for the second division. Jarrod played a starring role in midfield and put himself about, tracking his man and making some timely interceptions as the visitors threatened to take command. His cultured passing, something that stood out in England, but pretty much the norm in Australia, was on point in the first forty-five minutes, and it was his through ball that set Niko Toulaise away to round the keeper and score the opening goal.

The second half was very even until Jason Zalalas clattered into his man and was harshly sent off for his second game in a row, proving that a reputation does come before you in football. There were twenty-five minutes left to survive with ten men, but with Jarrod pulling the strings and marshalling the team just in front of the defence, it was difficult to tell which team had the full complement. A late corner saw defender Marc Edwards leap the highest and nestle a header back across the keeper into the corner of the net for 2–0, racing away to waste as much time as possible by jumping into the crowd.

This was as good a performance that Jarrod could remember being a part of. He was collared for an interview again as he walked off, Caleb giving him plenty of airtime in a very smooth interview. Jarrod was getting used to talking into a camera and had a confidence in talking with his interviewer that would get him plenty of fans on social media in the football community. The players saluted the home support and spread themselves out to meet the fans, with selfies and autographs for everyone. He noticed a big group of people surrounding two figures further up the main stand and walked further over to try and see who it was. He laughed when he saw it was Anna and Elin, getting more attention than the two teams who had just been playing.

Jarrod knew that the Matildas were now everyone's number one sporting team in Australia, enjoying the limelight just as the Olympic rowers, the swimming team and the Kookaburras, the national hockey team, had done over the years. It was the Matildas turn to shine brightly, and Jarrod could understand that, after their magnificent showing at the World Cup in the summer. Anna and Elin made their way down to see Jarrod. Anna gave her brother a hug.

"Not bad for a Division 2 team," she said quietly in his ear before retreating and giving him a wink. Jarrod narrowed his eyes and smiled, as Anna was again collared for selfies and signatures on shirts. Jarrod's star was definitely in Anna's shadow, but Jarrod felt nothing but happiness for her. Elin was getting as much attention, the whole world knowing these two sportswomen after their on-field kiss in the round of sixteen game between Australia and Sweden earlier this year. She was a very attractive woman too.

Anna and Elin were tucked up in bed by 10:00 p.m., after a search to find sheets to replace the overly warm doonas, and Jarrod was glad to see them happily installed. He had explained his punishing schedule to the girls, but he was saving his big secret of movie stardom for when the whole family was together. That would be in a matter of days. They were moving into the last week before Christmas. Mum and Dad would be coming down from Sydney to spend Christmas, and Marianne and the kids would be joining them later that day to bring the whole family together for the first time in years. Jarrod was excited.

51

Jigsaw

Anna was quick to get herself mobile, picking up her car from her friend Dana's place who had kindly looked after it while she was away, and she took Elin to the airport to pick up Mum and Dad. Jarrod had his personal trainer session early in the morning and then had to get to training with the squad in preparation for the midweek trip to Adelaide City. They would be leaving on the day of the game tomorrow and Jarrod was both relieved that he was around today to welcome his family and annoyed that he had to leave them straight away to head off to an away game. This was part of the landscape of being a professional footballer though, and it was everyone else who had to fit in with his schedule or he would potentially find himself out of favour at the club and deemed unreliable. There had been players in the past who had conjured up an injury to attend a wedding or to go on family holidays, but he'd also seen that backfire when the club made the player in question travel with the squad anyway. There was no way Jarrod would ever entertain such nonsense and the thought had never crossed his mind, despite having missed countless events and opportunities in the past.

Jarrod arrived back via the studios where he'd had another gruelling script session. He had adrenaline pumping through him after running through some exciting scenes from the movie, where the actors tried out some of their lines with actions instead of sitting around a table. The endorphins from training hadn't subsided and his excitement was high as he walked through the front door and into a lovely scene of his parents, his sister and her girlfriend, and Dana and Milena all sitting around the dining table enjoying a long lunch. Mum leapt up from her seat—she had probably positioned herself on the closest side of the table to the door—and walked to Jarrod, holding out her hands for a hug. She had tears in her eyes. It had only been a couple of weeks, but she could sense that she was close to having the whole family together for the first time in many years. Dad waited his turn in the background before going in for a hug, enveloping both of them with his arms. The rest of the table let out a cheer.

Dana and Milena had spent a couple of nights during the World Cup with Mum and Dad, and they had even been out on the tiles after watching Anna in a fantastic group stage game at the Docklands Stadium. Jarrod felt as though he had a network of people to trust already in Melbourne and was confident that Marianne and the kids would be able to leverage off that too. Things were coming together. The final piece of the jigsaw was picking up his family from the airport this evening. Jarrod had checked in with Marianne between sessions today and had received a voice message during his early morning workout telling him that the flight was running as scheduled from Hong Kong and that she was really looking forward to seeing him. Just hearing her voice sound so excited was a tonic for the rest of the day and he had been in a cheery mood ever since.

Jarrod took a seat at the table next to Mum, who had been busy already in the kitchen. She had baked some bread in the bread maker and had made a couple of salads with Elin while Anna and Dad worked out how to use the barbeque. There was plenty of food left over, which Mum got out of the fridge, while Dad fired up the barbeque using the control panel. Jarrod winced as he watched his dad flick through the screens and press a button, the flame coming on outside under the grill. Even Dad knew more about how the house worked. This was totally surreal.

It was time to head to the airport. Jarrod decided it would be best to go alone, just in case there was an overload of baggage, and Anna said she didn't want to cramp his style at the airport anyway. It was often a great time to catch up anyway, the journey back from an airport, and it was not a time to be overwhelmed with so many people after being stuck on a plane for hours. He took the route that he had taken a few days earlier to fetch Anna and Elin, even managing to do it without the in-car navigation. He was practically a local, he thought.

This time he was at the airport with plenty of time to spare and sat at a coffee shop knowing that he'd get a text or a call when they had got off the plane. He was nervous, and he could feel it. It had been six weeks since he had left them to head to Japan, and his family were now going to step into this new world that he had created for them. He could sense the pressure to deliver. Would this be better than living in Darlington? Would life be more difficult once he was announced as the new Harlowe Croft? Were the kids going to make friends easily despite not starting school until the end of January? Was this the start of the rest of their lives, or just another fleeting moment in their increasingly transient life?

Seeing Sebastian and Aneka was like a shot of happiness into his arm. Aneka, as always, was the first to race over to him and flung herself in for a hug. Sebastian played it cool. Jarrod could tell he had grown, both in height and in maturity, and he was almost as tall as Marianne. His wife strode down the walkway with so much style and spunk that Jarrod wasn't even sure it was her. She'd nailed it—he was instantly besotted with her once more. Jarrod felt complete again. Sebastian let his mum go in for the first hug and then grabbed Jarrod and gripped him tightly.

"Welcome home," he said. "Be prepared, it's hot outside."

52

Cheer

The party had grown since Jarrod had left the house. Anna had taken the liberty to invite some more friends over. There were a couple of Melbourne City girls, and friends from the Spanish class that she had been part of before the World Cup. Jarrod made sure that all the luggage was in the house and closed the front gate before taking the right luggage to the right rooms and showing the kids to their spacious rooms. Mum appeared up the stairs; she couldn't wait for them to come back downstairs and join the party. Aneka was so excited to see her, and Sebastian's face was beaming too. After a few trips up the stairs with some heavy suitcases, Jarrod corralled his excited family and led them downstairs to join the throng.

A cheer went up as Marianne appeared around the corner, followed by Mum holding Aneka's hand and Sebastian arm in arm with Jarrod. This was a truly lovely moment. They all fit around the table, after Dad had found how to extend it out, and Mum started to bring out more food that she'd been preparing and the kids excitedly dived in. By the end of the evening, Marianne had been hooked up with Meryl Hartigan, Anna's agent in Melbourne, and they had made plans for Christmas and New Year. Marianne, Sebastian and Aneka had been given strict instructions to keep the Harlowe Croft news under wraps. Jarrod wanted that to be a secret that he would reveal when the time was right, just as news was about to break, and he was relieved that the telephone conversation with Dad had been lost in time.

Jarrod stayed up way past the time he should have gone to bed, mainly to make sure that his family were happy with their living arrangements and that the kids were warm and cosy in their beds. He had missed the night-time routine of 'tucking in' his children, Sebastian with his intricate insight into the life of a teenager and Aneka with her incredible ability to recall everything that she had done during the day. The kiss on the forehead for Seb and the comically complicated handshake for Aneka were all he needed to know that they were happy and ready for sleep in their new home, and he walked through to join Marianne in their bedroom. She was hanging up clothes and deciding where things should go, pushing Jarrod's slim pickings to the side. Jarrod's timing may have been off, but he went in for an embrace from behind, moving his hands up the front of her dress to signal his intent. Much to his delight, his timing was spot on. She turned around smiling, put her hands on his shoulders and pushed him backwards onto the bed and climbed on top. They had missed each other's intimate company.

53

Grind

Leaving the door at 5:30 a.m. was tough. Everyone had slept, but Aneka had stirred and jumped into the warm spot left next to Marianne by Jarrod. The 6:00 a.m. training session was still on, upper body strength and tone the aim, but Malik knew that he had to take it easy today and they spent a lot of time discussing the best way forward to achieve the goals.

"We're aiming for the washboard," said Malik, as Jarrod left the gym. Jarrod lifted his shirt and tensed to show him he wasn't far away. Malik blew out his cheeks as if to mock him for being fat, but of course he was hardly carrying anything, just a little bit of middle-age baggage that he figured he'd never be able to shake.

Jarrod had never been a spectacular specimen but had been involved in modelling shoots with clothes on, but never without. He had a great posture that exuded confidence and masculinity, but with his shirt off, there was a distinct lack of bulk in the upper half of his body. Malik's daily grind made him feel bigger in the shoulders and in the chest, but he couldn't really see any difference. Harlowe Croft was known for being shirtless on beaches and in bedroom scenes. Jarrod was starting to feel a little inadequate.

The Adelaide trip went well. Despite playing with ten men for the majority of the second half after yet another red card, they battled well and held on to a point thanks to some fantastic goalkeeping and a couple of really bad misses by the home team. The team had a meal out near City's stadium and eventually checked in to their hotel at the airport at midnight. Jarrod was rooming with Jon Kosmidis, and they hit it off instantly. Jon had played in

Greece for ten years but was back home now in Melbourne. They talked into the early hours and made plans to catch up out of football time when they returned. Jarrod wasn't sure if he would have any free time from now on, but that didn't stop him making plans anyway.

54

Paella

Christmas Day was fantastic, and it spilled over into Boxing Day, with no Division 2 games, only the A-League proper having a couple of local derby fixtures. In the absence of the annual video call with Mum and Dad, Marianne instead brought up Pippa Robson on Zoom after first speaking with her folks in France. The kids loved it. Jarrod and Marianne looked on, holding hands in the background, as Michaela and Seb chatted coyly about their respective Christmas experiences.

The kids and Mum and Dad were in the pool all afternoon on both days, and Jarrod was delighted to see Sebastian and Aneka adapting to their new way of life and for Mum and Dad to be spending quality time with them. He always referred back to his solid upbringing when discussing his younger years, and he wanted his parents' influence to rub off on the kids so they understood that it was not just Jarrod telling them how it is or how it should be. Elin had been to her first training session with Western United. Danny Zorbas had been in touch to scold Jarrod for not pointing her towards South Melbourne. Anna was due to start in the morning back at the City Academy. They were picking up the keys to their accommodation too in the morning, so Jarrod had earmarked Boxing Day evening as potentially the last chance they would get to be all together.

Jarrod planned the evening beautifully. He had a huge selection of seafood still in its white polystyrene boxes in the second fridge in the garage and announced that they would be dining at 7:30 p.m. and Marianne joined him in the kitchen to prepare a banquet for the occasion. A huge fish on the barbecue, a salad laden with enormous prawns and firm avocado, and sashimi that Jarrod sliced himself using the delicate array of super-sharp knives that he found in a drawer in the barbecue itself. They made a big deal of the evening, each member of the family choosing a song to enter the room to as the paella pan gong signalled the start of the evening.

Sebastian had shaken off his shy and awkward self and strutted in to the tune of 'Highway to Hell' by AC/DC, while Mum waltzed in to 'Something Stupid' featuring Nicole Kidman. It was so Australian. Jarrod loved it. Elin stole the show, dressed up like a child of the seventies and dancing in to 'Super Trouper' by ABBA to great applause. The fish was lifted carefully from its foil onto an enormous plate and Dad peeled back the skin to reveal a perfectly cooked side of snapper, which he expertly divided between plates. The warm crusty bread and real butter was perfect, and they had an array of sparkling drinks, mainly non-alcoholic. Dad of course was making the most of it, sipping sparkling wine at the head of the table as the conversation grew. This was the best Christmas Jarrod could have imagined. He was just about to take it to a new level. He grabbed a knife and chinked it against his glass. Mum thought it was meant to signal a kiss, so went in for a smooch with Dad which had them all laughing.

"Christmas is a time for family, and I am so delighted to be spending this Christmas with my close family in such a fabulous setting," said Jarrod. He felt like a successful businessman who had gained all of this through savvy business deals, hard work and a sprinkling of luck. "I ... I mean, we ... have some news to share."

Sebastian and Aneka knew what this was about and raised the oohs to set the anticipation levels. Anna and Erin and Mum and Dad all looked nervously at each other, not knowing whether to be concerned or delighted. Dad stared at Jarrod with his eyes wide open.

Sebastian pressed play on the music system and the deep guitar of the 'Harlowe Croft' theme tune started up. Everyone was puzzled. The music faded away and Aneka unrolled a poster that Jarrod had been given. It was from the photo shoot. It had him standing by the car with his arms crossed, his gun pointed away from him. The graphics hadn't yet been added, but it was unmistakably Harlowe Croft.

"Oh my God," cried Elin. She was the only one to realise what was happening. "You're the new Harlowe Croft! I read about this on the plane. Craig Daniels was working on something else, and they were looking for someone to play him in the next movie."

Marianne was laughing; Anna, Mum and Dad still hadn't twigged. Elin raced around the table and hugged Jarrod, and then Marianne. She put her arms around both Sebastian and Aneka and was genuinely delighted.

"What's going on?" said Mum. "Harlowe Croft? I … I don't believe it!"

"So, you're going to be in a movie?" said a startled Anna. "You're going to be a movie star? My brother is going to be Harlowe Croft?"

Jarrod sat down and everyone joined him except Dad. He was a big fan of the movies. They had been around for years and were an institution, slightly sexist in a comedic kind of way, and thoroughly British. He stood there until he realised he was the only one standing and Mum tugged at his arm to get him to sit down.

"So, we're going to see some promotion for the new movie starting tomorrow," said Jarrod. Sebastian went around to everyone's glass to top them up with whatever they were drinking. "Life is going to be very different moving into the new year. This is going to be a real adventure."

He raised his glass. Everyone raised theirs and they toasted Jarrod's new direction.

"Those BetShed ads must have been a hit," said Anna, jokingly.

"When did this all come about?" asked Mum.

"You didn't think South Melbourne would be paying me enough to live like this, did you?" said Jarrod to Dad.

Dad was speechless and just chuckled to himself. He got up and went around to Jarrod and clasped him in a tight embrace.

"Oh, I am so happy for you," said Dad, choking up. "I didn't even know you were any good at acting."

"Don't worry, neither did I, Dad," said Jarrod.

"Straight glass, no water, no ice," he quipped, pointing at Jarrod's glass, finally remembering the phone conversation they'd had back when Jarrod floated the whole idea with him back in Darlington.

The conversation for the rest of the night was lively. Jarrod filled them all in on what he had been doing as part of the preparation, what the movie was all about and who the co-stars were. Elin asked if there were any bedroom scenes, and Marianne made everyone blush by saying that they were practising hard. What a total spin-out the evening had been. Sebastian was relieved to finally be able to talk about it. Elin was the most excited of them all as the movies were big in Sweden and she was a big fan.

55

Leathery

Jarrod woke to a phone call. It was Jacqui.

"Sorry to wake you so early," she said, forgoing the usual small talk about how his Christmas had been. "Just letting you know that the release of the photographs is at 11:00 a.m."

"Hi, Jacqui, yes, Christmas was great, thanks," said Jarrod calmly and quietly.

"You'll start to get calls from 7:00 a.m., I'd say," said Jacqui.

Jarrod looked at his watch as he slipped out of bed and made for the door. He had probably woken Marianne, but she was just happy to close her eyes again and rejoin her dream. He closed the door quietly behind him.

"The billboards go up tonight during the night," she continued. "But a couple of photos will be made available to a select band of press people in about fifteen minutes, and the official photos will be revealed to the world at 11:00 a.m. Are you ready for this?"

"I'll be ready," said Jarrod. "But I don't know if the rest of the family will be able to understand it."

"I'll be over at 9:00 a.m.," said Jacqui. "I'm just about to hit send to Hugo and our publicity team and then we're live! Make sure the front gate is closed."

"No one knows where I live, do they?" said Jarrod in surprise.

"There's no hiding once this is out," she said. "I'll probably be tailed right to your house. See you soon … oh wait, there, it's done. Sent."

Jarrod had no idea of the ramifications and was still sceptical whether there would even be any fuss about him being the new Harlowe Croft.

He felt the urge to clear up downstairs but walked into a spotless kitchen and a bread maker emanating the most delicious aroma. His mum had obviously been up at the break of dawn to make sure the kitchen was ready to go for another day, and he could hear her humming away outside as she cleaned the barbecue area, her headphones in and the non-cleaning hand waving around to the beat.

He left her to it, resisting the temptation to spring a surprise on her, and made his way to the office area that was up near the front door. Time to get up to date with his messages and news from back in England. He sat at the ornate wooden desk, a classic piece of furniture with a dark-green leathery surface and two large lamps that looked like solid brass arching over to light the area. He felt like the CEO of a major listed company in the 1980s.

He had a recent message from Duddy asking him to call at his earliest convenience, there was one on the encrypted messaging app Signal 7 from D.I. Allison of Scotland Yard from just before that, and a gap of maybe two hours before a flurry of messages from his Darlington teammates after they had notched a big result in the Boxing Day game.

He was keen to speak with Duddy, as it had been a few days, but went with D.I. Allison first and rang him on the app.

"Let me get to a better spot," said D.I. Allison. "Just in the café on the train on the way back from Southampton."

There was a short pause and some muffled shouts.

"Big win today, Jarrod," he continued. "What a day out. Can you believe we got Southampton away on Boxing Day?"

"Is now not a good time?" asked Jarrod.

"No," said D.I. Allison. "Now is the perfect time. I was trying to contact you."

D.I. Allison had seamlessly slipped from hard drinking Newcastle United fan to professional detective inspector in one short sentence.

"We've had some intelligence that Yannick Lefevre was in the country for a few days over Christmas. He slipped in at Aberdeen Airport on a flight from Norway, and we didn't pick it up until he left Newcastle Airport today. There's something brewing."

"Can you tell me?" asked Jarrod.

"I can't tell you anything concrete."

"Marcus," said Jarrod, using the detective inspector's first name for effect. "You need to tell me what you know. I need to know. My family need to know. What is it?"

"The word is that Yannick is part of a group of mercenaries who are heading to Australia," said D.I. Allison. "It's like a convention of nutters all getting together, drawn by some sort of pay day."

Jarrod didn't say a word. It didn't sound promising. D.I. Allison had obviously been on the cans today and was looser than normal with the information that he shared.

"We haven't yet linked it to anything he's been involved with in the past though," said D.I Allison. "But between you and me, it looks as though there's going to be some dangerous characters in Melbourne in the next forty-eight hours. We'll keep you updated with Mr Lefevre's movements, don't you worry, and we've got people on the ground over there too."

Jarrod's head was all over the place now. D.I. Allison's candid manner was most welcome, but what he was hearing was less than encouraging. And as always, it was so bloody ambiguous.

"Hello?" said D.I. Allison.

"Sorry, Marcus," said Jarrod. "I was just lost in thought for a moment. Is my family in danger?"

"I don't believe you are," assured D.I. Allison. "But just be wary."

"Just be wary?" said Jarrod, raising his voice before realising what he was doing.

"Yes, just let us know of anything unusual that happens in the next two days," said D.I. Allison. "You don't have a game until the day before New Year's Eve, right?"

"That's right," said Jarrod, impressed but concerned by D.I. Allison's knowledge of his A-League Division 2 fixture list. "Canberra United away."

"Okay," said D.I. Allison. "Give me a call when you're leaving to go to that game. But before then, if you see anything that looks a bit strange, or if you see your friend Yannick, you contact me on here, right?"

"Right," said Jarrod. "Thanks, Marcus."

"Okay, off to sink a few more with the lads. Honestly, young Marco Vetere's on fire at the moment. Scoring for fun. Howay the lads!"

And he hung up.

Jarrod looked up Duddy's name and called.

"Hey, Duddy," offered Jarrod, unsure whether it was the delay or if Duddy was pausing for effect.

"Jarrod, my good man," said Duddy in his slow and steady Scottish accent. "Wishing you season's greetings. I'd say you're not in your winter woollies over there."

"Ha ha, no, not at all," said Jarrod, remembering where he was.

"Been a while since we touched base," said Duddy. "I was speaking earlier today with Robert Biscotti from the movie company. He's keen for you to concentrate on making the movie and for it to take precedence over your football career in Australia."

"Woah!" said Jarrod. "That's news to me!"

"I went in to bat for you, Jarrod," said Duddy. "He doesn't understand football like we do, my friend."

"We discussed all this prior to me signing up," said Jarrod.

"Aye, but he's paying you an awful lot more money than South Melbourne," said Duddy. "You can perhaps see his point."

"Of course."

"Anyways," continued Duddy. "You're going to be all over the media today. That interview you did with Martin Parkinson just before Christmas is going up on social media, and there's a couple of photos they've asked me to leak to the press—they've just gone out and the celebrity websites are breaking the news right now."

"Yep, I'm up to date," said Jarrod.

"You'll no doubt get a bit of heat this morning from media outlets looking for interviews and sound bites," said Duddy. "Try not to engage with anyone until the photos are released a bit later, and even then, just decline to comment if you do end up in conversation."

"Okay, no problem," said Jarrod.

The short answers eventually got to Duddy.

"Jarrod, is everything okay at your end?" he asked.

"I'm worried," he said. "No, concerned. There's something going on here."

"Oh, like what?"

"I was just speaking with my contact at the police in the UK."

"D.I. Allison?"

"Yes, yes," said Jarrod, forgetting that Duddy was involved with the police in the initial sting that saw the illegal betting ring smashed, before all the guilty parties were released on some sort of technicality. Duddy had been asked by the police to facilitate Jarrod's surprise move to Newcastle, so it was more than likely that he would have been dealing directly with D.I. Allison.

"What did he tell you?" asked Duddy.

"He says that there's potentially some criminal activity happening right on my doorstep here in Melbourne, involving Yannick Lefevre," said Jarrod.

"Anything involving you?" asked Duddy. It seemed that Duddy was getting a little concerned too. Perhaps for the welfare of his prized asset, or that his client didn't need anything else on his plate right now.

"D.I. Allison didn't really give anything away," said Jarrod. "It was more what he didn't say."

"Jarrod, stay in touch," said Duddy by way of wrapping up the conversation. "Just enjoy your final moments out of the spotlight. See you."

Jarrod sat with his phone in his hand, feeling his blood pressure rising. He was going to be in a new stage of his life starting as early as 11:00 a.m. today. He sprang to his feet and made for the bedroom. He grabbed some shorts and a shirt and took them back downstairs and got ready. After popping his head in the kitchen to give his mum a hug and say good morning, he let her know that he was heading out for a quick run. It could be the last time he'd be able to do this.

56

Trepidation

Jarrod turned back into his road after half an hour through the quiet streets of Toorak and sprinted the last long stretch up to the house. He was half expecting a media throng at the front gate but was relieved to see no one there as he walked through the open gate. Sebastian was in the lounge room with his grandma, looking curiously at Seb's mobile phone. Apparently, Seb had rushed downstairs to show whoever was up.

"Look at this, Dad!" said Seb.

Jarrod walked over and stood behind them to look over their shoulders at the phone. There was a photo of Jarrod holding the gun, with sullen eyes, looking menacing, dressed in a sharp suit. The headline above was marked BREAKING NEWS and underneath it said 'Jarrod Black is the new Harlowe Croft' in big letters. This was it. At least they'd chosen a cracker of a photo, even though it was taken towards the end of the day when he was at his least alert.

"Look at my boy," said Mum. "Isn't he handsome?"

Fair point. He did scrub up pretty well, but he could tell it was well and truly Photoshopped and enhanced.

"Oh wow," said Jarrod, playing along as if Seb had been the first to find out. "The cat's out of the bag!"

Anna and Elin appeared, and Elin started to look around the kitchen for breakfast things. Mum was straight up, and they greeted each other with a hug. Mum knew where everything was already and offered to get the cooking started. Both Anna and Elin were due at training at 9:00 a.m., in opposite directions. Anna asked Mum not to fuss and she knew that Jarrod would have a cupboard full of cereal and that would be just what they needed.

"Who needs a lift?" asked Jarrod.

"Yes, please," said Anna. "Elin can take my car, and if you can take me, that will make it less of a rush."

"Done," said Jarrod with a smile. It was great being able to offer help to his sister.

"Quarter past eight," said Anna. "Be ready."

Jarrod walked back towards the front door and to the office area where he picked up his phone. He could see a long list already of missed calls and messages. As soon as he went to read the first one, the phone rang. It was a Signal 7 call, but from an unknown number. Jarrod sensed that he should answer it.

"Hello?" he said with trepidation.

"Hello, Jarrod," came the European accent. "Mr Lefevre here."

"You're joking …" said Jarrod almost to himself. The phone asked to be switched to video mode, a feature of the app that Jarrod had never investigated.

"Oh …" was all that Jarrod could say as the long and thin features of Yannick Lefevre appeared on his screen.

"I apologise for the early hour," said Yannick.

"What the fuck do you want?" asked Jarrod, surprising himself with his forthright manner and agitated voice.

"Jarrod, I would like to meet you to discuss a business matter," said the wiry Frenchman.

"No, thanks, Lefevre." Using his surname allowed him to avoid a personal connection with this man who had given him so much grief earlier this year.

"You have my number," said Yannick. "When you are ready to meet, we will discuss what we need from you."

"No, thanks," said Jarrod. "I'm really not interested in doing business with you."

Jarrod knew that he would be unable to leave the conversation with Yannick accepting that Jarrod wasn't interested.

"You don't have a choice, Jarrod."

"Goodbye," said Jarrod and hung up. His heart was racing. He stood there almost listening to the blood pump through his veins. The instant regret in hanging up dawned on him and he realised that he had a great deal more to say to this menace. How did he know about Signal 7? That was a private thing between Jarrod and D.I. Allison. Oh god, this was the last thing he needed.

JARROD BLACK - CHASING PACK

55

Mirror

"Hello, Jarrod," said Aurelio, once Jarrod had finally got round to answering his phone. "You're ignoring me."

"Not at all, Aurelio," said Jarrod honestly. "Phone's ringing hot."

"I can imagine," said his manager. "You weren't going to tell me?"

"I assumed you knew," said Jarrod, still being honest. "It was written into my contract. I guess it didn't mention what the business venture was, only that I wouldn't be able to commit to full-time training."

"It's certainly not what I expected," said Aurelio.

"Sorry, boss," said Jarrod.

"Promise me that it's not going to get in the way of your football," Aurelio continued. "I need to know that I can count on you."

"When I signed that contract with South Melbourne," said Jarrod, "I made that promise to you. I'm not ready to give up football. I'm not ready to go into coaching. And I'm not ready to throw it all away on a whim."

"It's hardly a whim," said Aurelio. "This is something massive."

Jarrod thought and paused for a few seconds.

"It's definitely bigger than I had anticipated," said Jarrod. "But you have my word."

"See you at training this afternoon," said Aurelio. "You're Jarrod Black the footballer as soon as you walk through those gates."

"Understood. And thanks."

Jarrod tried to put himself in Aurelio's shoes. He had chanced upon a major signing to bolster his midfield and had trusted in him by playing him right from the start. Now there was a cloud over his availability. It was tough not to feel in some way guilty for putting the club in this situation.

The realisation that life was going to be a whole lot different was starting to dawn on Jarrod. The simple logistics of getting from his house to training was potentially going to be fraught with danger. He'd already experienced paranoia on the way to drop Anna at the City academy, and he didn't dare get out of the car once he was there. After speaking with Yannick Lefevre, he was forever looking in his rear view mirror, expecting to see the beady eyes of the stick-like Frenchman glaring at him from the car behind.

He had spent the morning with the kids in the pool, in between checking his phone. It was indeed ringing hot, but there were only a select few people that he was willing to communicate with. Over lunch, Dad had let Jarrod know that he and Mum would be leaving in the morning. They felt that it was the right time to escape the madness. They offered to welcome the kids to Sydney at any time if it all got too much, especially in the holidays before school started. Jarrod was sad that his parents had made the decision to step into the background; he totally understood and was also relieved that he didn't have to pretend he would have time to spend with them.

It was now time to get to training and his latest message from Jacqui suggested that he might want to leave the car at home and let Johnny pick him up. There was no way though that he was going to descend into a pattern of letting everything be done for him, and he waved away the offer and said he'd aim to be at training a little earlier, to cater for any issues getting there. Sure enough, as the electric gate opened and he prepared to drive off, there was a wall of reporters and photographers waiting to pounce. Jarrod looked up through the windscreen and stared as the flashes started to go off. There was a respectful distance between the gate and the media scrum, and they parted slowly to let Jarrod through at a snail's pace, the photographers having enough time to whirr off a bank of shots on their expensive cameras and the reporters able to bark questions and peer in the dark windows to see who else was in the car or if there was anything juicy to write about. This was a well-practised scenario, it seemed, and it was a lot more civil than anything Jarrod had experienced in England.

There were a few photographers who ran after the car, but with the windows heavily tinted, they gave up after a few metres. All Jarrod could think of was how Marianne and the kids would cope if they had to go out. Or Mum and Dad. He was pretty sure that Anna and Elin would be well versed in handling the media after their time in the NWSL and at the World Cup.

58

Cringed

Jarrod was directed to the boardroom as soon as he arrived at the Lakeside. There was a meeting going on, and all the top brass at the club were there. Club president Sophia Theodoridis stopped mid-sentence when he was shown in; clearly, he had been the number one item on the agenda.

"The man himself," smiled Sophia.

Jarrod had shaken her hand at the first game, but her interest in him had since multiplied hundredfold.

"Please take a seat," she continued. "We were just discussing how we're going to capitalise on your newfound stardom and make this work for us."

Jarrod hadn't contemplated this and felt like a fool for not seeing it coming. He cringed, at least inside, at the sort of things this could lead to. It could be a shirt number change to 040, the agent number bestowed upon Harlowe Croft in one of the earlier movies, a themed match day where those in dinner jackets or formal dresses would get in free; Jarrod could already feel it in the air.

"Oh," said Jarrod, curiously. "I'm all ears."

"As you know," said Sophia, "we've taken a chance on you, bringing you to Melbourne at considerable expense, and now we're in danger of having our star player compromised by outside influences."

"I've already assured Aurelio …" started Jarrod.

"Yes, we understand your intentions are honourable," continued Sophia, walking around the boardroom behind the other members of the meeting. "But let's be upfront. This is going to take up a lot of your time, a lot of your energy, and you will have much more on your plate than simply playing and enjoying your time at South Melbourne."

"Right," said Jarrod, realising how futile any rejection would be to that last statement.

"So," said Sophia, turning to face Jarrod. "We would like to use this to our advantage too."

"What do you have in mind?" asked Jarrod, sitting back as if relaxing, but feeling anything but relaxed.

"Advertising, Jarrod," said Sophia. "Advertising is where we're going to use you. You're going to be the face of South Melbourne Football Club for the rest of the season. We're going to make sure every company in Melbourne wants to be a part of our success. Photo opportunities. Sponsor events. TV appearances, radio."

Jarrod was frozen. As if he would have time for any of that.

"Sounds doable," was all that Jarrod could muster while keeping a jovial manner.

"Good," said Sophia. "We'll let you know when we have something lined up. Thanks for your time."

Jarrod was dismissed as if he'd just been to see the headmaster. He managed to keep smiling and offered some goodbyes to the familiar faces around the table. As soon as he had closed the heavy wooden door, his face dropped, and he closed his eyes with a sigh.

The Canberra trip came and went without incident. Jarrod did as he was told and checked in with D.I. Allison as the team made their way together to the airport. There had been no further contact with Yannick Lefevre and nothing unusual. It seemed like the criminal underworld was on its Christmas break. Perhaps the nutters were in Australia for a holiday. Jarrod had often joked with Marianne about how her country of birth would slow down to a standstill in August, but in reality, Australia was very similar. Late December through to Australia Day was a very quiet period for the country. Football, though, continued, and the New Year brought in a few fixture changes for TV after LF Sports secured two further channels to show the games.

59

Partner

Life for the Black family was arriving at some sort of normality. Mum and Dad were long gone back to Sydney, Anna and Elin had moved into their funky apartment in Fitzroy and they were all in the groove of their respective football careers. Marianne had been networking regularly in the city to try and secure an opening in a sports management role or even in TV presenting, something that she had flirted with in the past in England. She was in no hurry though and was happy to spend extended time with the kids in the lead-up to them starting school. Seb was delighted to be heading to an all-boys' school after being wooed by the principal on their open day, but Aneka was distraught at having to join an all-girls' school in the opposite direction, finally being split up from her brother. Jarrod didn't understand why this had to be the way, but Marianne had been discussing it with some of her contacts and it was just the accepted way. Until the end of January though, the kids were living a quiet, detached life, which Seb described as being like in COVID lockdown all over again.

Jarrod's sudden shot to global stardom hadn't yet made too much of a difference to his life. There was of course a lot more media interest, and he was dragged from interview to interview at the behest of the production company. The club commitments did increase too, and he found himself in the company of drunk people at the end of home games in the corporate area, being the centre of attention of the sponsors and their partners. The punishing schedule he had endured in the lead-up to Christmas continued, and Malik was working him hard in an effort to bulk up his chest and give him more noticeable biceps.

The rehearsals, the acting school and the sessions with the stunt team were ramping up, and Jarrod was loving it. The people he was working with were definitely not buttering him up, and they were quite harsh in their criticism where he failed to live up to the high expectations. None more than the stunt studio, where the one-on-one sessions with teacher Alex were giving him a touch of anxiety. The ever-increasing difficulty of the tumbles and the falls was making him doubt himself, but they persisted until he got it right. Jarrod was slowly becoming the finished article.

In the week leading up to January 26th, the always controversial national holiday that signalled the end of the summer holidays, Jarrod took a call from Dalton Piercey. The call came in on the new super-encrypted app of the day, Tomov, on the new police-issue mobile phone he had been given once they had found out they were all in danger of being tapped. Jarrod was to meet at the unassuming Prahran police station for a briefing. He had a slender window that day and raced over after cutting short his rehearsals.

"Good to see you again, Jarrod," said Mr Piercey, looking both ways before ushering Jarrod behind the desk and up a long corridor into what looked like an interview room. Mr Piercey offered him a seat and sat opposite, as if in an interrogation.

"What can I do for you?" asked Jarrod, not having any inkling about what this was about.

"Today, we're assigning a security guard to you," said Mr Piercey. "You may have seen this coming."

It was Jarrod in fact who had asked for security over a month ago in a conversation with Jacqui. At the time it wasn't deemed necessary, but now, with the increased exposure for Jarrod and the increasing movements of the family around town, both the production company and the police had decided that a security guard would be a good move.

"Ah, that's great," said Jarrod. "Is this courtesy of the movie company or the police?"

"We were requested to find you someone by your production company," said Mr Piercey. "Although in a slightly unconventional way, the security guard is going to be an employee of a private security company who specialise in safeguarding high profile celebrities. Let's say, we have pulled a few strings to have this arranged at such short notice."

"Good to know the police can bend the rules," joked Jarrod. "Who is it?"

There was a bustling outside and a knock at the door before it was flung open, smashing into the doorstop before it made a hole in the wall.

"G'day, Dalts!" said a cheery voice and in strutted a man, no taller than Jarrod, wearing a green bomber jacket and smiling from ear to ear. "Sorry to barge in, I didn't realise you were in the middle of something."

Jarrod's instant reflex was to hope that this was not his security guard, but at the same time he was intrigued. He didn't seem the type to be behind the scenes.

"Good to see you, Bradley," said Mr Piercey with a smile, and they hugged. "Brad, I would like you to meet Jarrod Black. Jarrod, this is Brad Neylan."

Jarrod shook his hand, and Brad put his left hand on the handshake as if to seal an imaginary deal.

"Pleased to meet you, Brad," said Jarrod enthusiastically, still not knowing who he was talking to.

"Great to meet you too," said Brad. "You're a lot more good-looking in real life."

Jarrod stared, puzzled, at Mr Piercey.

"Oh, sorry," flustered Mr Piercey. "That grand entrance there was immaculately timed. We have secured Brad's services for the next six months to be the head of your security detail."

Jarrod held in a gulp.

"Looking forward to meeting the rest of the family," said Brad, slapping Jarrod on the shoulder. "We're going to be spending a lot of time together.

Nice motor you've got. I'll be driving from now on. Can I have the key?"

Jarrod looked at Mr Piercey, who gave a nod, and Jarrod handed over his keys. It seemed as though he was handing over the last remaining part of his freedom. It didn't take long though for Jarrod to warm to Brad. He had been a professional footballer with Newcastle Jets before moving over to play in Holland and ended up in the Championship at Blackburn Rovers. That was maybe five years before Jarrod ventured over to England himself, but as they got talking, they knew a lot of people in common. Mr Piercey sat back and listened as they talked for a good hour with the look of a man who knew he had made a great decision. He even went out to fetch them a coffee. Jarrod now had a partner in crime, and it took him back to his first days at Gateshead where he had instantly bonded with his best mate Reggie.

Jarrod was now running late for training. It was no stress though, as he had a new driver, and Brad seemed to know every back street between Prahran police station and the Lakeside Stadium. Jarrod was physically rattled by the time they pulled up in the car park. He hadn't seen driving quite like that since watching *Baby Driver* at the movies.

60

Badgering

The tough regime of training, rehearsals, game, fitness, acting school and stunt work was preventing Jarrod from spending any time with the family. He had talked previously with Marianne about this, and Jacqui had gone out of her way to extend her hand to help Marianne settle in. With an increase in the number of people wanting to talk with him and a more prominent public profile thanks to the advertising hoardings and the simultaneous increase in BetShed ads on TV, Jarrod was a man in demand from the moment he woke up until the moment he closed his bedroom door at night. He was feeling surprisingly alert though, and he had never felt so organised in his life. The family had Brad to call on at any time, and Jacqui was always around the house when Jarrod was there.

At training, an early evening session after returning from a midweek game on the Gold Coast, Sophia and manager Aurelio were in discussion as Jarrod got out of the car in front of the main entrance to the stadium building. They continued to chat and looked in Jarrod's direction, staring and talking until he got within earshot. He was asked to follow them to Sophia's office inside the building.

"You're looking good, Jarrod," said Sophia, closing the door behind her as the two men took a seat in front of her desk. Jarrod didn't see a need to respond.

"On that note," said Aurelio. "We're concerned with your weight loss. Have you noticed that you're getting knocked off the ball more often?"

"I'm feeling as good as I have for a long time, Aurelio," said Jarrod with a smile. It was true. He could feel the muscles in his arms restricted by the sleeves of his t-shirts, and his abs were starting to pop out like a six-pack. His waistline was a few centimetres smaller too and some of his clothes were starting to hang off him. There was consistent weight loss from week to week.

"You might be feeling good, but I'd hate to see you losing an important part of your game because you can't shield a ball or you come off second best shoulder to shoulder," said Aurelio. "Can you ease off a little on the weight loss?"

"You've not noticed how fast I am at the moment, though," said Jarrod, still smiling the smile of someone who was not going to take any of this on board.

"You're no spring chicken, Jarrod," said Aurelio with the hint of a smile. "It's not like you were the fastest player in the team."

"Thanks for your kind words," said Jarrod cheekily.

That was enough. Aurelio had got his point across. Sophia was happy that she didn't have to listen to Aurelio badgering her any longer and Jarrod walked out of the room with a spring in his step. It was true that Jarrod had been outfought in a couple of situations the previous evening, but his surprising turn of speed off the mark had given South Melbourne an extra dimension, and it was his jinking run into the box which had earned them a penalty to level the game late on and keep up the momentum in their search for a finals berth.

The heat though was something else. A Gold Coast evening in January, after a blistering hot day with no wind, was intense. Jarrod was compared, by the LF Sports commentator Denton Swift, to Karl-Heinz Rummenigge, the famous German captain, after his shirt was drenched after only ten minutes. It did though show his six pack, and the commentary veered off into a comedy routine about agent 040 and his golden Lamborghini. Jarrod shrugged off his heavy sweating, but he couldn't help thinking that his age had something to do with it, and perhaps his body was telling him something.

Marianne raced into the bedroom and launched herself on Jarrod, who was still stirring ahead of his early morning session with Malik. The beautiful morning sunshine and the warm conditions made it easy to be up and about early, and Marianne had taken the time to check her phone as she went to the bathroom.

"I've got it!" she shouted. "I've got the role!"

Jarrod was only half awake, stretching his heavy arms to the point of cramp and he was delighted to be accosted by his wife. She was naked, apart from the crop-top that she often wore to hide her post-op breasts, and that brief glimpse and her skin against his was enough to make Jarrod alter his schedule in his head.

"The golf job or the presenter gig?" asked Jarrod. He should have been a bit more on the ball.

"Both!" said Marianne excitedly. "Say hello to LF Sports' new golf reporter!"

The mention of LF Sports didn't dampen Jarrod's enthusiasm.

"You're going to be on TV?" he said, before realising that Marianne had told him all about it two days before.

"Yes!" she said. "News segments, golf show, written articles. Aren't I clever?"

Jarrod needed no more encouragement and rolled her over, pinned her arms to the bed and kissed her neck. Malik could wait. Things were falling into place. It was time to rehearse one of the more risqué scenes in *From the Gallows*.

61

School

It was the last day of January. Jarrod was feeling a little empty inside after dropping his sister Anna and her girlfriend Elin at Tullamarine the day before as they ended their A-League Women summer working holiday. He had got used to having them around; having family on their doorstep was an unusual and welcome situation. But the US was where Anna would be continuing her stellar rise to football stardom; Melbourne City's glorious run of wins was the opposite of Elin's tough time with league debutants Western United, who were in a battle for the wooden spoon with Perth Glory.

Sebastian and Aneka were ready to start school. Jarrod had already been out to his early morning training session and was back. Marianne was getting ready for her first day at work and the kids were comparing their uniforms in the mirror and laughing together. It was a picture of family life. Jacqui showed herself in, arriving with an extensive schedule of events for the day, before disappearing again, and Brad appeared at the back door after doing a quick scout of the perimeter. Jarrod was dropping off Aneka and Brad was taking Sebastian. This would become a routine, only punctuated when Marianne was settled in her job and could be a little more flexible. Sebastian was looking forward to the car ride with Brad, and the two had really hit it off in their brief time together.

Brad had returned before Jarrod and was already helping himself to a cup of coffee from the state-of-the-art industrial Italian coffee machine. He was pouring out the milk, taking it slowly to make a pattern of the Angel of the North, the badge of Gateshead FC. Jarrod walked into the smell of enticing aroma and Brad was just placing the two cups on the table.

"Made you one," said Brad, showing him his masterpiece in the froth which made Jarrod smile.

"I could get used to this," said Jarrod, taking a seat. This was a rare moment of relaxation.

"We're not due at the studio for forty-five minutes, time to enjoy one of life's pleasures," said Brad. He'd even put an almond biscotti and a sachet of sugar on the saucer. "I couldn't remember if you took sugar or not."

The two of them enjoyed a chat for twenty minutes, the house quiet and the sun streaming through the side window giving the house a religious feel. Just as the conversation was moving on to how their respective former clubs were doing in the Championship back in England, Brad stood up and announced that it was time to go. He seemed to have an in-built clock that belonged to someone in the military.

First stop was the studio, where Brad dropped Jarrod at the door and drove off at speed, stopping abruptly at the security gate where he appeared to be getting a ticking off for driving so fast. Jarrod looked on and shook his head before hurrying through the door and being met by Jacqui who guided him to where they were going through the rehearsals. This was a scene where Croft would be fighting with one of the bad guys under a slow-moving train. It was like the opposite of a scene in any number of action movies where the fight happened on top of the carriages. This was all about keeping low and springing into action in the small gaps between carriages. Clearly there were no trains or carriages today, so there were a few helpers with cushions running along the set which signalled the timing of when they had to duck, crouch or even lie completely flat. It was intense. The director, Donny Valdez, who Jarrod had only met once, was on scene to see if the concept of a fight scene under a train would be feasible, He didn't give any indication of whether he thought it was a success or not.

To Jarrod though, this was a lot of fun. It was like a game of Whack-a-Mole, and he copped plenty of cushions to the head when he didn't make it down in time. He could also feel his body was much easier to manoeuvre and his new slimmer shape was handy when he had to make himself as flat as possible. Both Jarrod and the two 'baddies' who were having to follow his every move were heaving in the chest when they came up for a break. They gave each other high fives. This was great teamwork, and Jarrod felt right at home.

A quick bite to eat, wheeled in on a trolley as if they were on a plane, and they were right back into it, moving on to a small room where they all ran through the next scene. In this one, Croft had been captured by the main villain, Stelios Banfelt, and was negotiating his release. The script editor was in the room with the actors and there were a number of people offering their input. This was where Jarrod was struggling a little, and the physical demands of his lifestyle meant that he would often switch off during these sessions if he wasn't the centre of attention. This time though, his attention was completely fine. One of the actresses playing the evil Banfelt's daughter was there, and she was just stunningly beautiful in the face, even without make up and wearing the daggiest of tracksuits. Jarrod felt as though he was trying to impress her, like a peacock would to impress a mate, and as a result he was switched on and full of verve. He realised what he was doing at one stage and slumped in his seat in horror with his hands over his face.

62

Terror

Brad was there right at the door in the car when they had finished. He had a bottle of Evian for Jarrod, which Jarrod sipped and then gulped down, memories of his Switzerland trip only six months ago coming flooding back. Brad was even looking after his hydration needs, how good was this? Brad had patched things up with the security guard at the gate and exchanged a joke and a handshake as he went through, announcing he had a special cargo, pointing to Jarrod. Jarrod smiled and gave a nervous wave. As the gate opened, Brad floored it, and the wheels spun and they left in a cloud of smoke, Jarrod's hands clamped to the side of his seat. They were at the Lakeside in no time, and much to his amusement, Jarrod was early—that journey would have taken him twice as long if he'd been driving. Again, Brad drove right up to the door. Whether that was policy for his security agency or it was Brad's thing, he seemed to delight in getting as close to the door as possible, this time getting up onto the kerb and just missing the bollards to drop his special cargo right by the door.

This was his domain, where he felt the most comfortable, and he put his heart into training whenever he was there. The boys at South Melbourne had taken the news that they were training and playing with a movie superstar very well and Jarrod expected nothing less than some proper ribbing and gold old-fashioned banter to keep his feet on the ground. This time they'd excelled themselves. The free kick wall that they used, a row of six metal life-size 2D figures, had been adorned with the faces of former Harlowe Crofts on each of the heads, and one of them had a dinner jacket on, complete with shirt and tie, and the face was Jarrod's. The players all sung the jangly theme tune as he ran up for his first shot and burst out in a roar when he found the top corner and ran in to kiss his alter-ego in the defensive wall. It was pure comedy gold, and Jarrod felt safe and secure at the football club, surrounded with good football people.

Sophia collared him on the way out and ran through some commitments that she had planned for him. There were some that he knew he couldn't do, but in the main they were achievable and not too corny. He knew the club should benefit from his situation and wasn't averse to helping out where he could. The light was starting to fade, and Jarrod had promised to be back home to catch up with the kids for a swim after they'd had dinner. They'd fill him in with the news from their first day at school. He made sure Sophia had Jacqui's details before he left and let her know that she could talk with Jacqui to find available times in the days and weeks ahead. Jarrod skipped outside, relieved to see the car waiting for him, although it was waiting a little further from the doorway. Brad must have got tired of waiting or maybe had to move to let someone else through.

He made his way over to the car, the exhaust showing that it was on and ready to go. He noticed someone in his peripheral vision and glanced over to see a man in dark clothing coming up alongside him. When he reached the car, the passenger window was being lowered and Jarrod looked in before grabbing the door handle. He stopped. Frozen to the spot. There in the driver's seat was Yannick Lefevre, beckoning him in. His first thought was to rip open the door and lunge at Lefevre, but he could see that he had a gun in his right hand, held low so no one outside the car would see. He put his head down further and saw who was in the back. Marianne was in the middle, Seb was sitting upright and still, Aneka had her head under Marianne's arm as if to hide from view. They all stared at Jarrod. They weren't moving and their eyes were a mix of resignation, fear and pleading. Another man sat in the rear seats in the boot, his arm over the back seats, a gun in his hand pointing loosely at Marianne. By now there were two burly men behind him, standing close enough to suggest that he should get in the car, and Yannick patted the seat beside him. Jarrod had no option and calmly got in.

"Where's my security man?" asked Jarrod. He reached behind and touched Marianne's knee and felt Aneka's hand clasp to his wrist. A click came from Lefevre's gun and Jarrod moved his arm back by his side.

"Your man Brad is with us in the rear," said Lefevre in his heavy French accent. "Are you with us, Brad?"

The man with the gun in the rear seats, who was hunched over slightly from being in those awkward seats, gave a kick and Jarrod heard a muffled groan.

"Where are we going?" asked Jarrod.

There was silence as Lefevre pulled away slowly and they made their way out of the car park. Jarrod's heart was racing. He didn't dare speak. He glanced over at Seb and gave him a wink, which at least removed the absolute terror from his eyes. It wasn't long before they were parked in front of a big house on the seafront of what looked like Port Melbourne beach, with the surf life-saving club in the distance. A second car parked behind them. Three men got out and one of them opened the rear door to let Marianne and the kids out, while Jarrod opened his door slowly and got out. Aneka switched from Marianne to Jarrod while Seb grabbed on tightly to his mum's hand. They walked with trepidation over to the front door, which was slightly ajar, and walked in, up the hallway and into the cathedral-like living area at the rear of the house.

Jarrod resisted saying "for fuck's sake" when the host appeared from the kitchen. It was a face he'd seen before. In fact, only six months ago he'd had a similar meeting with this man in the suburbs of Newcastle. It was Viktor Andreyev.

"Please, sit," he offered in a very friendly tone. It was clear where everyone was meant to sit. Jarrod in the comfy chair opposite the host, Marianne and the kids on the big sofa that was facing the two chairs, but quite far away.

It could have been a scene from a world leaders' conference where Obama and Putin discussed their respective issues in front of the cameras. Viktor was very professional and polite, and made sure the family had drinks and snacks on the table in front of them.

"First of all, I apologise for the manner in which you were brought here tonight," said Viktor. "My associate Yannick did try to make contact, but our request perhaps wasn't firm enough."

"Why am I … why are we here?" asked Jarrod calmly.

"Straight to the point, Jarrod," said Viktor, reaching down and taking some of the mixed nuts from a bowl that sat between them on a low coffee table. "We're here to help you understand your role in a small project that we have on the horizon."

"A small project?" asked Jarrod. Viktor let a peanut drop out of his clenched fist into the palm of his other hand and threw it into his mouth from a distance. Seb would have been impressed with that had he not been sitting there terrified.

"Your team is heading for the play-offs; this is an exciting time for South Melbourne FC," said Viktor, seemingly ignoring the question. "When you are in the final of the play-offs, there is a job that I would like you to do for me. It won't bring any harm to anyone but will make the result of the game a little easier to predict."

"Not this again," said Jarrod abruptly. If this had been a meeting of world leaders it could have rocked the boat and had diplomats ejected from embassies. "I am absolutely not interested in being part of this. I'm more than happy to turn a blind eye to this whole conversation and not a word will be said. Please, I don't understand why I would be considered as a candidate for your scheme. Surely you could find someone a little more discreet. Someone not in the news?"

Marianne shifted uncomfortably in the sofa.

"Jarrod," said Viktor slowly, raising his eyes up to meet his. "You caused us a lot of issues last year, and our business was heavily affected by your actions."

He was referring to Jarrod's involvement in smashing the illegal betting syndicate in Europe. Surely, though, Viktor understood that Jarrod was working with the police.

"We have had to get closer to the police in England," continued Viktor. "We have people on the inside in the right places. Remember that Signal 7 is now owned by Chiya Incorporated. We hear everything."

Jarrod was gobsmacked. He had no idea. That's how Lefevre had got his number and that went a long way to explaining how and why Viktor, Murtaka and Jens Lermann all walked free after being initially pinned as the leaders of the betting syndicate. They had access to police communication and used it to their advantage. Jarrod felt violated after all those sensitive conversations with D.I. Allison. Just running through those conversations in his head, he felt dirty.

"Clearly you will not be able to involve your good friend Marcus in this one," said Viktor, referencing D.I. Allison by his first name for extra effect. "Plus, we will be compensating you handsomely for your involvement in this … scheme."

"Money is of no interest to me."

"What your movie company pays you will be peanuts compared to what we will pay you," said Viktor, letting another nut drop from his fist. "We are not dealing in the junior dollar values that you are dealing with at the moment. This will change your life. And you can walk away, and we will never need your services again."

"The answer is still no," said Jarrod, trying his best not to cross his arms.

"Remember that your beautiful wife and children are here today. They are as involved in this as you are," said Viktor. That was enough of a veiled threat to really put the wind up Jarrod. He could see Aneka burrowing her head even further into Marianne's arms and he knew that they really had no choice in this.

63

Liberal

As this was all unfolding inside the prestigious beachside residence, security guard Brad was still bound up in the boot of the car. He was alone. He'd taken a few kicks from the kind gentleman in the back with him on the journey from the Lakeside, and had been tied by his hands, knees and ankles. His hands were bound around a support strut for the back seats of the car, so he wasn't going anywhere. It was starting to piss him off. Little did he know, and little did this unpleasant mob of gentlemen thugs know, but Brad's security agency had been alerted to the situation. He hadn't checked in by phone or text in the usual window, and it was standard practice in these scenarios to send out a crew to track down the phone, and hopefully the employee. The big lummox that had been liberal with his right shoe since he had taken up residence on the floor of the car had taken Brad's phone from his jacket pocket, and he was now outside the car talking with Lefevre and another of the henchmen at the front door.

Brad's discomfort, with his shoulder starting to go numb, was the trigger for him to jolt his body, which exposed the smallest gap in the rope that was firmly wrapped around his wrists. He'd always been quite flexible in the wrists after breaking them both over the years and started to pump his hands together. He had some movement and could just reach the rope with his mouth. Using his teeth in the same way that a stubborn shoelace might be freed from a tight knot, he teased the rope from side to side. He looked like a dog with a toy. Somehow the rope loosened ever so slightly, and he slid his right wrist down the left wrist and with a great deal of burning and rubbing, freed his right hand with a determined heave. He stopped so the car wouldn't move too much. The traffic was surprisingly heavy anyway, so any noise or movement wouldn't be noticed from the outside.

He quickly freed his left hand and struggled successfully with the expertly tied knot in the rope around his knees. The one around his ankles was quite easy to remove. He was completely free, his shoulder spasming as he crouched onto his knees. He could see the three men chatting away. Brad's work phone had been taken, but his personal phone, a sleek model that certainly didn't feel like a phone, was still in the secret zip pocket of his trousers. He quickly looked up on his phone, zooming in on the map to see the actual house number, what the nearest Uber Eats restaurant was, and expertly placed an order of a chicken korma with rice and pappadums. This was clearly something Brad did very often. A loud voice and some laughing from outside was enough to put him back in his foetal position, with the ropes placed around his knees and ankles as if he was still bound. He'd have to wait this one out.

He checked in with his employers and was told that a crew was waiting in a nearby street. It wasn't long before the familiar tinny whine of the Uber Eats moped came into earshot. He could hear everything. The click of the stand as the driver parked up, the rustle in the thermal bag on the rack and the whistle as he or she walked up the driveway to the house. Brad popped his head up and could see the three men standing, looking menacing, spreading to form a human shield in front of the Uber Eats delivery guy. This was his chance.

Knowing the model of the car he was in, releasing the door to the boot would be pointless as it would give off a bleating sound, so he slowly reached around and flicked one of the back seats down and crawled over it and around to the back side door, closest to the road, flicking off the door lights in the middle console. He slowly opened it and dropped out onto the road. It must have looked quite a sight to the passing motorists.

He got to his feet and closed the door softly and inched his way to the back of the car. A removalist van was roaring along the road and just about to pass, and he took his chance to dart out from behind the car and into the next door's driveway. He walked up the driveway until he was out of sight of the front door and scaled the Colorbond fence, dropping into the no man's land at the side of the house. He quickly walked up to the back of the house, where the bi-fold doors were open to give some breeze on this warm night.

With a glance inside to assess the situation and a quick clench of the fist to himself for good luck, Brad strolled in through the back doors until he was standing in front of Viktor and Jarrod.

"Here's what's going to happen, sir," he said calmly. Jarrod looked at him with bewilderment. Viktor listened calmly. "I'm going to leave with Marianne and the children and we're going to forget that this whole thing ever happened. I'd let this happen if I were you."

Viktor's eyes were wide, and he looked to be understandably agitated. Marianne took the prompt and stood up immediately, grabbing Aneka's hand and putting her hand on Seb's shoulder. They started to walk towards the back door. Brad signalled which way they should go.

Jarrod took the prompt too and stood up. Viktor stood up and calmly walked in front of Jarrod, facing him to block his way. This was tense. Brad had seen enough and, in an instant, launched himself at Viktor and took him out with the most impressive of tackles to the midriff, something that would have drawn a roar from the crowd on State of Origin night. The thud as he hit the ground was huge. Jarrod had taken a few of those from Alex at stunt training and they didn't tickle. Brad was up straight away, knowing that such a noise would alert the heavies outside. He was making for the back door before Jarrod could react and Brad had to grab him to get him moving. Brad hoisted Aneka over the fence and linked his fingers together for Seb to vault over and instructed them to run out the front and to the right. There was no time to help Marianne. It didn't matter, she had already bounced up the fence and over and was away, following Aneka and Seb.

Jarrod and Brad walked slowly to the edge of the house and saw the remaining two heavies catch sight of Marianne as she sprinted out of the neighbouring driveway, and they left the Uber Eats guy at the front door and gave chase. Brad waited a second and ran through the front garden and jumped through the surprisingly thick hedge, giving Jarrod the signal to follow him. They could see Marianne running as fast as she could behind Aneka and Sebastian, with the two heavies in pursuit. Brad yelled after them, which caused the goons to stop. They were confused for a moment and Brad yelled again: "Jarrod's here!" They turned and raced back.

The security truck from Brad's firm appeared in the distance and screeched into a driveway in front of the kids. Jarrod could just make out Jacqui from a distance, leaping out of the side of the van and directing the kids and then Marianne to get in. The heavies were closing in on Jarrod and Brad. Two more, Lefevre one of them, had just burst through the door.

"Run, Jarrod," he said quickly. "Go that way, around the block," he said, pointing in the other direction.

"What about ..."

"RUN!"

Jarrod did what he was told to do and sprinted off in the opposite direction as if he was chasing a through ball down the wing to make a cross before the ball went out. Brad went around the other side of the car and jumped in the back door that he had left slightly open. He reached into the driver's seat and clicked the doors locked. The two henchmen arrived and tried the doors and started to kick at them and thump at the windows. Jarrod's insistence for tempered glass was a good decision at this point. Brad was trapped, but he could see outside that the security truck was coming up the road, and he could also see Viktor Andreyev hurrying out of the front door with a young lady and calling his men to get in their cars. The banging stopped and Andreyev's car screeched out of the driveway as the security truck arrived.

Jacqui appeared at the window of the car.

"Are you okay?" she asked.

"Never been better," said Brad, reaching over and clicking the unlock button. He got out.

"Where's Jarrod?" asked Jacqui frantically,

"He'll be back in a minute or two," said Brad. He walked over to the front door where the Uber Eats delivery guy was still standing, frozen to the spot.

"Hello, mate," said Brad. "Chicken korma with pappadums?"

The delivery guy nodded and handed over the bag.

"And here's something for your trouble," said Brad, handing over a five-dollar note that he'd found in his secret pocket next to his personal phone.

64

Pappadum

Jarrod had sprinted his heart out to get as far away as possible. He calculated he was probably halfway to doing a circuit and would take the next left. He slowed to a walk, his chest burning after what was surely his quickest 800m ever. He was heaving for air, so much so that he couldn't hear the car coming along the next street, and he turned the corner just as a dark-coloured car slowed up beside him. Jarrod dropped his shoulders, resigned to the fact that he'd failed to get away. The back window went down. Viktor was sitting in the back seat. If it had been Stelios Banfelt from the Harlowe Croft movies, with a fluffy cat on his lap, it wouldn't have been out of place.

"We'll be in touch, Jarrod," he said.

Jarrod kept on walking and didn't look. He had personal trainer Malik's voice in his head, telling him to look; one of the first rules of self-defence was to look confidently in the eyes of the aggressor.

"You have no choice," continued Viktor.

Jarrod stopped and turned to look at Viktor. For someone who had been crash tackled to the floor only a few minutes ago, he looked unflustered. Jarrod could see the figure of a young lady beside him, her face concentrating on her mobile phone. It was the model from the photo shoot. The Russian. It was either his daughter or his mistress. Damn it, that's how they'd really got into his phone. The car kept moving and edged past. Jarrod could see Lefevre driving. The window went up and the car gathered speed before hooking a right turn and disappearing out of sight.

Jarrod started to run again and turned the corner at the end of the street to make his way back to complete the circuit.

The security team did a quick walk through the house and determined that no one was inside. Marianne and the kids got out of the truck as Jarrod ran up the road from where they had just driven. He was still gasping for breath but went in for the hug with Marianne and the kids.

"You're all right, you're all right, I'm so sorry," said Jarrod between heavy breaths.

They walked over to the front door where Brad had unpacked the meal and had tucked a napkin into his stained and ripped shirt. He offered Sebastian a pappadum which he took, and they started to eat the curry together.

"What just happened?" said Jarrod.

"We're living in the fast lane, that's what just happened," said Brad, with a piece of chicken hanging from a thread from his mouth. It dropped onto his white shirt, and he looked at it for a moment and chuckled.

Jacqui had the spare key to Jarrod's car. It would need a bit of attention after taking a few size twelves to the side panels, but it was drivable. Brad thanked his security colleagues and they left. Brad drove; Jacqui sat in the passenger seat. Marianne and the kids were in the same positions they'd been in earlier in the night and Jarrod was crouched in the rear seat like a banished child. They were home in a matter of minutes and piled out of the car and through the front door. The kids' school bags were where they had left them earlier in the night. Jarrod went straight to the bag he'd had in Japan and rummaged through a side pocket, eventually finding a business card. It was Akio, the inquisitive Japanese reporter he had met in Tokyo.

Jarrod asked to borrow Brad's remaining phone. He needed to be off the network. He called the number and waited an age for the ringing to start.

"Akio speaking," came the reply; at least, that's what Jarrod thought he said, as it may have been in Japanese.

"Hello, Akio, Jarrod Black," said Jarrod, unsure as to whether the reporter would remember him. The delay was quite pronounced.

"Hello, Jarrod," said Akio. "I am so glad you called. I will be in Melbourne again tomorrow and I would like to meet up again. You are on my radar once more."

"Oh, wow, yes," said Jarrod, knowing that he would be asking the first favour. "Listen, I think you may be on to something with your story. We can help each other out. First, I need a big favour."

"Fire away," said Akio, using a turn of phrase that underlined his command of the English language.

"I would like you to send a text to my friend Marcus," said Jarrod. "It's urgent. And I'd like him to call this number straight away. It's not my phone. Does it come up with the number at your end?"

Jarrod could tell Akio was checking his phone.

"Private number," said Akio.

"One minute," said Jarrod, and raced around to the kitchen to ask Brad what his number was. Brad took a minute before it came to him. Jarrod repeated the numbers into the phone. Akio repeated them back.

"Plus 61?" asked Akio.

"Plus 61 and drop the zero," said Jarrod. "Okay, that's the number for Marcus to call. Now, Marcus' number."

He put Akio on speaker and flicked through his contacts. He had Marcus' phone number as well as his Signal 7 number and read it out. Again, Akio repeated it back flawlessly.

"Plus 61?" asked Akio.

"Plus 44, drop the zero," said Jarrod.

"I'll do that now. Just a text?" asked Akio.

"Yes, and say it's important. Ring me when you get to Melbourne. Just use this number," said Jarrod, knowing very well that he wouldn't have any time for this.

Jarrod walked back into the kitchen where Jacqui was setting the table and Brad was cooking up a storm, having raided the cupboards. Jarrod handed the phone to Brad with a smile, warning that it would ring very soon. Brad's floury hands weren't mobile-phone friendly, and Jarrod placed it on the bench next to him.

Jarrod found Marianne sitting on Aneka's bed, still holding Aneka whose eyes were red. She started crying again when she saw Jarrod. Marianne smiled at Jarrod and hugged Aneka even closer. Jarrod walked across to Seb's room. He had his book open and was frantically writing. Jarrod stood behind him and glanced at what he was writing. It was an introduction to himself as the first page of his English exercise book. He glanced up at Jarrod and Jarrod put his hand on his shoulder. In answer to the question 'describe your parents', he had written in the small space 'Mum is on TV and Dad is an action movie actor'. Not one mention of football. After the evening they had just been through, it was no surprise. Seb must have thought that his action movie actor role spilled over into real life.

There was a call from the kitchen. Phone for Jarrod. Jarrod rushed downstairs and grabbed the phone from the bench where he'd left it. It had a white fingerprint where Brad had answered it. It looked like gnocchi was on the menu, and it felt like a celebrity chef had taken over his kitchen.

"Dinner in ten," said Brad, with the look of someone you wouldn't dare be there for in eleven minutes.

Jarrod retreated again to the study area near the front door.

"Marcus," said Jarrod, hopeful that this was indeed D.I. Allison on the other end of the line.

"Jarrod," said D.I. Allison to confirm it was him.

"Did you know any of this was going to happen?" asked Jarrod, getting into a rhythm and trying to spill his words out all at once. "Viktor

Andreyev, Yannick Lefevre? Why are these people not in custody? Why are they involving me? Why are they bringing my family into it? Help me here, Marcus. I'm freaked out."

"Jarrod, Jarrod," said D.I. Allison. "Slowly."

He paused before continuing.

"We believe that Viktor Andreyev is planning to hijack a game, possibly a finals game. Those games are usually games that could spring an upset, but he is using all of his possible avenues to make sure the result of the game is a banker. All of his associates will be in on the plan. Murtaka Chiya still wants her funds to take over at Newcastle United. LF Sports need the money to keep ploughing into Australian football—they can't go on throwing cash at something that doesn't make any money yet. And you'll not be surprised to know that there are many, many people involved. Does that sound like anything you know?"

"Marcus, I was effectively kidnapped by Lefevre," said Jarrod with not a hint of drama. "All my normal lines of communication with you are compromised, and now Marianne and the kids are involved. Can't you wrap this up? What more proof do you need of laws being broken? Do you want someone to be killed?"

"This is the end game," said D.I. Allison. "We just need to tie all the perpetrators together and this is our biggest chance to blow it out of the water."

"That's what you said last time," said Jarrod, reminding D.I. Allison that he had been placed in this uncomfortable position already once before. It showed great faith in the acting skills that D.I. Allison, the Metropolitan Police and Interpol had in him.

"No one gets hurt this time though," said D.I. Allison. "This is a crime that leaves no casualties."

"Apart from the poor team who has a result written in ink before the game starts," said Jarrod. "Apart from the fans who travel thousands of miles to see their team. Apart from the player whose wife and kids are traumatised and get kidnapped."

"Jarrod, this is possibly the only time we're going to speak with each other before we move in on this," said D.I. Allison. "As you say, communication lines are looking less private that we thought. We need you to be with us on this one. Wait for Andreyev to be in touch—he will— and agree to be involved in return for leaving Marianne and the kids out of it. He is a professional businessman who does professional deals. And he says he is a fan of yours. He might be even more so after you gave him a good touch-up tonight."

Jarrod was shocked that D.I. Allison knew that. Before he could question it, D.I. Allison changed tact completely.

"Good win for the Toon last night again," he said. "Smeltzy saved a penalty and we won 1–0 at Aston Villa."

Jarrod relaxed. He knew that D.I. Allison could defuse any situation with football talk. He had wanted to question him why Andreyev would want to work with Murtaka again after they seemingly used him as a fall guy last time. The friendly football talk stopped him.

"How will I contact you?" said Jarrod, shutting down the deflection straight away.

"We'll contact you," said D.I. Allison. "Don't try and use anything on your phone, or anyone's phone. This one you've got now—whose is it?"

"This is my security guard's," said Jarrod.

"I'd get him to throw it away if I was you," said D.I. Allison. "We'll contact you. That police phone is compromised too. Dalton Piercey will be close by at all times. You probably haven't noticed the undercover guys. They're out there and keeping you safe."

That was the end of the conversation. Jarrod had just been placed in the exact situation that he didn't want to be in. It was fraught with risk, against all his morals, and he didn't have time for this shit. He stood holding the phone to his ear even though the call had ended. Then he grabbed a luminous pink sticky note, wrote the name Akio on it and stuck it above the study desk. He would need to find out what the Japanese reporter knew.

He walked back into the kitchen. It must have been ten minutes. Aneka was helping Brad plate up, and Jacqui was filling everyone's glass with water. Marianne walked in arm in arm with Sebastian and they all sat down at the table. It was late, it was dark. As Brad went to sit down with a chopping board full of garlic bread, he stood up instead and raised his water glass.

"Thank you, family," he said. "That was something that we would all like to forget. So, let's forget that ever happened. We've all just come in from school and work, and everything is super normal. Cheers!"

Marianne smiled and there was clinking of glasses.

"Aneka," said Jarrod. "What was the highlight of your day at school?"

The evening went as any evening in any dining room in Australia would go, with parents catching up with their kids' school day and kids asking their parents about their day. Jacqui and Brad clinked glasses and smiled at each other.

65

Flurry

The end of the regular season was a week away and South Melbourne only needed a point to be assured of a finals berth. A win though would give them second place and a distinct home advantage in the finals. With Easter out of the way and school holidays on again, Jarrod enjoyed being around the kids for fleeting moments in between rehearsals, stunt work, personal training and training with the club. Brad and Jacqui were as much a part of their family as anyone else, and it was not unusual to see Brad helping out Seb with his homework or Jacqui playing in the pool with Aneka when Jarrod came in.

The chaos some weeks ago now in Albert Park was a distant memory, although Brad had alerted Jarrod and Marianne to Aneka being quite clingy whenever he escorted her anywhere. Perhaps she had been spooked by that episode, but in reality, it had shaken them all, and Jarrod often talked it through with Marianne when they were in bed at night. Marianne had landed what she considered a dream role. She was part of the LF Sports golf team on a casual basis and had fallen into a technical role with the Golf Australia Victorian office when an event manager moved overseas and the position became available to those in the know. She seemed to be very happy with the work-life balance but had yet to be involved in a major TV event. That would be coming at the end of the Easter holidays with a flurry of events that would take her around the country as a co-host of the nightly golf show.

The kids had made a lot of friends, despite Seb taking a few weeks to get used to having no girls at school, and the invites had already started to come in for birthday parties, some of them a little more ostentatious than he remembered back in Darlington. Having a burn in the park on their bikes and a barbecue didn't seem to cut it, and there was expectation for gifts—all very foreign to both Jarrod and Marianne. With Brad taking the heat off by playing chauffeur to the kids and Jacqui on hand to help out after hours, the family were starting to enjoy Melbourne. There was always the looming finals series in the back of Jarrod's mind which would bring with it extra challenges, thanks to Viktor Andreyev and his cohorts, but the longer they went without contact from Lefevre, the further into the background that was pushed.

Jarrod was at the studio, running through another tricky scene with one of his co-stars, Raphael Finn, who played a senior colleague of Harlowe Croft in the movie. The two of them were having fun learning the script and were mastering it, Jarrod having to use his best English accent and Rapha having to use a deeper and huskier voice than his normal tone to deliver the lines convincingly as an older man. The scene involved Croft taking off his hat and throwing it onto an antique hat stand; the character had forgotten that the hat had a razor brim and it sliced through the wood like a chainsaw through a tree. The ridiculousness of the scene in such a big budget action movie tickled them both and there was a lot of laughter. There was a flurry of activity suddenly and a large man with an entourage of young and beautiful assistants appeared on set. He walked up to Jarrod and held out his hand.

"Good to finally meet you, Jarrod," said the man. "Robert Biscotti. We've spoken many times before."

Jarrod recognised the name and after linking a few thoughts in his head, put the connections together and realised this was the producer of the Harlowe Croft movie.

"Oh, wow, yes," said Jarrod, unable to think of anything relevant to say. "Very pleased to put a face to a name."

"Yes, quite," said Robert. "Now, we have some dates regarding filming that have just been thrown around. Your football team finishes the season this week, I hear." He was obviously not a football fan, and Jarrod wouldn't be surprised if he didn't know how the season worked.

"Yes," said Jarrod innocently. "The regular season finishes on the weekend, and then we have two weeks of finals."

"Oh," said Robert, his face dropping. "That might conflict with our dates. I'm sure you understand the huge logistical task that this whole project involves. We have actors, staff, make-up, camera operators, film equipment, catering, accommodation, all that and more to organise. Many millions of dollars of expense. I hope you understand that."

"Of course," said Jarrod. "A football game only goes for ninety minutes. The rest of the time, I'm all yours."

Of course, that wasn't entirely true. He had training and club commitments, and if they didn't finish in the top two, or it was top vs second in the final, then he'd have to travel to at least one away game in the finals series.

"Is your team in the finals?" asked Robert, starting to catch on.

"I'd like to think we're there," said Jarrod with a smile.

"Oh," said Robert, with the tone of a man who usually got his way.

"You should come along to a game," said Jarrod cheekily. "You might enjoy it."

"Good day, Jarrod," said Robert. And with that he turned with a smile and led his entourage on to his next appointment. If he'd had a cape, he would have swooshed it in the air to accentuate the dramatic exit.

Jarrod and Rapha looked at each other and smiled.

The finals series was non-negotiable. For a player to miss out on the pinnacle of the season, that was just not the way it was. The top four of the second division would play off in a finals series to find out who would join the champions in the A-League. In any other league in the world, the play-offs would have involved teams two to five, but this was Australia and they always had to have a Championship series to go with the first-past-the-post Premiership winners. If the Premiers won the Championship, then the losers of the play-off final would be promoted. It just didn't make sense, to Jarrod anyway, and the final could be a rather meaningless game if it weren't for the winner getting a bye into the latter stages of the Australia Cup.

Jarrod had also kept a close eye on Darlington's results, as best he could with the workload and the time difference. They had been flying earlier in the season, suffered a winless streak before Christmas, but had steadily risen back to the top six with only three games to go. After winning promotion to the Football League before Jarrod arrived at the club last year and then gaining promotion via the play-offs to League One in their first season, this had been a meteoric rise. The club had grown in stature, they had made plans to buy back their impressive twenty-five-thousand-seat stadium that had been in other hands since the original club was wound up ten years previously, and the fan base had grown exponentially with some very shrewd and attractive marketing ploys.

Jarrod had regular updates from the club, June and Pauline from the club staff and teammate Steven Horton keeping him up to date with the gossip. The Football League show aired on LF Sports every Monday night, which sometimes featured Darlington in their one highlight from League One, and there was plenty of action online that Jarrod didn't have time to watch. Anton Broman was pushing for top scorer in the league and Peter Van Vloten was earning rave reviews. There were definite parallels with his season in the A-League Division 2, but Jarrod still had a twinge of jealousy at missing out on another incredible season at Darlo.

The manager of Darlington, Gary Hollister, who had put faith in him to bring him in last season to guide them to promotion, had been in touch recently and had hinted that Jarrod could easily return to the Arena for the play-off games once the season had ended in Australia. That was the stuff of fantasy though, with Jarrod's movie commitments all-consuming. It did though stir emotion in him, and he had found himself drifting off in thought in a script read-through earlier in the week and got caught out by his co-stars. The scenario of heading back to England for a week or so to help his club win promotion again to the Championship was played around in his head. The reality though of his situation would make it near impossible. He hadn't called Gary to discuss it. Not yet anyway.

66

Pizzazz

The final game of the season was at the Lakeside, a 5:00 p.m. Saturday afternoon kick-off, which was mirrored around the country in every game in Division 2. It was billed as a Super Saturday, with LF Sports increasing their capacity to show every game live with the ability to jump between games when action occurred elsewhere. Interest in the final day was high. The top flight A-League games had all been rearranged for the Friday or the Sunday, so the focus was squarely on the second tier. There was interest at both ends of the table, with two teams in danger of being relegated back to the National Premier League and a complex combination of possibilities at the top. The broadcasters would be lamenting the fact that Sydney Olympic had missed out on the finals after a horror run, and their Sydney neighbours APIA Leichhardt were in danger of missing out too. Wollongong Wolves would take out the crown with a win, and a win for South Melbourne could take them into second depending on the other results.

Jarrod was at the stadium very early, Brad screeching up to the door to drop him off, but he wasn't the first one there. There was a red carpet leading into the main entrance, roped off with fancy red ropes going through golden bollards, and a gold banner read 'Agent 040 welcomes you to the Lakeside'. As the automatic door opened, there was a throng of tall gentlemen dressed in dinner jackets receiving instructions from an event co-ordinator. Jarrod groaned inside and scurried inside past the camera crews that were setting up. He went straight to the changing room and a few of his teammates were already there getting changed or getting physio treatment. A loud cheer went up. There were photos printed out and sticky-taped haphazardly to the walls; there was even a screenshot of the BetShed ad on the wall where Jarrod would usually get changed.

Jarrod smiled. It was universal, the joking and banter that went with football, and he was secretly delighted that his teammates had again given him plenty of stick about his newfound fame.

"Have you seen the helicopter?" asked Harry, Jarrod's midfield partner.

"Yeah, fuck off," said Jarrod smiling.

"Nah, straight up, mate," said Harry. "They're going to get you to land in the centre circle with the ball for kick-off."

"Ha ha, as if …" said Jarrod, before looking around and seeing everyone looking at him. They all had the look of genuine concern. It only took a few seconds though for them to burst out laughing and pile in on Jarrod, lots of hair rustling and elbows to the side.

"You had me going there," said Jarrod. "Only for a second though."

That was a great way to start the pre-match preparation. When Jarrod left the changing room to make his way to the field for the warm-up, he passed a photographer and did a double take. It was Akio, decked out in the official A-League media bib and accreditation. Akio smiled and nodded. Jarrod stood and watched as he walked past him, without a word. There was applause as Jarrod and a few others made their way onto the field for the warm-up and the crowd was already looking healthy. As he made his way to the other side of the field, he heard someone shout his name. He looked up and walked over.

"Jarrod, my good man."

It was Robert Biscotti, with Stevie Mosseman and Jacqui. Jarrod couldn't believe it.

"Robert," said Jarrod, unsure of why they would be here at all. "You came to see a game!"

"Of course," said Robert. "I have to keep an eye on my lead actor and see that he is conducting himself in a manner befitting Harlowe Croft."

"You didn't have anything to do with all that pizzazz at the front entrance, did you, Robert?" asked Jarrod.

"Your beautiful club president Sophia asked us along," said Robert. "She may have asked us for some props and backdrops. Just wait until the fortieth minute, Agent 040."

Jarrod screwed up his face.

"Now, Jarrod, while I've got you," continued Robert. "Our filming starts this coming Thursday. Hot off the press."

Jarrod looked incredulously at Jacqui whose hand reached slowly for her face then stopped. She simply closed her eyes.

"Full steam ahead," said Stevie. "This is where we bring it all together."

"Okay, thanks for the news," said Jarrod. He turned and ran off back to the rest of his teammates who were assembling ready for the warm-up. He was cursing under his breath. These people just had no concept of a life outside movies. And why would he want to know that piece of information right now? Was it meant to destabilise him and get his mind off his game? Did Robert want Jarrod's team to miss out on second spot and have to travel away for the semi-finals with a high chance of losing? Highly unlikely, but that's exactly what it felt like and Jarrod was angry.

With a three-man central midfield and with Jason Zalalas managing to avoid any more sendings-off, South Melbourne were humming. Their opponents, South Hobart, were battling themselves for a top four spot, and a draw might see both teams qualify. Jarrod though was keen to make sure. After greeting Grant Howett when they found themselves covering the same part of the field in the opening minutes, Jarrod made a statement with a strong challenge on Grant that got the crowd buzzing and his teammates clapping their hands in approval. The battle of the Souths heated up immediately and South Melbourne took the lead after only seven minutes, left winger Ari Papandony finding himself free at the far post with time to control and shoot low past the goalkeeper for 1–0. The floodgates threatened to open, Jarrod hitting a shot from distance which just cleared the bar, before Harry De Fonte mishit a shot from a deep cross and the ball ricocheted off a defender and into the net for two. The fortieth minute passed thankfully without incident.

The second half was more of the same. The South Melbourne fans were in full voice and thoroughly enjoying the show, whereas the small band of South Hobart fans who had travelled over were getting more and more agitated. Scores from elsewhere were being flashed on the scoreboard, and Jarrod could sense that their opponents would become more and more desperate and determined to rescue the game. Sure enough, just as South Melbourne were looking at their two-goal lead and wondering whether to stick or twist, a midfield run drew two players leaving a gap for the central defender to race forward unchallenged and smash a ball home from a long way out. The small band of Tasmanian fans erupted, the players forgoing the celebration to regroup at halfway ready to go again.

Jarrod could almost hear Robert cheering that goal in and urging a second. That wasn't to be the case though and South Melbourne held on, thanks to some expert game management in injury time to eat up the extra four minutes. The Lakeside Stadium was bouncing, the music came on, the players celebrated and then shook hands with their unlucky opponents, who now knew they had missed out on the top four. The pitch-side interviews were done, and the players saluted the fans who had remained in the stadium. The floodlights were dimmed, and a spotlight trained on Jarrod, as the music changed to the jangly bass of 'Harlowe Croft' and the crowd started to clap to the beat. Jarrod didn't know what to do. In the end he simply waved awkwardly and made his way off the field into the tunnel. There was no getting away from this charade.

The players were all in party mode in the changing room and Jarrod was happy to join in with the celebration for the cameras, somewhat of a tradition in Australian football. Beer in hand, they all sang along to 'South Melbourne, blue and white forever' although Jarrod had never heard the song before so was only singing along to the bits that repeated. He felt good about today. The passion was still there, although he still didn't quite feel that he was hitting the heights as he had done with his Darlington teammates.

The players all congregated in the bar area of the stadium that was now empty of fans before being ushered out by one of the cleaners and told to go and greet the remaining fans outside. As they were walking towards the front entrance, Jarrod could see the gold Lamborghini being winched onto a truck—they'd gone to town here tonight. Jarrod noticed Dalton Piercey, the federal police officer, chatting with a club official. Jarrod walked closely to him and made sure he brushed into him, knocking his elbow. Mr Piercey turned and acknowledged Jarrod with a nod of the head, but there was clearly no contact going to be made between the two. Something was brewing and Mr Piercey's presence was as reassuring as it was concerning for Jarrod.

67

Dominance

South Melbourne demolished their semi-final opponents in the first of the finals games, their second place securing the home advantage with a near-capacity crowd of well over eleven thousand packed into the Lakeside Stadium. Niko Toulaise had struck the post twice in the first half against third-placed Adelaide City, and it threatened to turn into 'one of those games'. That was until Nicky Stolic raised the roof with a shot from halfway that looped over the visiting keeper to open the scoring early in the second half. It was one-way traffic after that; Jarrod got on the scoresheet with a tap-in for the second and Niko grabbed the third and fourth goals late on to give the scoreline a true reflection of their dominance.

There were no cheesy gimmicks at this game, no movie producers willing his team to lose, and still no sign of Lefevre or Andreyev to throw that spanner in the works. It had been surprisingly uneventful for a semi-final and the fans had been in fine voice all game. Aurelio congratulated Jarrod on a good game and apologised for doubting his ability to keep focus while the rest of his life was going crazy.

It certainly was going crazy. Shooting of the movie had started two days before in the Dandenong Ranges out on the Eastern edge of Melbourne, and Jarrod had gone up there with Jacqui on the Wednesday night after training, with a first briefing at 11:00 p.m. Brad's remit was to look after the family, and Jarrod was secretly happy that they were the focus of his attention, and he could have a break from this high-octane character. Jarrod was housed in a trailer, just as he had expected from watching American movies, and he was woken by a flurry of activity at 6:30 a.m. as the crew all arrived and the final alterations were made in the cold light of day on sets that had been assembled over the last week. There was a hint of rain, and the catering area had a tarpaulin over it that was rustling in the wind. That made Jarrod get out of bed, throw on the clothes he wore after training the night before, and go and join the crew and a couple of fellow actors for some breakfast.

It was a different vibe to a football team. Jarrod felt a little paranoid as he didn't know anyone there yet and said only a few cheery hellos without engaging in conversation. That was until Jacqui turned up, grabbed a plate and pushed in beside him to start briefing him on everything and everyone he needed to know. She introduced him to the catering staff, making sure he knew they were the most important people on set. She directed him to a white picnic table where three men were sitting and made more introductions to the sound engineers. As they sat and ate their gourmet cooked breakfast, more people arrived, more familiar faces from the studio in Melbourne. This was a coming together of two different worlds—those whose creativity made this possible and those whose knowledge and skill would execute the ideas into a movie. It was exciting.

Jarrod had his first real-life session in make-up, not the ten-minute spruce-up that he'd experienced for his previous punditry appearances. He was very surprised by the number of products that were used on his face. He had his eyebrows shaped and groomed and the make-up artist took photos of his face from all angles, presumably to make sure it was made up the same way each day. There was eyeliner and lip colour, and his hair was held in place by the most industrial of hair sprays. He walked out over an hour later feeling a million dollars, but a little concerned that he looked like a middle-aged drag queen.

The first scenes were filmed, and of course they were out of order and didn't follow on from each other, which Jarrod wasn't expecting. Donny Valdez and his co-directors were fussing over Jarrod and making sure that he followed their direction to the tiniest detail. He had to walk with his back straight; Harlowe Croft had a specific way of holding his posture and he had to tone down the Australian accent he had picked up since moving back. This took the acting out of it, and Jarrod immediately understood where he would and wouldn't be able to bring some improvisation and personal touches into the movie. The scene he did with Rapha as daylight was beginning to wane was the most enjoyable; the two actors got on well and were enjoying the moment for what it was—two guys having a chinwag in someone's back garden.

The first evening all together on location was enormous. It must have been a tradition of the trade, but everyone was up for a big night. The catering team had a fantastic evening meal prepared once Jarrod had showered and caught up with Marianne and the kids on the phone. It was tempting to stay in his cosy little mobile home, but a rap at the door from Jacqui got him out of his doze and they went over to join the rest of the cast and crew. The camera crew were shooting some night-time scenery, but the rest of the crew who were staying over were getting louder and louder as the evening wore on. Jarrod was offered a red wine by the caterers and accepted. It was no box wine special from the bargain bin either—this was serious wine and it accompanied the roast chicken meal perfectly. It felt like camping, but they all had the same sense of achievement from a big day of work. Donny gave a speech as they all sat around a crackling fire at the side of the catering area in the cool autumn evening. The stars were out, and it was a great time for yarns, as Jarrod listened to some old heads cracking on about incidents they had encountered on previous movie sets.

A few spots of rain were enough to curtail the evening and everyone pitched in to clear up and get all of the white tables clear, ready for breakfast in the morning. If this was the life that he was going to lead for the next month or two, there were definitely worse places to be.

Filming was scheduled around Jarrod's availability, and the following day, after another early start at sunrise, Brad arrived on site to pick him up. Jacqui and Brad had to coordinate Jarrod's movements carefully so he would be on time wherever he went, but Jarrod could see that they were flirting with each other. As Jarrod was sitting waiting to see if he had to do one last take, he could see Brad sitting in his car and Jacqui leaning in for the kiss. Jarrod would use that knowledge to his advantage in the future, he thought to himself, smiling.

He was rushed back to the Lakeside Stadium for training, and this was rushing even by Brad's standards, but as always, Brad managed to find a crafty shortcut and they ended up pulling right in front of the door with two minutes to spare. Jarrod had freaked out as they neared the stadium and he realised he was still fully made up, but a swift dowsing with water and some vigorous rubbing with a towel got the majority of the make-up off and he was ready to step back into the world of football.

68

Jeopardy

With the semi-final wrapped up, and a night at home with the family, he was about to embark on the busiest Grand Final week that he could imagine. Brad buzzed him at 5:30 a.m. on the Sunday to be up on set for the 6:30 a.m. start. The continuous early starts with personal trainer Malik had programmed Jarrod's body clock to be up and about well before then, and he bounced out of the front door with a spring in his step, ready to face the week.

Jarrod checked his messages and email on the way up and was happy to see that Darlington had made it to the play-offs in League One back in England. Benson Gadriga, the player signed from obscurity at the start of the season, and who Jarrod had dislodged from the team after only one game, had been the hero, scoring a late goal at Wycombe Wanderers, but succumbing to a nasty leg break after colliding with the post as he slid the goal home. The goal had given Darlington hope with a hard-earned three points, and the scores from the other games went their way and they had secured sixth spot on goal difference. That leg-break though added to a mounting list of serious injuries at the club. According to the BBC football website, they were running out of midfield options at such a crucial time, and they had been written off already as no-hopers in their play-off semi-final against a team who had finished fifteen points ahead of them. This coincided with an email from Gary, his manager at Darlington, enquiring as to Jarrod's availability to return to the UK for two weeks once the A-League season was over.

Jarrod was lost in thought. He whirled scenarios around in his head and became restless in the passenger seat.

"You okay, Jarrod?" asked Brad. He had quickly become Jarrod's right-hand man and was a party to every phone call he took in the car as it came up on loudspeaker. He could also sense when things weren't quite right.

"I'm getting that feeling when you know you should be somewhere else," said Jarrod.

"You mean back in Darlington?" asked Brad, glancing at Jarrod for a reaction.

Jarrod was startled.

"I've still got plenty of contacts back in England, you know," continued Brad. "You're big news over there, and with the injury situation and all that …"

Jarrod felt almost violated, as though Brad had been reading his thoughts.

"So, I feel almost obliged to be over there to help," said Jarrod, regaining his composure. "What an opportunity for the club."

"But what an opportunity for you here," said Brad. "Why would you want to put all of that in jeopardy for a couple of games where you could get thrashed?"

"No, you're right. You're right. Not my problem."

Brad looked ahead at the road and looked thoroughly unconvinced that he'd heard the last of that idea.

Shooting for the day wrapped up early and there was a big screen up in the catering area ready to watch the second A-League Division 2 semi-final. Jarrod hadn't even asked for this, and it was a pleasant surprise to know that some of the crew were big into football. They'd never mentioned it before. This was fourth-placed Bayswater City travelling to Premiers Wollongong Wolves. This would be the equivalent of Darlington's upcoming play-off semi-final against high-flying Peterborough United. David vs Goliath.

The whole crew was going for the Perth-based team, as they wanted to see the final held in Melbourne, even though a home win would give South Melbourne instant promotion. It was surreal to be watching the game with real football fans who knew a great deal more than him about the A-League and the history of the teams playing. Jarrod was stoked—football really was slowly becoming the number one sport in the country.

A performance of pure backs-against-the-wall defending by the visiting team saw the game go into extra time locked at 0–0. The huge crowd at WIN stadium was still roaring their team home, but they had wasted a host of good chances and the game was still beautifully poised. In a moment of unexpected drama, the Bayswater central defender intercepted a ball on the edge of his area and galloped forward. He paused to let the cavalry catch up, feigned to pass the ball back and then took off again towards the penalty area. A step-over that Messi would be proud of then sent his opposing defender to the floor and he advanced with huge strides to smash the ball sweetly with his left foot, sending the ball rocketing into the top corner of the goal. The corner of the stadium containing the visiting fans erupted, the catering area erupted; it was an incredible moment. The Bayswater players jumped on their goal scorer and milked as much time as they could from the moment.

The final whistle, when it came after more close calls, saw an outpouring of emotion on the field in Wollongong, the Bayswater players out on their feet, but finding the energy to celebrate with the coaches and substitutes. Jarrod received pats on the back and encouraging words from the crew before dinner was called and the big screen was turned off.

69

Risk

Jarrod was up early, unable to sleep with all the crazy ideas in his head. He also had a raft of messages that had come in overnight and his fear of missing a vital email led him to fire up his laptop at 4:40 a.m. Before he got to his emails, he noticed the Twitter page, still up from the last time he'd logged on, was showing a long list of angry tweets from Wollongong Wolves supporters and suspicious A-League fans. There was a suggestion of some sort of collusion to manufacture the result last night, and the Wollongong players were under the microscope for all of the chances they had missed. Jarrod's heart was beating fast. This looked so much like something he might be embroiled in next week for the Grand Final and the decider to see who goes up to the A-League from Division 2.

He checked his emails for replies from his own emails he had sent the night before from his phone before bed. The first was from Duddy, who simply replied "you'd be crazy" to the question of whether he should come back to England to help Darlington make it through the play-offs. There was also one from night owl agent Mr Leonard who suggested that he should concentrate on his movie after the Grand Final and ride the huge wave of good fortune he was on. He did notice a P.S. at the end though that said, "I know what you're like though."

There was also an email from Teco Angelou, manager of Matsumoto Yamaga where Jarrod had played towards the end of the season. They had secured promotion as expected to the J-League last season; Jarrod had been following it closely after he had left. They were building a squad to make an impact, and Teco attached an offer to the email, and asked if he would consider it. He'd even send over a delegation to meet him to discuss terms if required.

The offer attachment was in Japanese, but the second page was a translation. There were some big sums of money mentioned. Jarrod was taken aback. He had thought he'd made himself clear to Teco previously, but the wily manager had seen through Jarrod's firm position and had presented him with a ridiculous offer to play at the top level in Japan. He remembered his few days in Kashima with Mum, Dad and Anna way back when he was looking for a professional contract. Coupled with the short and very successful spell he had last year, this was definitely something that Jarrod found attractive. It would be a great way to complete his career.

There was a soft knock on the door before Jacqui bustled in, looking cold. It was only 5:30 a.m. and she was immaculately dressed, ready to face another crazy day ahead.

"Sorry for barging in at this hour," she said. "That email you sent last night had me worried though."

It was true. Jarrod had thrown around the vague idea of heading back to Darlington before he'd finally gone to sleep. It was like throwing grenades and not bothering to find out if they had gone off. It was almost as though he'd done it in his sleep. He couldn't be sure if he'd sent one to Jacqui.

"Shit, sorry," said Jarrod, knowing that he would have been the reason for Jacqui being here so early. "I was just lost in thought last night."

He prepared himself for a scolding. She instead reached in and kissed him on the cheek.

"Jarrod, you do understand the situation at the moment, don't you?" asked Jacqui semi-rhetorically. "We have millions of dollars of people and equipment here, all here for one reason, and that reason is to make a movie. The best movie ever. Your first movie. What an opportunity."

"I know, I know," said Jarrod. "You must think I'm the most ungrateful person."

"I do understand though," said Jacqui, holding his gaze for an uncomfortable length of time. "But you'll be jeopardising the whole movie if you disappear for ten days. Everything I've worked for, everything I've been preparing for years, it would all be put at risk."

Jarrod swallowed, trying not to make it sound like a gulp in the quiet trailer.

"I'm asking you not to throw this all away, Jarrod," said Jacqui, putting her hand on his. That signalled the end of that conversation. She suddenly drew back her hand, sat up straight and reached into her bag, one of those leathery satchels that a university lecturer may have. She pulled out the run sheet for the day. This was something that she was doing for all the key actors, on top of the standard call sheet that included all the equipment and technical jargon.

"Get ready," she ordered, albeit with a smile. "You have an interview at 6:15 with *Vue* magazine. I saw them arriving when I got here, lovely lady Cecilia. You've got a live cross with the morning show with Stefan Karlsson afterwards and you'll only have a forty-five-minute window following that to get through make-up in time for the first scene."

Jarrod just sat and tried to take it all in. Jacqui clapped her hands and got him off his seat and rushing around, before disappearing into the bathroom for a shower. He had just been schooled. There was no way he had any time for flights of fancy to England. This was serious. This was why he was being paid eighteen million pounds.

70

Volatile

The week continued at the same pace. He had time in the car with Brad on two occasions as he returned home to head to training and had a night at home and was then whisked off to an impromptu photo shoot with George Baillie as the demand for publicity ramped up following his morning show appearance. The PR firm, Axis 151, was bombarding Jacqui with requests for Jarrod's time, and she was doing a great job of managing what got through to him.

On the pre-dawn drive out East for the final session of shooting before the weekend's Grand Final, Jarrod took a call from a private number, something he didn't normally do, but the time of day suggested that it might be legitimate and important. As always, his phone went straight to loudspeaker, on extra loud, and Jarrod could hear a man's breath, so it was definitely a real call.

"Hello?" said Jarrod, meekly.

"Ah, Jarrod," came the Eastern European accent of Viktor Andreyev. "I'm so glad you took my call."

Jarrod looked at Brad and gritted his teeth before putting his finger to his pursed lips. This was a personal conversation meant only for Jarrod, but he had talked over the possibility of this call with Brad already.

"Hello, Viktor," said Brad. Jarrod looked at him with staring eyes. Brad was driving, so had his eyes on the road.

"Bradley Neylan," said Viktor slowly. "There's a voice I will never forget. I was hoping you would stay for a drink when I saw you last in Albert Park, but you seemed in such a hurry."

"I was hoping never to hear your voice ever again, Viktor," said Brad.

"My dear Bradley," said Viktor condescendingly, though very well for someone speaking in their second language. "We had an agreement. Didn't we? You remember where you were heading before we … before we rescued you?"

Brad glanced over at Jarrod with a look that suggested there was a lot of explaining to do. Jarrod cradled his head in his fingertips, looking forlorn.

"Follow these instructions carefully, Bradley," said Viktor. "Turn left at Dorset Road and travel for 500 metres. You will see a black four-wheel drive with a black number plate parked in a road on your left. Park in front of the black car and Jarrod will come and join us for a short ride. We will return with Jarrod after fifteen minutes and you can be on your way."

Jarrod was staring at Brad, wondering what he was going to say. Jarrod had no idea where Dorset Road was, but he was sure that Brad knew. Before either of them had time to talk, the phone call ended, and the quiet music returned to the radio. Brad swerved into the left lane when he realised that he was almost at the turn. Luckily there was no one on the road at this early hour. They continued along the straight road that ran past service stations, fast food outlets and factory units until they saw a conspicuous black car parked in a single-lane street off to the left of the main road. Brad swerved into the street and pulled up slowly behind the black car.

"He said in front," said Jarrod.

"He'll have to make do with behind," said Brad.

Jarrod took off his seat belt. He patted Brad on the knee.

"See you in fifteen minutes, I guess," he said.

He opened the passenger door and went to get out. Brad grabbed his arm.

"I'm sorry, Jarrod," said Brad. "I'll explain it all later."

"Yes, you will," said Jarrod, and with that he got out of the car, closed the door and started to walk up to the black car. A hand opened the rear door on the passenger side and Jarrod walked up alongside to peer inside, expecting to meet the gun-toting heavies he had met in Albert Park. He was relieved to see only Viktor Andreyev in the back seat and got in and closed the door. Brad looked on anxiously behind, his hands still on the wheel.

"Thank you for meeting with me again," said Viktor, who beckoned his driver to start away. "Perhaps this is more appropriate one-on-one."

Jarrod last saw him the night Brad crash-tackled him and they made a swift exit.

"Good to see no damage was done after I saw you last," said Jarrod. Why he was showing any sort of concern and entering into small talk with a known Russian gangster, Jarrod had no idea himself.

"Yes, dear Bradley did knock the stuffing out of me, I do admit," said Viktor, raising a smile. "He always has been quite direct. Anyway, you are here as you have a job to do. And this time you will be doing it."

There was not a hint of a threat in his voice, he was just stating facts.

"In this case," continued Viktor, handing Jarrod what looked like a binoculars case, "you will find a bottle. It is a bottle that is typically used for smelling salts. Your physio will have some in his bag. It is nothing unusual."

"Okay," said Jarrod, taking the case and unzipping it to see inside. He opened the case and as described, there was a small glass bottle in the shape of a maple syrup container without the comedy handle, albeit a little smaller. It was clearly marked as smelling salts. "Does this do what it says on the label?"

"I suggest that you don't open it," said Viktor calmly as Jarrod feigned to unscrew the lid.

Jarrod stopped and put the bottle back into its protective moulded case, as though it was a grenade.

"This is a volatile mix of substances," said Viktor. "It is odourless and will fill a room in seconds. The active ingredients are a sedative and a mild nerve agent that can cause the slightest of nausea in some people. The effects will last an hour, maybe two at the most."

Jarrod couldn't believe what he was hearing. Active ingredients? He didn't say anything for a moment, trying to process what he was hearing.

"And what am I doing with this bottle?" asked Jarrod, knowing full well that he would not be using it for any wholesome reason.

"This bottle will be opened in the home dressing room on Grand Final day," said Viktor with a practised answer. "You can open it and leave it under your seat or put it anywhere really. No need to spill it, just open the bottle. You can leave the room if you choose, maybe go out early to warm up? It is safe, you will need to trust me, but it will have an effect temporarily."

Jarrod was always one of the last out of the changing rooms, so that wouldn't really work, but he got the idea.

"And why am I doing this?" asked Jarrod. "I'm going to poison my own team?"

"Oh no," said Viktor. "Don't think of this as poison. It is simply something to dull the senses temporarily."

Jarrod closed his eyes and shook his head, breathing in heavily. He was struggling with this.

"Right, is that all I need to do?"

"That is the only task I am asking you to do," said Viktor. "But the result of the game MUST be a win for the visiting team. You will not know who is working alongside you, but you MUST make sure that your team DOES NOT win this game."

Jarrod was looking at Viktor now with his mouth slightly open. Not only was he asking him to poison his teammates, but he was to try and influence the game if the poison wasn't enough to sway the result in the first instance.

"Of course, there is a substantial financial reward for your assistance," said Viktor. "You may be in line to double your money from your movie career."

He said all this straight-faced. He wasn't being unrealistic, and he wasn't being flippant.

"A payment will be made into your bank account upon completion, with a description of Zion Films. That should make the transaction justifiable. It will be six million pounds, but we are relying on you to take this to its conclusion."

Jarrod was lost for words. Viktor didn't know how much he was being paid, but this was still a huge amount.

"The takeover at Newcastle United could be underway in a matter of days," he said by way of conclusion. The suggestion that dirty money could be used to buy his beloved Newcastle was as outrageous as it was tempting. He'd love to see that happen—the club had finally rid itself of its previous parasitic owner, but it had no funds to invest seriously in players, and it was still a club treading water above the relegation zone. It didn't happen last time, thanks to Jarrod and D.I. Allison, but he could be the one who made it happen. The 'fit and proper' test of EPL owners would be quite a coup if it came off. He was torn. Viktor had hit a raw nerve.

There was no signing of a contract, only a handshake between the two men. The car had done a loop and the driver parked in front of Jarrod's car, where they had left fifteen minutes earlier.

"Give my regards to your family," said Viktor, this time with a suggestion of menace. "And please let Bradley know that I owe him one. He's a good man."

Jarrod could feel his face reddening and he felt hot. His mind had gone blank, and he said nothing as he left the black car out of the rear door. He closed the door behind him, and the driver started away immediately. Jarrod stood and watched. Brad eased his car forward until Jarrod was in line with the front passenger window.

"What are we waiting for?" said Brad.

71

Tempo

Today was the day. Grand Final day. It had definitely lived up to the billing of a Grand Final week like no other. After the big day of shooting on the Friday had been curtailed for Jarrod so he could go and join in with his final training session of the season at the Lakeside, he felt as ready as he could be. His mind though was on so many other things. He had a weapon of chemical warfare in the drawer of the table in his study. He was embroiled somehow, again, in a match-fixing scandal that was about to unfold. He had Matsumoto chasing his signature for a massive opportunity in the J-League. He was sought after by Darlington to come back and help them through their injury crisis. Manager Gary was looking for an assistant manager. He'd even heard from old coach Des Davis once more, fluttering his eyes about a role at Hartlepool. With the movie producers making it quite clear that they were not impressed with his constant disappearing to training and games, Jarrod quite rightly felt like a wanted man.

He had taken solace though in his training, and the final session yesterday was a lot of fun. Specifically timed to be a dry run for Grand Final day, the squad had all eaten together around 2:30 p.m., then enjoyed a light training session, an hour of media commitments followed by a high tempo practice game at the same kick-off time as today's Grand Final, a 5:30 p.m. start at AAMI Park. The change of venue was swiftly dealt with early in the week when it was clear that demand was going to outstrip supply at the Lakeside. With the top A-League division having their Grand Final on the Sunday, also in Melbourne, there was a lot of buzz about the city and many football people were in town to make the most of a big weekend of football.

Jarrod started the day with an early morning walk with Marianne, an opportunity to catch up after a disjointed week. Marianne was buzzing about her new career in the media and was filling him in with the details of the kids' busy school and social lives. She was also excited for Jarrod to be playing in a Grand Final in his first season in Australia. Marianne was good like that. She followed the football, albeit loosely, but having Brad around a lot was helping her keep up to date with everything South Melbourne and A-League Division 2. By the end of the walk, Jarrod felt as though he knew his wife once again and they walked the last half a kilometre hand in hand like love-struck teenagers.

When they returned, Jarrod was close to telling Marianne all about the meeting that took place in the back of Viktor Andreyev's car. Aneka put paid to that though, bounding down the hallway and launching herself into Jarrod's arms. She was as excited as anyone about today. She had taken a big interest in football this year and was a member of the school team and the local football club. The legacy from last year's massive Women's World Cup was still being felt throughout Australia and participation numbers, especially in Aneka's age group, were at an all-time high. Aneka led them through into the kitchen where Sebastian was frying eggs and Aneka had only just finished a stack of pancakes. Jarrod and Marianne made a massive fuss. They were genuinely impressed, and Seb and Aneka were loving the attention and the top-quality time together with their parents that they had been missing. Anna and Elin were there, Mum and Dad had arrived, and it was a big family reunion all over again. What a great way to spend the morning of the big game.

72

Bottle

Brad was over in the early afternoon to pick up Jarrod. After a false start when Jarrod forgot the case that contained the bottle, Brad dropped him to the Lakeside, and would later pick up Jacqui from her place nearby and return to fetch Marianne and the kids to take them all to the game. Jarrod felt nervous. Primarily for the football, but he also had a huge decision to make. Was he going to plunge himself below the line and go against all his principles and morals and sacrifice a place in the top flight for an underhand deal that would make him even more rich than he felt he was right now? Was he resigned to doing this? Could he look himself in the mirror and trust his judgement ever again? Jarrod was a Socceroos player. He represented his nation. He was very proud of his country too. Surely, he couldn't go through with this. His communication with the police had been all but severed, and there was a veiled threat to his family, but he knew that it was something he couldn't go ahead with.

The Bayswater City team were already at AAMI Park when the South Melbourne coach rolled into the car park, and they pulled up alongside this intriguing stadium. It was like an Ikea version of the Centre Pompidou in Paris and had that immediately out-of-date architecture that would never have looked modern. Still, it was a rectangular stadium, and Jarrod had been looking forward to his first club game at this scene of many memorable A-League games over the years.

The players filed off the coach and past a throng of young fans, most of the players breezing past with headphones on, but Jarrod stopped and gave them what they wanted. Nicky Stolic joined him, and they both stayed until everyone had a signature, a selfie or a handshake. This was Grand Final day.

Jarrod was a specialist at play-off finals, and he had enjoyed success in his last one not even a year ago. He knew that it was a big deal for the fans, for the league and for everyone in football around Australia.

The players went straight to the field, taking in first the marvellous surroundings, before walking on the edge of the field to feel the lush grass. They then walked in through the tunnel and made their way to the changing rooms. Jarrod hung behind and patted his pocket to make sure the small bottle was still in place before catching up with Jason Zalalas. They heard a voice from behind.

"Gentlemen," said the voice. They both turned around. "Good to see you both again."

It was Bella, the referee who had taken Jarrod's phone number in a game a few months ago. Jason smiled. Jarrod looked and forced as much of a smile as he could muster.

"Jason," she said, turning to the South Melbourne captain. "I have asked Kennedy, the captain from the Bayswater City team, to come meet on the field at 4:00 p.m. for a chat and I'd like you to join us. That's in ten minutes."

Jason smiled again.

"Sure," he said, and walked off.

Jarrod had the impression that Bella wanted to speak with him too. She grabbed his hand and led him into the referee's room, the next door on the left. Jarrod heard the door click as Bella closed it behind her. Jarrod turned and Bella stood very close, facing him. This was weird. If she had poisoned spikes coming out of her trainers right now, it would not have surprised Jarrod one bit.

"Jarrod," she said. "Today is a big day for me, and a big day for Australian football."

Jarrod had the urge to recoil before steadying himself.

"This game is going to be quite a spectacle today," she continued, moving closer to him, her eyes darting around his face. "I would like you to trust me with some of the decisions, even if they may not entirely go your way. We have instructions from above. I trust we're on the same wavelength."

She had her hand on his chest now.

"We must celebrate tonight," she said, moving her mouth close to his. "We will both be happy whichever way the result goes. Viktor will make sure of that."

Jarrod had already had an inkling that Bella was another one of the key pieces in this elaborate scheme, and that confirmed it. His mind was whirring, almost to the point of his physical body disconnecting with his thoughts. He had to think fast. Bella went in for the kiss and Jarrod had no choice but to let it happen. She was all over him in a flash, her hand was up his shirt, and she was pressing herself hard up against him. The bottle in Jarrod's pocket dug into him. He swiftly pulled it out of his pocket and managed to get both hands around Bella's back. His hands fumbled to open the child-proof lid and he made sure he offered more back with the kiss to cover his move. The lid unscrewed, he quickly tipped the bottle into Bella's pocket and screwed the lid back on. He hadn't taken a breath since he'd done it, and in one move, slipped the bottle back in his pocket and prised Bella off him.

He tried not to breathe. He looked at her in the eyes, trying to engage her.

"Listen, I've got to get back," said Jarrod, in almost a whisper.

He bundled past Bella, who was red and blotched under her neck and clearly flustered. He could feel himself going red with holding his breath and prayed that the door wasn't fully locked. It wasn't. He casually opened it and looked back at Bella who was straightening her tracksuit. He smiled and she smiled back.

"You've got to meet Jason and Kennedy, remember."

The door closed behind him, and he gasped for air, trying to be as quiet as possible. He checked the bottle to make sure the lid was tight and followed the sign for the gents' bathroom, just around the corner. This was a totally mad situation. He washed his hands with soap and looked at his face that was a little blotched from the over-zealous effort he had put in with Bella. His mind was racing. He walked back into the hallway and out into a reception area.

There were staff everywhere and the atmosphere was starting to get the big match buzz. He asked the receptionist for a piece of paper and a pen and asked if she knew where the police control room was. He took the pen and the sheet of A4 paper and stood at the reception desk to write two notes on it, before creasing the paper between his fingernails and expertly ripping it in two. He handed the pen back with a smile and made his way to the South Melbourne changing room. A quick detour via one of the catering rooms, and he came out with a polystyrene box, the kind that would hold a hot serving of fish and chips.

He walked into the changing room, passing Jason on the way out.

"Look out for the ref," said Jarrod. "She means business today."

He went over to his spot, which had all his gear laid out for him. He was normally one of the first ones in the changing rooms and the last one out, and it didn't go unnoticed.

"Jesus, Jarrod," said fellow midfielder Ari. "Bit hungry, were you?"

"Empty, honest," said Jarrod, shaking the empty box and putting it down on the floor next to his bag. He started to get ready. He was all thumbs. There were a lot of nerves in the changing room, so Jarrod wasn't out of place with his slightly nervy disposition. A few of the players had already gone out and he took his chance to get the case out of his bag and put the bottle in it. He then put the case in the snack box and laid one of the notes on top of it. The other note he put in the pocket of his warm-up top, and he went back to getting his socks and boots on. Most of the players were gone now. Jarrod shared a joke with Jason, asking him whether he'd been eaten alive by Bella. Despite the strict rule of no mobile phones in the changing rooms, he picked up his phone and flicked through the apps to the Find My application and it popped up as Jarrod was talking. He glanced to see where his kids were. He could see Seb was at the front of the main stand next to the tunnel, where he usually positioned himself when he had to be at a game early. Jarrod waited for Jason, and they went out together, Jarrod carrying his snack box as if he'd brought the leftovers from lunch at the Lakeside.

He spotted Seb straight away. Jason ran out to great applause while Jarrod walked over to Seb, put the box in his hands and put his arms around him. He talked into his ear, telling him he had an important job to do and where to take the box, and that it was for Dalton Piercey. He asked Seb to repeat the name to him, and wasn't convinced, so watched him type it in his phone. After he'd checked it, Jarrod took the phone and did a selfie with him. It looked like a player giving his son a hug and taking a photo, all innocent and wholesome. Jarrod watched as Seb walked off slowly with the box, scanning the aisles to find the quickest way. Jarrod turned and sprinted onto the field, another round of applause rang out and Jarrod could finally concentrate on getting ready for the game. He was the last one on the field and the warm-up was called immediately.

Bayswater City had an unusually large following. They had enjoyed a big investment in players this season, benefitting from the Harper-Thompson rule of increasing the salary cap for those geographical locations with less teams in the top tier. Being from Perth, with Perth Glory the only team from Western Australia, they were effectively incentivised to achieve promotion. The investment appeared to be working until the last third of the season when the wheels came off and they only just scraped into fourth spot. The league had also allowed them to secure two late signings from the A-League proper, with two high class midfielders joining from teams who had missed the finals series. That paid dividends on their visit to Wollongong the week before when they came away with a smash and grab win at the Premiers. There was uproar throughout Australian football though. Sokkah Twitter was peaking with conspiracy theories and suggestions of foul play. The Meadowbank Ultras fan movement was calling for an investigation and

A-League Memes was in overdrive.

The warm-up was just what Jarrod needed to get his head in the game. The team headed off the field together, leaving the Bayswater players still going through their warm-up. They passed Johnny, South Melbourne's number one fan, and he got a lot of attention from the players. Dalton Piercey was in the tunnel, looking concerned. Jarrod caught his eye but didn't engage him. Jarrod held out his hand to shake Dalton's and the second of the notes was now in the police detective's palm. Jarrod was pumped now, and he went around to each of the starting players in turn in the changing room and gave them a rev up, slapping arms, grabbing shirt fronts, and being generally enthusiastic about what lay ahead. He was worried that the churning in his stomach might be something to do with the mystery liquid in the bottle he had briefly opened but put it down to nerves. It was great to feel nervous before a big game, and he felt like he was a teenager again, running out for his debut in a League Cup tie back at Carlisle United.

There was a knock at the door and the players filed out. Bella walked confidently through the players with her refereeing team and on her signal, the two teams walked out to a huge welcome from a capacity crowd. Jarrod saw Akio, the Japanese reporter, again with all the official A-League media accreditation badges and bib. Just how he got the official gear was a total mystery. He was concentrating but nodded as Jarrod walked past. Jarrod was taken aback by just how much noise there was—it had been a while since he had played in front of this many people. The teams lined up for the national anthem, the camera panning across their faces as they sang. Jarrod was caught out by the amended words again and smiled when he realised.

The stadium was rocking, and the kick-off was the crescendo. The opening five minutes of the game were played at a terrific pace. Jarrod decided to tuck into a deep-lying midfield role until the pace started to abate, playing almost alongside central defender Brendan Maley. Bayswater were like a swarm whenever South Melbourne got possession, and they coughed up the ball immediately. Jarrod felt that the game needed a steadying influence, so he picked his moment and let his midfield opponent take a circuitous route around him and teed up an almighty challenge. The clean tackle saw the ball and the man end up against the advertising hoardings and got the home crowd to their feet in admiration. Bella was quick on the scene, calling Jarrod over. Jarrod looked at her. She was a picture of concentration, but her face was whiter than he remembered. The crowd was groaning at the thought of an early yellow card for one of their playmakers.

"Are you okay?" said Jarrod, with his inside knowledge of what Bella could be feeling right now.

"It's early in the game," said Bella. "And you can think yourself very lucky."

Jarrod recoiled, using his best Italian body language to express his exasperation and disdain. As he did, Bella tumbled forward. Jarrod's instinct was to reach out to catch her, but she caught herself mid-stumble.

"Lads, ref's not good," said Jarrod, rushing in as she collapsed forward. He caught her before she hit the ground. Two of the Bayswater players were nearby and helped Jarrod get her on her side and waved the physios on from the other side of the field. The ambulance people were on the field promptly and moved the players back as they tended to the referee. The players all retreated to the halfway line, took on water and looked on with concern. The Bayswater captain, Kennedy Bakaraglou, asked the ambulance people if they should create a human shield around the ambulance people and the referee team, but he was waved away.

A good five minutes passed; Aurelio was giving his players a team talk after their initial ten shaky minutes, urging them to value possession and make the ball work for them. Bella sat up and got to her feet. She walked with the rest of the referee team towards the tunnel at the halfway line and applause rang out as she started to jog. She got to halfway and walked off, straight down the tunnel. This was serious, and the murmur of the crowd was getting louder. Speculation as to what would happen now was circulating, and there was movement amongst the officials. Eventually the fourth official removed his tracksuit and was wired up, and a reserve fourth official was found from the South Melbourne back-room staff and the game was ready to restart.

South Melbourne steadied their ship after the frantic opening, and the game settled into an absorbing encounter. Bayswater were dangerous on the break, but South Melbourne were dictating the play. A raking ball from captain Jason Zalalas found striker Costa Hrysanthos on the right side of a swift attack, and his control was perfect. He advanced to the byline and chipped the most delightful ball in for Ari Papandony to connect with a flying volley, but the Bayswater keeper made an acrobatic point-blank save to preserve the goalless scoreline. The momentum was swinging towards South Melbourne, and the fans and players could sense it.

Jon Kosmidis found himself deep in his own half, mopping up after a glorious tackle from Marc Edwards to snuff out a Bayswater attack. He looked up for the long ball, then turned inside and went to roll a slow ball to Brendan. A sudden movement from the Bayswater striker caught him in two minds though and he went to pull out of the pass but had already touched it lightly, right into the path of the lurking Kennedy. He took the gift and galloped into the box with defenders closing in for the kill. An early shot, though, with his wrong foot caught out Georgie Vargas in the home goal and the ball sailed over him and into the unguarded net via the post for an outrageous opening goal. The City fans erupted. That was the sort of goal that away teams dreamt of when they were under the cosh, and the chants started as the jubilation subsided.

"Going up, going up …" they chanted. It rang around the ground for the next five minutes as South Melbourne toiled to get back in the game.

The half time whistle sounded. Jarrod was keen to get into the changing rooms so they could address the obvious issues and get set for the biggest forty-five minutes of the season. In the depths of the stadium, just as the tunnel turned into a corridor, with the changing rooms on either side, he saw Dalton Piercey off in the other direction, with a group of police officers, an ambulance person and Bella, who was sitting in a seat, still looking grey. Jarrod walked over. Dalton looked at him, but Jarrod was simply curious to see how Bella was.

"Are you okay?" asked Jarrod, echoing the question he had asked on ten minutes. Bella looked up at him with deep sunken eyes.

"Thanks for asking, Jarrod," said Bella. "Feeling a lot better. I don't know what came over me. Maybe it was something I ate."

"Glad to see you're okay," he said. Considering he had her tongue down his throat a couple of hours earlier, it couldn't have been something she ate. Jarrod turned and jogged back to the changing room to join his teammates. Again, he passed Akio on the way into the room, who gave him a nod, but said nothing. Jarrod doubled back.

"What's going on, Akio?" asked Jarrod.

"You tell me," said the Japanese reporter, much less friendly than he remembered. "You are playing a very dangerous game."

Jarrod had the feeling that he was out on his own now. Akio was probably the most clued up about what was happening; Dalton Piercey could only see what he could see and act upon the knowledge that Jarrod had shared with him before the game. Would they see a host of dramatic arrests during the game as Jarrod had seen at St James Park last year? The mood in the changing room was positive. Aurelio was calm. There was a change of formation, the manager keen to strike early. Ari would move from midfield into attack, and Jarrod would push up as an attacking midfielder. It was a 3-4-3 formation. Attack, attack, attack! The players were excited. The last time they played like this, they had turned a dour 0–0 into a four-goal win. It was business time.

73

Precision

The knock on the door by the fourth official sent the players racing to the corridor in a frenzy of positivity. They were itching to get out there and put it right. Jarrod was doing his best to pump up his teammates, but that was tempered when he saw Viktor Andreyev and Jens Lermann at the edge of the tunnel, glaring at players of both teams as they walked past. They saved an extra-hard stare for Jarrod as he walked past. He squeezed his water bottle as hard as he could, showering himself and both of them with water. He walked past Dalton Piercey again and gave him the pleading eyes and open hands. He was ten metres away from two of the most corrupt people on the planet and he was choosing instead to tend to the referee. Do your job, man!

The second half was only five minutes old and already South Melbourne had hit the bar and the post. It was one-way traffic, but they just couldn't get the vital goal to bring them level. Niko Toulaise was getting all the service, but the visiting goalkeeper was equal to everything. The crowd was working up into a fevered state. Jarrod was linking up beautifully with Costa up front, but the strikers were crowded out by the intense defending of the Bayswater team.

This was some of the best attacking football the crowd had seen all season, the flowing moves and Ronaldinho-like precision through balls keeping the majority of fans off their seats. Jason Zalalas swept across right in front of Costa, but he couldn't sort his feet out in time and the ball was sliced wide. Almost from the goal kick, Ari picked out Niko, who held the ball up for Nicky Stolic to smash one at goal from distance. Again, the goalkeeper did well to palm the ball away, the rebound hacked away from

Costa's feet. Jarrod was now playing in a front four and Bayswater couldn't get out of their half.

The sight of the visiting striker changing course to head for the corner flag with still ten minutes to go was disheartening. This would be the longest ten minutes plus stoppage time that either team had endured. A volley from distance by Niko and a goalmouth scramble were the only highlights of the last ten minutes as some high-quality gamesmanship came into play. The three minutes of stoppage time allowed goalkeeper Georgie to come up and join the attack, but it was all in vain. The final whistle sounded, and all South Melbourne hands went on heads. What a glorious opportunity to put another Victorian team into the big time, and they had lost out at home against an out-of-form team that only finished fourth in the competition by the skin of their teeth.

Caleb Powell, the LF Sports reporter, almost apologetically commandeered Jarrod for an interview as the Bayswater players celebrated. Commentator Denton Swift chimed in on their chat to say he couldn't understand how they hadn't scored. There was an air of disbelief. Jarrod was as professional as he could be, but he knew that his team had blown a great chance. In his mind, he felt that he had done everything he could have possibly done, but he knew that he was up against more than just the opposition. For all he knew, there could have been many players on both teams, the officials and even the VAR, ready to pounce to sway the game in favour of Bayswater. In the end, they didn't need any of it, so it seemed. The Bayswater fans were chanting the 'Harlowe Croft' theme tune in the background, which at least drew a smile from him. Jarrod was keen to speak with Jon afterwards though. That was a very lousy way to cough up possession for the goal, and he felt guilty for looking for a scapegoat for the defeat when it was probably due to the visitors having the better game plan.

Marianne and the kids were there to console him as he walked into the members' area after the game. Jacqui rushed in and gave him a hug. Mum, his biggest fan, saved her hug until last and it made Jarrod feel a whole lot better. Today was meant to herald a new dawn for the South Melbourne Football Club, and instead they had been condemned to another year out of the division where their fans felt they deserved to be.

74

Dividends

Jarrod walked through the gate and made his way over to the catering area. He had his head down. He heard someone clapping, then a second person, and before long, everyone there was applauding and cheering. Jarrod looked up and smiled as he walked into the crowd and received hugs and had his hair well and truly ruffled. He had played a great game yesterday and the football-mad crew knew it. Two of them had their South Melbourne scarves on and looked a little worse for wear, but there were teary smiles through bloodshot eyes all round.

By 8:00 a.m., with a little help from make-up, life had returned to its crazy normal. Jarrod found himself doing a scene involving his neck being wrapped in one of the bad guy's legs and trying to reach a gun that was just out of reach. It was eerily similar to the moment he'd had yesterday in the referees' room at AAMI Park, although this time he had a burly man's backside in his face as opposed to a fit woman's lips.

There was a break around 10:30 a.m. and Jarrod went to check his phone. Dalton Piercey was standing next to the table where Jarrod had left his phone and hat. Brad was with him.

"Shall we find somewhere private?" asked Dalton.

Jarrod led them through the muddle of wires and tables and over to his trailer, and the three men climbed in and sat around the table.

Dalton took out his mobile phone and placed it on the table. He hit the button to dial and a call to an unknown number started. It was D.I. Allison.

"Thanks for organising, Dalton," said D.I. Allison when he eventually spoke. "Obviously we need to be very careful with contact directly with Jarrod."

"Hello, Marcus," said Jarrod. "You've been absent for a while."

"What Jarrod means is 'Hello, Marcus, thanks for keeping me safe'," said Dalton.

Jarrod looked at him, puzzled. Jacqui walked through the door and joined them. It didn't seem that Jacqui should be excluded from the conversation, so they continued.

"Thanks to you, Jarrod," said D.I. Allison, "we now have Andreyev on a plane back here to England. We've got enough evidence to push for a conviction. Based upon his role in yesterday's events, we have the necessary links with Lefevre and a number of additional people of interest involved in yesterday's game. The AFP have also taken in two of your teammates for questioning, along with the referee from yesterday's game."

"What about the betting?" asked Jarrod. "I believe some people have made a lot of money out of the result from yesterday."

"That is a given," said D.I. Allison. "And we have Interpol on that. Some big amounts of money changed hands with betting companies yesterday and there will be some rich people or organisations this evening. That's not our concern though. The main thing is that you're okay and that you'll be able to return to the UK to give evidence to the court in Andreyev's trial."

Jarrod looked at Jacqui. Her eyes were wide open, and she had a worried look on her face.

"When does the trial start?" said Jarrod. "I mean, I'm in the middle of shooting a movie here."

"It could be as soon as next week."

"Wow," said Jarrod. "You'll have to liaise with my colleague Jacqui when the time comes."

Jacqui tilted her head to one side and raised her eyebrows. She looked forlornly at Jarrod.

Dalton wrapped up the call, and then explained what was happening in Australia in terms of Andreyev and Lefevre.

"We have Lefevre in for questioning right now," he said. "We're trying to make the link between Andreyev and various figures in the Melbourne underworld. He'll hopefully be on a plane tomorrow to join Andreyev in London for a good grilling."

"So, am I in any danger?" asked Jarrod.

"You should be out of immediate danger," said Dalton. "Any dodgy betting would have paid handsome dividends yesterday and we will be tracing the money the best we can in Australia, but we expect that the majority of bets will have been done overseas anyway."

"What about the referee yesterday, Bella?" asked Jarrod.

"I think Bella has been involved in this before," he said. "She had a reputation of being someone who makes things happen at the right price in her early days, but she had served a lengthy suspension and seemed to be back on the trajectory to the top of the game. Perhaps this time though she was given a good incentive. She'll be in big trouble for this one when or if it gets out."

"There's a lot of money being thrown about," said Jarrod. "They offered me six million pounds."

Dalton sat back in the seat, fortunate that his was the only one with a back rest.

"They offered you six million pounds? Ten million dollars?" he said eventually.

"That's right," said Jarrod. "Andreyev owes me, big style!"

"Ha ha," laughed Brad. "I don't think you'll be seeing any of that."

They all smiled.

75

Jackpot

Sydney FC had taken out the A-League crown with a late winner against Melbourne City. The week then resumed at its furious pace. Filming was in full swing, and with no training and no games to get in the way, the movie was progressing well. He spent two nights at home with the family and enjoyed a proper catch-up with the kids. Marianne was as happy as he had ever known, her new career with the major sports broadcaster in the country coming as a major coup to help her settle into Australian life. Seb had started with the Melbourne Victory academy, thanks to some string-pulling from Brad, and had a rekindled interest in football after making the school team. He still kept in touch with his friends back in England through Zoom calls and could be heard chatting with Michaela early in the morning. Aneka had cemented herself in a group of friends at school that was starting to pay dividends on the social front. With Brad on hand, whenever he was not with Jarrod, and Jacqui playing a big part in their family life too, Jarrod knew that he was already a long way to becoming settled in his home country.

South Melbourne called him in for a meeting on the Sunday evening. They were interested in signing him up for next season. Jarrod had given up all hope of returning to help Darlington get through the play-offs. There had been no contact from D.I. Allison or from Dalton Piercey since Sunday and he had been exploring more media opportunities in Australia now that football was no longer taking up the rest of his time. South Melbourne would have to negotiate with Darlington again to secure another loan period, and it would make sense, with the production of the movie to continue into the start of the following season. With A-League club Western United having finished surprisingly at the foot of the league, they had become the first ever top flight club in Australia to be officially relegated, meaning that any Melbourne team in the second tier would have an increased salary cap for the following season. With two teams going up to increase the numbers further in the top division, this was a golden opportunity to strengthen the team and make a big run for promotion.

The meeting went well; president Sophia and manager Aurelio were on the charm offensive, and he even saw club supporters Johnny and Temuri in the car park on the way in. The club was desperate for success in the A-League, and their positivity and drive rubbed off on Jarrod. They even offered to pay extra salary to Jarrod, and Jarrod was left to think about it for a couple of days. He could use the extra wages to do something philanthropic, something he'd thought about since signing the movie deal. Or maybe he could start to buy shares in Newcastle United, with the club currently under the stewardship of the supporters and a potential takeover coming soon.

Jarrod called Gary, his manager at Darlington, when he returned home. The team were due to play in the first leg of the play-offs in a few hours, and he would simply wish him the best.

"Hello, Gary," said Jarrod.

"Good to hear from you, Jarrod," said Gary. "If you were ringing me to say you'd touched down at Teesside Airport, I'd be really happy."

"Ah, unfortunately not," said Jarrod. "Just ringing you to wish you and the lads good luck this afternoon with the game. You confident?"

"We're always confident, my friend. Peterborough finished miles in front of us, but if there's a bunch of lads who can do this, it's these Darlington boys. The offer is still there to work with us next season. A player-coach role would be perfect for you. Your A Licence came through, I expect."

"Oh shit," said Jarrod. He'd forgotten all about that. He was waiting for the results of the video analysis he had submitted, and he'd completely lost track. "Let me check that."

"Ha ha," laughed Gary. "You've obviously got a lot on your plate at the moment. Good luck with it all. We'll catch up soon, okay?"

"Thanks, Gary," said Jarrod. "I'll be in touch, don't you worry."

Jarrod logged on to his emails and did a search to find any emails from the FA. Sure enough, there was an email from St George's Park asking him to attend a graduation ceremony to present him with his A Licence. He had missed the cut-off to respond to the event next Thursday, but at least it was official, and he had attained the required score in his final assessment to become a fully fledged football coach. His thoughts were fully on the future now. Surely it was the next logical step to get into coaching and to build his reputation under a good quality manager. He sat staring at his screen for a while until he heard a key in the door behind him. Brad had returned with Jacqui, and they had brought Dalton Piercey along. This looked ominous. He was a little puzzled to see them, but led them through to the kitchen, where Brad started up the coffee machine and tapped out the old coffee grounds from the filter.

Dalton placed his phone on the table and started a call.

"Thanks for organising again, Dalton," said D.I. Allison. "Jarrod, are you there?"

"Hearing you loud and clear, Marcus."

"Here's the latest," said D.I. Allison. "The trial starts on Thursday. We need you to be here by Wednesday morning at the latest. You will be needed for ten days."

Jarrod could see Jacqui putting her head in her hands. This would be horrific news for the movie. Brad came over and put his arm around her.

"What am I going to do about the shooting of the movie?" asked Jarrod.

"That's for you to organise with your people there, I'm afraid," said D.I. Allison. "We can organise you a flight tonight or tomorrow morning."

It was time for quick decisions.

"Tomorrow morning sounds good," said Jarrod. He looked at Jacqui who had started to bite her nails. He reached out and put his hand on hers.

"I'll get it set up. I'll liaise with Jacqui at your end," said D.I. Allison.

"I'm here," said Jacqui, her voice almost breaking.

"Great," said D.I. Allison. "I'll let you know when everything is in place. You might like to check the news too in about half an hour. You might have a bit more work on your hands, I'm afraid."

Jacqui and Jarrod looked at each other and shrugged.

"And Jarrod," continued D.I. Allison. "I just saw the news about LF Sports—looks like they've hit the jackpot and signed up for another five years with the A-League."

"Really?" said Jarrod with total surprise. "Where could they have got the money?"

The call ended and all four of them grabbed their mobile phones and started to look for news. Sure enough, on The Roar website, there was a picture of Jens Lermann above a breaking news item about his company signing up for five additional years of the A-League Men's and Women's, the FFA Cup and all international matches involving the Socceroos and the Matildas. The increased deal showed just how much football had grown in stature over the last few years and what it was worth. It also showed to Jarrod just how much money had been gained from last Saturday's play-off final result.

Jacqui received a phone call. She looked stone-faced and opened the back door to take the call in private in the garden. She returned after a few minutes with a concerned but excited look. Her mood had definitely been lifted.

"You're not going to believe this," she said. "Stevie and Robert have been taken in for questioning over some financial irregularities to do with the movie. We're going to need to close down production for a few days."

This was getting weirder by the minute. Her phone rang again and she excitedly answered it before running outside again, talking loudly.

The front door opened, and Marianne came in with the kids. Aneka ran to give Jarrod a hug while Brad and Seb exchanged their own elaborate handshake.

"Hello, everyone," breezed Marianne. "What did I miss?"

76

Departures

Jarrod's phone rang. It wasn't even five in the morning. His flight wasn't until 9:30 a.m., so he was probably due to get up. It was Akio, the Japanese reporter who seemed to have relocated to Melbourne with his eye on the big story. Jarrod picked up his mobile and crept out of the bedroom.

"Akio, my friend," said Jarrod softly. "What can I do for you?"

"Jarrod, I am so sorry for calling you this early."

"I was up anyway," said Jarrod, only half truthfully. "What's up?"

"I wanted to give you a warning of a story hitting the news today. I have rock solid evidence of Jens Lermann and Murtaka Chiya being in business with Viktor Andreyev."

"That's not really news," said Jarrod, confused by what he was hearing.

"No, but your movie producers, Mr Mosseman and Mr Biscotti, are involved too," said Akio. "Were you aware of that?"

"Are you sure?" asked Jarrod, incredulously. "I mean, they've never shown anything but indifference about my football here in Australia."

"They're involved," said Akio. "I have had a tip-off and I'm on the case right now. Once this story hits, we should be able to follow it up with another that will bring you into the frame and blow this into the public arena. I'm sorry to involve you, Jarrod."

"No worries, Akio," said Jarrod. "Thanks for the pre-warning."

"See you soon, Jarrod," said Akio and Jarrod hung up. So, that was a twist, Stevie Mosseman and Robert Biscotti could be involved in the whole scheme. What on earth was going to come out next?

Jarrod was desperate to speak with D.I. Allison but knew that could wait until he got to England. Right now, Jarrod had to get moving. He was a little out of practice after four months in the same country, but his efficient packing process came back to him as he tip-toed around the room and quietly gathered his toiletries from the en-suite bathroom. He had a glance in the mirror. His eyes were a little sunken, but he looked pretty good for 5:00 a.m. He heard a car pull up outside and then twenty seconds later heard a key in the front door. Brad was here already. He could hear him walking into the kitchen and then the tapping of the coffee filter on the edge of the bin. A creature of habit.

Jarrod slipped into bed next to Marianne and gave her a cuddle. She stirred and ran her fingers through his hair, arching her back. The temptation was there to move in for a little more, but he knew that time wasn't on his side. He settled for a kiss and left Marianne to her sleep. He crept into both kids' rooms to give them a kiss. Aneka woke up and gave him a hug, Seb just rolled over and Jarrod gave him a kiss on the forehead. A coffee was waiting for him when he got downstairs, Brad trying his best to be quiet, but his voice wasn't the quiet type. Jarrod wheeled his suitcase while Brad took Jarrod's hand luggage, and they went out the front gate. There was a bank of photographers blocking the way, and Jarrod's car was, perhaps accidentally, blocked in by cars.

"Quick," said Brad. "Get in my ute."

They raced down the street to where Brad had parked his souped-up truck. He popped the tray lid and Jarrod flung in his suitcase, and they jumped in. Before the photographers had a chance to react, Brad's extreme driving techniques kicked in and he wheel-spun out of the parking spot, turning 180 degrees and firing like a bullet away from the chasing mob, down the street.

"Shit, my passport's in the other car," said Jarrod. Brad took an envelope out of his jacket pocket and handed him his passport with a smile.

The panic to get away from the media scrum was over and Brad's driving simmered down as they doubled back and hit the freeway. What an escape that was. Brad warned Jarrod that it would be more of the same at the airport and let him know that there would be no messing around when they got to Tullamarine. Jarrod did his check-in on his phone and made sure he would have as little hold-up as possible before getting to the safety of the airside section of the departure area.

They were ten minutes away. Jarrod's curiosity got the better of him. "Brad," he said. "How long have you and Jacqui been an item?"

Brad feigned a sharp turn by running his hands along the steering wheel without turning it. Jarrod's heart jumped.

"I really like Jacqui," said Brad, laughing. "Let's just say that we've clicked. And you're the man who has brought us together. So, thanks for that."

Jarrod didn't know what to say. So, he changed the conversation. "So, tell me about your relationship with Viktor, then."

Brad feigned again, but this time Jarrod knew what he was doing.

"Do you mind if I don't tell you?" asked Brad. "I'm not particularly proud of that point of my life. Let's just say, I didn't mix with the right people, and ended up knowing a lot of the police force around Melbourne. Is that enough of an answer for you?"

"You worked for Viktor?" asked Jarrod.

"Hey, look at that bird," said Brad, pointing to a hawk that was hovering in the distance before descending on its plunge to grab some unfortunate animal on the ground. They both watched as the bird disappeared from view. That was as far as that conversation was going and Jarrod was happy with the non-answer he got.

"You'll be working with me when I get back?" asked Jarrod.

"Of course," said Brad, smiling. "You've got a movie to shoot, and I've got to protect your family from the paparazzi. Just make the most of your time away from all of this. I've heard you've got some serious minders at the other end. We'll all be here when you get back."

They wound around the final bend in front of the departures area and there were a lot of people. They both scanned the area, but luckily it was just rush hour and there weren't any media types amongst the throng. Brad seemed to know all the policemen at the drop-off zone and was waved into the spot right in front of the door. They both jumped out; Brad popped the lid again and got Jarrod's suitcase out. The two clasped in a warm embrace.

"Thank you for everything, Brad," said Jarrod. "And look after my family."

Brad saluted like a soldier and Jarrod scurried off, in through the door to the check-in desks as Brad got the hurry-up from the police. The journey was underway.

77

Assistant

The Quick Pass to get him through immigration was a godsend, judging by the queue, and the ability to check in at the business lounge was even better. Time to relax and unwind ahead of the long journey via Doha to Manchester. He found a seat in front of the big screen showing the morning news and filled a plate with fruit to enjoy as he watched. It was great to see a story about LF Sports and their new TV deal for Australian football leading the news, but the second story was breaking news about production being halted on the latest Harlowe Croft movie in Melbourne. Jarrod saw himself on screen and sat and slurped through his watermelon without a care for who was watching him or whether he was spilling it down his shirt. The timing to get out of the country was impeccable. He could feel eyes watching him even in the sanctuary of the lounge.

The arrival into Manchester Airport was efficient and he quickly made his way to the train station to catch the trans-Pennine train. He was expecting to be met by some sort of security person, but shrugged as he walked through the automatic doors into the fresh air outside the terminal. Memories of his last time at the station came flooding back. This time he was in a rush but not as much as he had been this time last year. A gentleman sitting by the exit of the carriage, once he'd boarded the waiting train, caught his eye and smiled—perhaps security was here after all. Heading through Huddersfield gave him goose bumps. He wrote a quick text to Peter Van Vloten, as directed by Gary in their phone conversation from Doha Airport, as the train raced through Northallerton station. As advertised, Peter was there at the station to pick him up. Despite only having played a short time with Peter, it felt like Jarrod was home.

"Tell me about Sunday's game," said Jarrod as they negotiated the tight car park.

"Do I have to?" asked Peter. "We were looking so good in the first half, despite being without five or six players. We just fell apart in the second half. Freddie gave the ball away for the second, so unlike him. 2–0 down after the home leg isn't the best."

Jarrod had only read what he could on the BBC website and the snippets he picked up from social media. Two goals behind going into the second leg looked insurmountable, but Jarrod had this opportunity to play, and he was going to take it. They arrived at the Arena in just a few minutes, and Jarrod was surprised not to be dropped right in front of the entrance. This wasn't Brad driving. Different person, different scene, different country, different life. They walked in through the main entrance together and Jarrod was immediately accosted by the head of media, Pauline. They hugged for what seemed like a minute. The commotion brought other people out of their offices and rooms, and a crowd formed around Jarrod. He was being peppered with questions, quick-fire, just like the media scrum outside his house.

Gary appeared and beckoned Jarrod over to join him in Pauline's office. Pauline closed the door behind her. Gary patted Jarrod on the back. He leaned on the desk, right next to the magazine that was still there with Craig Daniels on the cover. Jarrod stood up and patted the magazine. Pauline and Gary looked at it, puzzled, and then laughed.

"Jarrod Black," said Gary. "Am I glad to see you."

"I hear you're missing a few players for tomorrow's game," said Jarrod. That was an understatement.

"Now that Dec Hines is ruled out, I think we can find a spot for you in the team," said Gary. "But look at you! There's nothing left on your bones. Are you sure you're going to be able to cope with ninety minutes against the big blokes in Peterborough's midfield?"

"They'll get nowhere near me," said Jarrod. "What I've lost in size, I've gained in speed and agility."

"I hope you're right," said Gary. "I saw the highlights of the Grand Final you played in, and you should have won that one."

Jarrod was impressed that Gary had tuned in. Of course he would though, it was his job to know about the players in his team.

"I guess I'll be staying with Peter at my house?" asked Jarrod.

"Seems the most logical," said Pauline. "I think he'd like his landlord to check a few things too."

"When are we leaving for the game?" asked Jarrod.

"Meeting here at midday tomorrow," said Gary. "I understand that you'll be making your own way after the game."

"I'll need to speak with D.I. Allison," said Jarrod. It would make sense if he was due in court the following day in London. "I'm a little sketchy on details at the moment."

"Tell me, Jarrod," said Gary. "How do you find the football in Australia?"

Jarrod wasn't sure of the angle that Gary was taking, so he was just honest.

"Look, there aren't that many big names playing in Australia," said Jarrod. "There are a few, but they're in Australia for the lifestyle and the sunshine. The football is really good though. The skill level is high, and the raw talent is coming through now that the second division is underway. They could use a few more quality coaches though."

"Glad you brought that up," said Gary. "I never did fill the assistant manager role at the club. We've been a little light on the ground since Des moved to Hartlepool. I'd like to formally offer you the role of assistant manager from next season, regardless of which division we end up playing in. I've seen how you take in everything when you're around coaches. I like that. You're developing a style in your head, and I'd love to be able to help you develop it."

"I'm flattered," said Jarrod. "You know that I'm interested. I've even got the coaching badges now."

He paused, trying to think of the right thing to say.

"But I'm locked into a movie role right now," he continued. "And that's going to keep me in Australia until well after the start of next season."

"The offer is there."

Gary handed an envelope to Jarrod, who declined to open it, and instead put it in the front pocket of his hand luggage. Gary looked at the clock on the wall.

"Training in ten minutes," he said. "Are you up to it?"

"Try and keep me away," said Jarrod.

He had a broad smile, and his face was still lit up as he left Pauline's office with Gary.

78

Bicycle

The journey to Peterborough was quick and easy. Away games for Jarrod in Australia involved a coach to the airport, waiting around in an airport lounge and then more travel at the other end. This was especially true when they were playing outside the main capital cities. The midday meet gave Jarrod time to recover from the long journey the day before; he also popped in to say a quick hello to an excited Pippa Robson, and it allowed him to catch up with D.I. Allison by phone to firm up plans for Wednesday evening and Thursday's appearance at the Central Criminal Court. As predicted by Pauline, Peter had a list of items that needed attention in the house, most of which needed handyman skills well beyond Jarrod's means. Jarrod replaced a few light bulbs and trimmed back the branches of the tree that were scraping against the roof. It was so good to be back doing normal things in his own house, up a ladder, getting his hands dirty.

The London Road stadium was like a big warehouse from the outside as they drove into the car park. It was a tidy stadium though, and the players had a quick walk on the field to get a feel for the playing surface. It was impeccable, trimmed to perfection and without any hint of deviation when they played the ball to each other. No rugby league played on this surface. The hairs on Jarrod's arms were sticking up. He was being swept away by the emotion of being back. He'd slipped back into the squad as if he hadn't been away. The faces were all the same, and the training session the previous day had allowed the players to get used to having Jarrod back as the focal point in midfield once again.

Kick-off was still a long way away, but they had their meal together as a squad and Jarrod caught up on what he'd missed during the season and tried to tune in again to the Crazy Gang style of humour that he missed so much. The BetShed advert came up as well as the 'Harlowe Croft' theme tune. Keeper Wes filled in Jarrod about the goal of the season contenders, and it looked nailed on for Ghali Barbera, after he beat eight players and scored with a lob in a home game on Boxing Day.

The extent of the injury crisis was evident from the team sheet that Gary passed around after lunch. At least Raynor Gunn was declared fit enough to make the bench, but without a host of players, they were looking at the youth to make an impact. Young Steven Horton was drafted in on the right of a three-man defence in place of the unlucky Mitch Short, and Julien Favot was in attack. These were players who had not figured at all this season, but Darlington had to throw caution to the wind and go on the offensive. The sight of Dario Reilly, a fellow old-timer like himself, playing out of position on the left of the defence was a big surprise.

The afternoon was such a tonic for Jarrod. He didn't want it to end, but there was a vital match to be played and the squad left in twos and threes to the changing rooms.

The floodlights were on. The crowd was almost at capacity, and Jarrod was nervously pacing around the changing room. Benson sat watching from the corner of the room on his crutches. Gary gave them a real heartfelt final team talk, the photo of their fans from that game at Luton the previous season was up on the wall, and Gary referred to it to make his point that this one was not just for the team, but it was for everyone involved in the club. The players were pumped up and made their way to the tunnel before being led out by the referees. This was universal. It was almost the same atmosphere as the game he'd played in at the Lakeside ten days previously. A hand came out of the crowd, and he instinctively shook it before turning to see James Bain, the Socceroos player who lived in the area, smiling at him, wishing him good luck.

The away end was full, under the low roof, and the noise was tremendous.

Kick-off brought the noise to its maximum, and the first touch for Wes in front of the away fans brought a massive cheer. The game started like a chess game, and it was difficult to see how Peterborough would let this slip. Darlington chased the ball to no avail, until finally Connor Naughton nipped in and stole the ball from the Peterborough defender. He grappled with his opponent and stole a yard on him, before being hauled to the ground as he shaped to move the ball onto his left foot for a clear shot at goal. The inevitable red card for the defender sent shock waves around the stadium. Darlington's chances had increased dramatically. Jarrod could feel the tension from the home fans, and it gave him an immediate energy hit. The free kick was wasted, but it wasn't long before they used their extra man to take the lead, a corner headed back across goal for Anton Broman to bicycle kick the ball into the bottom corner. What a goal!

The first half was end-to-end stuff. Peterborough were still creating chances, but the attacking formation adopted by the visitors was giving them a lot of possession. It was Darlington who struck next to bring the scores level on aggregate. Jarrod and Peter combined beautifully in the middle of the park and Peter slid the ball through for Connor to run on to. His low shot beat the keeper but hit the post. Julien though was on the spot to tap the ball into the empty net. With away goals not important, the game was now on a knife-edge. The half time whistle was greeted with a massive roar from the Darlington end.

The second half started in similar fashion. Wes went full length to palm away a rocket from distance, and Dario cleared one from under the bar. Just one goal from either side would do it. Jarrod found himself hassled off the ball by one of the two big midfielders, a hulk of a man who was just missing the metal teeth to be the classic Harlowe Croft villain. He had been so instrumental in Sunday's game at the Arena, but the sight of Jarrod sprinting with all his might to slide in and win the ball back was greeted with applause from the bench and even from the Peterborough fans. Peter was getting a little frustrated with Dan Collier on the wing who wasn't offering the right angle for him, but when Jarrod played the ball to Dan, he followed his pass and ran around him to receive the ball back on the overlap. Instead, that created a hole for Dan to run into, and he played the most exquisite ball into the area for Anton to dive onto and send a bullet header into the goal in front of the Darlo fans for 3–0. The celebrations were long, but there was way too much time left to resort to time-wasting at only one goal ahead. Gary waved them forward, wanting more.

Sure enough, Jackie Thomas played in Julien down the right and the cross was perfect for Anton to reach out his left foot and hook the ball back across the keeper into the goal. The game was won. The unthinkable had happened and Darlington had come back from 2–0 down to win 4–2 on aggregate with a superb hat-trick from their target man Anton Broman. The celebrations were huge at the final whistle. The players were punching the air and clapping along to the chants, Jarrod in the thick of it. Darlington were in the play-off finals for a third season in a row. It was an unbelievable feat. And they'd done it with such a threadbare squad and a movie star from Australia who had only just arrived on a plane and had made all the difference. It was the stuff of legends.

There was no time for celebration though, and D.I. Allison was outside the changing rooms when the players started to file out. Jarrod clasped hands with the detective inspector, and they shared an impromptu hug. They made their way out of the stadium, D.I. Allison running Jarrod through the good and the bad points of the game from a spectator's perspective. They would still be talking about it when they arrived at the hotel in London.

"Jarrod," he said, after handing him a piece of paper with the running schedule for the following day. "Expect this to be quite a trying few days. I'll pick you up in the morning."

79

Graduation

The week was indeed quite traumatic. Jarrod had a starring role in the court case against Viktor Andreyev. At one point he was stared down by the smooth-talking Russian, but Jarrod refused to avert his gaze and stared right through him. The accusation was an accessory to murder. The gunman who had shot Newcastle United star Andre Rambouillet last year had already been sentenced to thirty years' jail for the cold-blooded killing, but Andreyev had so far escaped the law having had an arm's-length involvement. The prosecution was craftily using his illegal betting syndicate involvement as a potential scapegoat for his involvement in the murder and D.I. Allison explained to Jarrod that if they didn't get him for murder, they would be able to nail him to the betting syndicate. There was always the possibility of not making either of the charges stick, but both D.I. Allison and Jarrod knew that he was definitely part of both.

The court appearances made it difficult to link up with Darlington for training, and it was only when a session was adjourned before lunch that Jarrod quickly organised to catch the train north and be at the Arena for the evening session. There were players coming back from injury, but the squad still looked threadbare. The play-off final was on the Saturday of the long weekend, and that was only four days away. Raynor looked the most likely to be fit in time, but regular striker Will Telfer was already ruled out. This was going to be another tough game, and the Sheffield Wednesday team they were up against had just disposed of Reading by six goals on aggregate in a most one-sided of semi-final matchups.

Jarrod found himself having quite a bit of free time on his hands in London, due to the relatively short days in court, and he was able to take up the offer of interviews from various outlets, on the proviso that the court matters were not part of the discussion. His interview with Four Four Two was fantastic. They were doing a piece on players who were peaking at the end of their careers, and it made Jarrod feel a million dollars to be compared to some of the greats around the world. The magazine *When Saturday Comes*, one of his favourites over the years, was interested in the angle of playing in two different leagues in the same season, and *Empire* magazine was simply interested to hear about his short journey from footballer to movie star. A few phone interviews with the national newspapers also came through, all organised by the PR company in Sydney, and Jarrod was getting comfortable and practised at what constituted a good answer.

Thursday morning brought news that Stevie Mosseman and Robert Biscotti had been cleared of any wrongdoing. From Jacqui's account of what happened, they were absolutely furious to be implicated in any shady betting dealings. It was as though someone had set them up. They were ready to recommence shooting for the movie as they had all the crew, cast and equipment already on site, eating into the budget. Jarrod asked Duddy to cover for him. Apparently, Jarrod had a 'family issue' in Sydney and would be away for a few days. It left Jarrod feeling very uncomfortable, at least for fifteen minutes. He could rely on Jacqui to smooth things over and stall the producers for as long as was needed. It was a tissue of lies that would be completely blown out of the water when news came through of Jarrod playing at Wembley on Saturday in front of an international TV audience and a massive crowd.

Jarrod's involvement in the trial of Viktor Andreyev concluded before lunchtime and Jarrod couldn't get out of London quickly enough. D.I. Allison was travelling home, and Jarrod was surprised that they were able to leave so early without any debriefing. D.I. Allison's driving was from the Brad Neylan handbook, and he had them out of central London without delay and they hovered well over the speed limit up the M1. Just after Leicester, Jarrod noticed that they were heading west instead of north, and the motorway had ended. The name Burton-upon-Trent came next, and Jarrod realised that they were heading for St George's Park.

"I heard you had an appointment," said D.I. Allison.

"How the hell did you know?"

"June told me," said D.I. Allison. "And it's worked out well."

The car park was almost full when they arrived. They were an hour later than the official kick-off time for the graduation ceremony at the on-site Hilton hotel. Jarrod had pulled up the invitation on his phone and could see that it went all night after the official presentations. They walked in and Jarrod explained his circumstances to the receptionist at the trestle table in the lobby, who took his details and walked into the main room of the building to check with a colleague. She beckoned both of them in and found them two spaces at a table right at the back. Jarrod scanned the room. He could see faces from the courses he'd attended over the years. They were just coming to the end of a series of speeches, before launching into the certificate presentation. The timing of their arrival was incredible.

All graduates were called up one by one; there were around twenty present and a few absentees. When Jarrod's name was called, he made his way through the tables to the stage, heads turning as he went, and was presented with an A4 envelope. The photographer snapped away and Jarrod joined the wall of graduates at the back of the stage. There were massive names in there, recently retired internationals, not only from England, and other seasoned professionals from the Premier League. This was a proud moment for Jarrod, a totally unexpected experience.

Jarrod was emotional when he got back to the car. D.I. Allison quipped that he was just upset to have to pass up an evening of networking with fellow future managers. In truth, Jarrod knew that this was a big moment in his life. This was the first graduation ceremony of any kind he had attended, and that feeling of accomplishment mixed with the realisation that he could step into the next stage of his footballing life at any time made his eyes glass over and he was lost in thought.

D.I. Allison and Jarrod had enjoyed five hours in the car together, arriving at the Arena at 6:30 p.m. The training session had just started, and Jarrod was in a hurry to join it, but took the time to hug D.I. Allison again.

"See you on Saturday?" asked Jarrod.

"Funny you should say that," said D.I. Allison. "I'm due back down on Monday, so it's a definite maybe. I've got to make sure you get on your plane too, so, yes, I'll see you there."

"You didn't have anything to do with all this, did you?" asked Jarrod, narrowing his eyes.

"Your luck was definitely in with the trial," he said. "The movie producers ending up in custody, well, there are rumours doing the rounds of who set them up."

Gerry Lincoln, the Darlington owner, was passing on his way into the Arena. He stopped and looked and bounded over when he saw them.

"Jarrod," he said excitedly. "Bloody marvellous to see you. Detective Inspector, I don't know how you did it, but thanks so much. You deserve a medal."

That was enough to tell Jarrod that D.I. Allison indeed had a lot to do with him being in England right now, and that he might not be the straight-laced policeman that he had thought he was. Jarrod threw a puzzled look D.I. Allison's way, and the detective inspector clicked his fingers and pointed at Jarrod.

"See you on Saturday."

80

Manor

Jarrod had been here before. It was twelve months almost to the day since their dramatic League Two play-off win, and the club had achieved the most incredible feat of reaching the play-off final three seasons in a row. No other team had done that—it wasn't really a feat, a feat would have been automatic promotion, but it was an exciting end to another over-achieving season for this collection of misfit footballers, young talent and old heads. Jarrod was so delighted to have made it back for the whole experience, the meet at the stadium, the coach journey, the hotel, the dinner the night before, the breakfast, the pre-game session. All of that he figured he would miss due to the trial, but somehow again the cards had fallen in his favour.

Aside from Peter running late and getting them to the Arena ten minutes late and incurring a handsome final-day fine, the Friday went as smoothly as he remembered. They were booked in to stay at the same hotel as last year, and owner Gerry was lord of the manor again at dinner, making sure that the players knew exactly what their job was. It was all about the fans. It always had been since he took over at the club. It was a club that tried to do things the right way with the involvement of the supporters in every major decision. Jarrod could just imagine Gerry at the latest fan forum: "Right, I can get Jarrod Black back to help us in the play-offs, who's with me? I might need to call in a few favours."

Jarrod was not surprised at all to see adverts for *Harlowe Croft: From the Gallows* plastered all around the outside of Wembley and along Wembley Way. With BetShed ads sprinkled among them, it was spooky to see his face at every corner as the coach neared the stadium. Jarrod was a sought-after star in the UK, the new Agent 040, and he was starting to understand how big this was becoming.

81

Holster

"Ladies and gentlemen, please turn off all mobile devices as we will shortly be departing the terminal," came the announcement. Jarrod still had a few minutes of the extended highlights to go, and he was keen to see the last two goals. His polo shirt smelled of champagne and beer. It had been a glorious climax to an amazing ten days in England, and Darlington were now in the Championship.

"Sir, can you please turn off your tablet?" insisted the flight attendant. Jarrod obliged. He'd see the rest later. For now, though, he had the wonderful memories of the game running around in his head. The lap of honour with the play-off trophy, celebrating the winning goal, embracing Gerry and Gary, and singing along with the fans. The celebrations in the changing room had been curtailed when D.I. Allison appeared to give him a hurry-up, and Jarrod had to make a swift exit, his teammates doing a guard of honour in various stages of undress as he raced off to make his plane at Heathrow.

The screen started up in the back of the seat in front. It was an advert. It was Jarrod, coming out of the water, no shirt on, with a hunting knife in a leather holster, flicking his head to send droplets from his hair into the sunshine. He remembered how many takes they had to do to get the right one. It was real. It was happening. Jarrod Black had become Harlowe Croft.

ACKNOWLEDGEMENTS

Jarrod Black is back, and thanks to Popcorn Press and Fair Play Publishing for continuing the story of Australia's favourite football fiction family. It's great to see more fiction making its way into the world of football writing. It's evidence that our country has a great depth of writing talent just waiting to be unearthed.

A tip of the hat to the coronavirus that gave me the time to put together this story in the first place—the one positive to have come from the pandemic.

Thanks to the #SokkahTwitter community for the entertainment and for making social media a happy place to visit.

A shout-out to the Sydney FC community for being so fantastic during a season of ups and downs and cementing my love for the club.

And a big thank you to Michelle for being with me along the way; many more football trips to come. I can't wait.

Once you have read this book, I would love some feedback. Feedback on social media is fantastic, positive feedback on Amazon or Goodreads is priceless. Even a message will let me know that the book is being consumed and enjoyed, and propel me to complete the next in the series of unashamed football novels. This is an adventure that has no limits. Stay tuned for more!

ABOUT THE AUTHOR

Texi Smith is a part-time writer of fiction as well as a reporter for TheRoar.com.au where he writes regularly on Australian football, and for whom he has been fortunate to cover the 2022 World Cup. In-between, he has a full-time IT consultancy, he has run ten Sydney Marathons, he plays football in an Over 45s league, referees, and is dad to two teenage children.

Originally from Newcastle in England, he has lived in Sydney for more than 20 years.

Jarrod Black Chasing Pack is his fifth novel and the fourth in the Jarrod Black series of unashamed football fiction. The fifth was about Jarrod's sister, Anna Black.

MORE REALLY GOOD FOOTBALL FICTION FROM POPCORN PRESS

Game

The Gaffer

The End
of the Game

Anna Black
This girl can play!

Jarrod Black

Guilty Party

Jarrod Black

Hospital Pass

Introducing

Jarrod Black

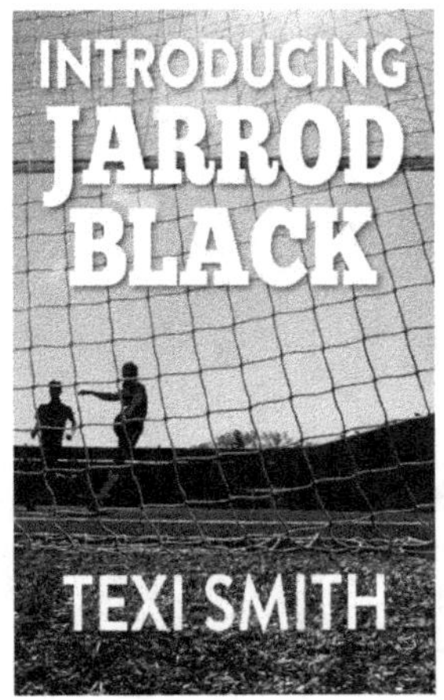

Coming soon

The Yawning Giant

Mark Bowman

POPCORN
PRESS